A Particle
of God

First published by O Books, 2009
O Books is an imprint of John Hunt Publishing Ltd., The Bothy, Deershot Lodge, Park Lane, Ropley,
Hants, SO24 0BE, UK
office1@o-books.net
www.o-books.net

Distribution in:	South Africa
	Alternative Books
UK and Europe	altbook@peterhyde.co.za
Orca Book Services	Tel: 021 555 4027 Fax: 021 447 1430
orders@orcabookservices.co.uk	
Tel: 01202 665432 Fax: 01202 666219	Text copyright Teddy Bart 2008
Int. code (44)	
	Design: Stuart Davies
USA and Canada	
NBN	ISBN: 978 1 84694 172 6
custserv@nbnbooks.com	
Tel: 1 800 462 6420 Fax: 1 800 338 4550	All rights reserved. Except for brief quotations
	in critical articles or reviews, no part of this
Australia and New Zealand	book may be reproduced in any manner without
Brumby Books	prior written permission from the publishers.
sales@brumbybooks.com.au	
Tel: 61 3 9761 5535 Fax: 61 3 9761 7095	The rights of Teddy Bart as author have been
	asserted in accordance with the Copyright,
Far East (offices in Singapore, Thailand,	Designs and Patents Act 1988.
Hong Kong, Taiwan)	
Pansing Distribution Pte Ltd	A CIP catalogue record for this book is available
kemal@pansing.com	from the British Library.
Tel: 65 6319 9939 Fax: 65 6462 5761	

Printed by Digital Book Print

O Books operates a distinctive and ethical publishing philosophy in
all areas of its business, from its global network of authors to
production and worldwide distribution.
This book is produced on FSC certified stock, within ISO14001
standards. The printer plants sufficient trees each year through
the Woodland Trust to absorb the level of emitted carbon in
its production.

A Particle
of God

Teddy Bart

BOOKS

Winchester, UK
Washington, USA

CONTENTS

The only way to know God in His wholeness is to approach Him from both directions simultaneously — by loving one's fellow man—in whom resides a particle of God in the form of the human soul—and by loving and listening to the personal God Who resides in one's own soul. In doing this, we come to recognize that the God in others is really the God in us, and therefore we all are truly one.
Kabbalah

You are energy in physical form. Or, to use a spiritual concept - you are a soul within a physical body - a particle of God.
Wallace D. Wattles
The Science of Getting Rich

The soul of man is a particle of God.
Seneca

I become a transparent eye-ball. I am nothing. I see all. The currents of the Universal Being circulate through me. I am a particle of God.
Ralph Waldo Emerson
Nature

This book is dedicated to my angels,
helpers and guides who
helped me remember.

Prologue

"Bingo! I've got me a winner!"

"Oh, Dr. Malak," the hefty nurse named Rita said, laughing. "You say that every time we deliver a healthy baby."

Dr. David Malak performed his post-delivery procedures and handed off the wrinkled pink infant to another nurse named Clara who wrapped the baby in a blue blanket and presented it to its mother.

"Here's your boy, Mrs. Rabinowitz."

Rachel Rabinowitz carefully took the bundle in her arms. For a moment she just looked at him with that special love known only to mothers who have regained a child after losing a child.

A man wearing a brown suit, white shirt and nondescript necktie cautiously approached the bed. Rachel looked up at him with tears of joy, and said, "Look Jake, we have a son."

Jacob Rabinowitz kissed his wife on the cheek. Then he carefully parted the corner of the blanket covering the baby's face and greeted the new life with a tender kiss on the forehead.

Jacob said, "We'll name him Joseph, after your father, Yoseff, may he rest in peace."

"And I'll call him Yoseley," Rachel said with a tired smile.

Dr. Malak entered the room to check on Rachel's condition and have another look at the baby.

Rachel said, "I wish you to have such a beautiful son one day, Dr. Malak."

"That would be nice, Mrs. Rabinowitz," Dr. David Malak said, as he left the room followed by Clara and Rita, his two nurses, chattering to each other about where to have dinner.

Jacob sat in a chair beside Rachel as she nursed Joseph. Feeling a bit uneasy, he reached over and turned on the small radio on Rachel's bedside table.

"This is Edward R. Murrow, speaking to you tonight from

Berlin, where, last night, the Nazi's worst crackdown on the Jews brutally..."

"Jake, please turn it to something more pleasant," Rachel asked.

He fished around on the dial and brought in another station.

"The Pirate's Rip Sewell is on the mound. At bat, the Cub's Phil Caveretta. Sewell winds up, throws, Caveretta swings… and it's the old dipsy-doodle!"

"Jake! Please!"

Jacob twisted the knob on the dial and stopped on the next clear station.

"Now here's a fresh new star all the way from Tennessee singing her rendition of the number one song in England. Here's Miss Dinah Shore and *We'll Meet Again*."

Rachel's eye's widened. She looked over toward her husband, and said, "Look Jake… the baby is smiling!"

"Don't be silly, Rachel. It's just gas."

Rachel ignored her husband's comment. She focused on the small face with a blissful smile staring somewhere above.

I wonder what he knows? she thought.

Chapter 1

Joey Robin lay on the sofa watching the *Tonight Show*, wishing Jay Leno was Johnny Carson.

No one hosted like Carson did, he thought. *He had wit, charm, timing — all the gifts. He was the best. Taste… that's what Carson had.* Joey exhaled a deep sigh, shook his head, and thought, *ah, what the hell. No one cares about taste anymore.*

Joey felt himself getting worked up again. He had been warned not to let that happen. He clicked off the TV, placed the remote on his chest, and starred at the ceiling.

Where has my life gone?

For nearly to forty years, Joey Robin had been a radio and television talk show host in Memphis. In the '70's, '80's and '90's he was known as "Mr. Memphis." His plaques, certificates and awards, for best 'this' and best 'that', lined the walls of his study. He was the embodiment of the Rodger Miller song, *Kansas City Star* — a celebrity, respected and admired within a radius of fifty miles. Beyond that: anonymous.

Joey's on-air style was a throwback. Aspects of his heroes, such as Merv Griffin, Jack Paar, Steve Allen, Johnny Carson, and others whose star was the reflection of the light they shined on their guest, melded with his own unique manner and technique. Except for a few such as Larry King, Charlie Rose, and Terry Gross, that conversational style didn't sell anymore. Program directors wanted conservative opinionated hosts who superciliously spout their far-right social and political conviction, and if you don't agree, you're an idiot! Or worse — a liberal!

Like Richard Cory, in Edward Arlington Robinson's poem, everyone who met Joey Robin thought he was happy and fulfilled.

As they did with Cory, they misjudged Robin. His interior life was in constant turmoil.

Joey Robin harbored a deeply-guarded unrequited love affair

with fame. While loving his work and basking in the local adoration, he had always thought himself good enough and deserving enough to have become a national star.

During the past ten years or so, as he aged well into his '60's, with the odds of his attaining his dream of stardom a long shot at best, the issue of who gets sprinkled with stardust and why, and who the gods pass over, and why, had become like a tumor on his soul.

Nine months ago Joey was fired.

So Joey Robin involuntarily adopted the life of severe discontent — his work aborted, his dream unrealized.

Being Joey Robin had been his whole life. Being Joey Robin subordinated all other interests. His life force was talking into a microphone, looking into a camera.

And now that he wasn't Joey Robin anymore, it was as if he had lost his life. He was living without a life. He didn't know how to be himself. He had no self other than when he was "Joey Robin... you're on the air... go ahead please." Now, he was a hollow vessel, dashed on a barren shore; a dead man resting.

He laid there, the TV flickering, his pained mind wondering.

Why, dear God. Why? Why was I denied the big time? What could I have done? What should I have done that I didn't do? Where has my life gone?

"Honey, you coming up?" he heard his wife call, interrupting his self inflicted misery.

With his eyes still glued to a spot on the ceiling, Joey answered, "In a minute."

"Okay, but don't fall asleep on the sofa. Remember to lock the door. And take your medicine. Good night, honey."

"Good night, Cris," Joey muttered, hardly audibly.

Joey and Crystal had been married for forty-seven years. They met when Joey was a disc jockey in Ashville, North Carolina. She was nineteen. He was twenty-three. Now he was seventy. And she was still nineteen.

His eyes closed and he dozed for several minutes. Awakening in a half-sleep state, he slowly rolled off the sofa saying, "Oy!" with each muscle ache, before he was standing upright. Wearily, he made his way up the stairs and into the bathroom where he gently closed the door to prevent the light from waking Crystal.

He swallowed his Lipitor, his Lisinopril, a baby aspirin and an Omega 3 fish oil capsule in one swig of bottled water, turned off the bathroom light, tiptoed to the bed and carefully slipped under the blanket, trying his best not to disturb Crystal.

He leaned over to softly kiss her goodnight on the forehead but his lips found only her pillow. As if shocked by a cattle prod, Joey fell back with a thud, his head coming to rest on his pillow, his eyes filling with tears. He sobbed uncontrollably. He beat his fists against the sheets and cried, as he had cried every night for the past month.

"Oh Cris, I miss you so much!"

His whimpering became deep sobs. Eventually, he was enveloped into the sanctuary of sleep and the plane wherein he could be at peace, where he could be Joey Robin again.

Chapter 2

The interview with Johnny Carson was going splendidly. Joey had established that eye connection with the 'King of Late Night Comedy' that happens rarely. But when it happens — and it happens exclusively among seasoned pros — both host and guest make interviewing magic. They read each other, anticipate one another, and react to one another as if they are two halves of one person. The audience was howling. Joey Robin was in broadcasting nirvana.

Suddenly, in an instant, Carson's face changed expression. He looked haggard: spent. His glow vanished. The link between him and Joey broke and froze in freeze frame. The sound from the audience stopped abruptly, as if someone pressed the mute button. Then the picture started breaking up.

Joey felt cold, alone, isolated. The sound from the ringing phone grew louder. He didn't want to hear it. He pressed his hands to his ears.

Stop ringing!

But the ringing continued to gain decibels in proportion to the diminishing clarity of Carson's image.

Then, Carson was gone but the phone kept on ringing. Joey reached behind him and grappled for the receiver.

Joey Robin, you're on the air, what's your question? he almost said automatically. But he wasn't Joey Robin anymore. So he just said, in a sleepy voice, "Hello?"

"Joey?" the up-beat, familiar voice said. "Did I wake you, sweetie?"

Joey cleared his throat, sat up, blinked several times, and said, "No, kid. You didn't wake me. You interrupted my interview with Johnny Carson, that's all."

A slight pause. Then, she said, "I was just calling to check on you. Are you okay, Joey?"

The question was simple, but sincere. She really did care that he was okay.

For over twenty years, up until the station dumped his show, Rose Barbelo had worked with Joey Robin. Her full name was Angelina Rose Barbelo, but she didn't like being called Angel for short, so she professionally went by her middle name.

Off the air, when the two of them were alone, or when she was visiting the Robin home, Joey called her 'kid', which may have been the result of his viewing *Casablanca* too many times. But on the air, or when making a serious point, or in front of others (except Crystal), she was always Rose.

Joey had hired her as an intern. She learned fast, worked smart and was devoted to Joey's well being. When his production assistant quit, Joey put Rose in the job. When he had a 'my way or the highway' argument with his producer, Rose was the natural replacement. He began using her to play off of, like a Gelman on Regis; a silent foil, a human prop, a stooge. She didn't mind. It made the show better; it made Joey better — her twin motivations.

One day, when a guest didn't show up, he put Rose on the air to chat with him. She was a natural, playing the sidekick supporting role to absolute perfection; a rare and precious commodity in a business where everyone wants to be the main attraction: the top banana. And no one knew the value of an Ed McMahan or a Dean Martin or a Rose Barbelo more than the showbiz-savvy Joey Robin. In no time, she was his co-host.

Eventually, she became a local personality in her own right. When Joey got canned, Rose was offered her own show on a competing station. The show became a ratings winner. Within a year of airing locally, a national syndicator picked it up. Seemingly overnight, *Pathways with Rose Barbelo* became a national sensation. Rose Barbelo was more than a star; she was a brand. Barbelo Productions spanned all elements of media. This year she came in third among the *Forbes Magazine* annual 'Celebrity 100 Power List' with an estimated income of $240 million, and was noted throughout the world for her philanthropy through her charitable foundation.

"Do you want me to bring you something to eat?" Rose asked.

"Don't you have a meeting or something to go to, kid?" Joey asked, and then wished he hadn't said it like that.

Actually, she had back-to-back meetings scheduled on her calendar plus a photo session before her 11:00am call time for her show, but she let the barb go. She knew him too well: empathized with his suffering too deeply, and owed him too much to take offense or give him even more guilt than he had.

"Naw, I'm open. Say, how about I bring us a bagel. You got coffee? I've got an idea I'd like to talk with you about," she said warmly.

He was grateful she didn't come back at him like she was capable of doing when someone is rude. Rose hadn't gotten where she got without moxie.

Joey would have loved having a bagel and coffee. He would have loved seeing her, seeing anybody, actually. But he knew she was extending herself in loving friendship, and that she had more to do than sit in his depressing home watching him being depressed.

"I'll take a rain check, kid. I have several things I have to do this morning. Busy day. Wow! It's nearly nine! I'd better get showered and dressed. Tomorrow maybe?"

Rose figured if she had a dollar for every rain check she took from him for nearly a year, she could endow The Rose Barbelo Foundation herself.

"Sure, sweetie. Maybe tomorrow. You take care. Call me later if you can."

"I'd rather call you Rose," he said in a Groucho Marx voice.

She had heard the joke a million times, but she gave Joey a laugh as a gift. Even though Rose had attained huge stardom — the kind of stardom Joey had always dreamed of — a part of her felt like she was still riding side car and he was driving the bike. Oddly, in spite of her solo success, she felt most comfortable when she thought of herself in her previous supporting role as Sancho along side Don Quixote.

"See you, Rose. I'll be watching you. Say, who've you got on today?"

It was not a small talk question. Joey was immersed in Rose's success even though, cognitively, he never quite comprehended why her program, *Pathways* — focusing on matters pertaining to body, mind and spirit — became such a huge success. Rose had always been about spiritual high-mindedness: the greater good. Joey had always been about showbiz; what ever worked.

Nonetheless, he harbored no thoughts of envy, resentment or jealousy. Conversely, he was thoroughly proud of her. Her success validated him. She was his completion; the closest he had come to the big time; his other self.

Rose hesitated, and then answered. "I don't want to make you sad."

"Sad? Me? Chuckles the Clown? Never! Who've you got on?"

"A fascinating guy named David Malak. His latest book is about people who have had a premonition of their death," she answered.

"How does he know they had a premonition of their death if they're dead?" Joey deadpanned.

Rose chuckled and said, "They told someone before they died, silly."

"Oh." Joey said without missing a beat. "Actually, I believe in death premonitions. It starts with a twenty-two year old pisher of a program director telling you you've got to pick up your pace, insult the guests, and have a conservative point of view. Shortly after, you say, 'I won't do that,' you're dead."

Rose laughed full-out. "Now *that's* funny," she said.

Joey had typically covered his discomfort with anything dealing with death by deflecting the topic with humor; an idiosyncrasy that always puzzled Rose.

"Oh, one more thing, I almost forgot. I'm having a drink with

Crystal after the show today. Anything you want me to tell her?" Rose asked.

A hundred lines raced across Joey's mind in an instant - some funny, some sad. He decided to go for funny *and* sad.

"Yes. Ask her how to get the dryer to turn off. It's been running for three weeks. All my socks and underwear are stir fried," he deadpanned.

"I'll be sure to ask her. Bye, love," Rose said, and clicked off.

The Carsons, the Griffins, the Paars, the Allens — both Steve and Woody — all had that ability to create a joke by mixing misfortune and self-deprecation with reality and truth. The dryer wasn't actually running for three weeks, but his real life state of affairs — his helplessness, his uselessness, his feeling of being a visitor in his own body — was framed pictorially in the dryer shtick. That had always been one of his talents as a talk show host. Albeit now fallow, he was pleased he still had the ability to produce that feature of his former self.

He felt guilty that he didn't dream about Crystal but dreamed, instead, of interviewing Johnny Carson.

First I lose my show, and then I lose my wife. Two cancellations in one year! And which loss lies heaviest in my subconscious? He paused a second with an expression like Jack Benny when confronted by a mugger and asked, "Your money or your life?" After concluding the answer, he whispers to himself, *What a shmuck I am!*

Guilt or no guilt, since his show was dumped, all his dreams were about interviewing, or trying to get an interview, or being in the company of someone he'd like to interview. His dream life was about his love life.

Mindlessly, he went upstairs to the bathroom, oblivious to the fact that since Crystal moved out, the room had taken on all the physical and aromatic characteristics of a men's locker room. The mirror above the sink was splattered with spit-out mouthwash and toothpaste; the countertop was slippery from dripped aftershave;

the once-fluffy bath towel that hung over the shower stall the day Crystal left was still there but was now rigid like peeled tree bark. It, along with the washcloth on a hook in the shower, smelled rank.

Joey showered, shaved and brushed his teeth — seven were his; the rest were made in a dental laboratory.

In the bedroom, he dressed in a blue denim shirt, khaki trousers, and a beat-up pair of brown loafers. He walked into the second bedroom, the one he used as a study, and fired up his laptop to check for e-mails. When his show was up and running he averaged over a hundred e-mails a day. Lately he was averaging about two or three of any importance, and they were usually from Rose with a joke, an idea, or just a thought. Today he had none.

He spoke to the screen as if he were on the air:

If I would have simply accepted the will of Fate and been grateful for the many years I did what I loved doing every day when that twenty-two year old pisher told me they were canceling me; if I had just said, 'Oh well, it was wonderful while it lasted'; if I would have just flowed with the story, and walked out like a mensch into the rest of my life, I wouldn't be here alone now. I would have woken up slowly with Cris, had coffee, talked about today, yesterday, tomorrow, and then maybe gone out for a walk, gone out for some breakfast, read, sat, just enjoyed some time alone that we never had before. Why did I let it cripple me? Why did I allow it to cripple us? Why did…

"You've Got Mail!" The voice from the computer said.

Wonderful! I wonder what's on Rose's mind now.

Joey clicked 'Read' and read the message. He blinked, widened his eyes, and read it again. Involuntarily, his shoulders quivered. He read the message again.

DO YOU WANT TO DIE?

Chapter 3

Rose, you never did know when to give it up. But this is a little over the top, don't ya think? I mean, surely there must be a punch line coming. Or, then again, maybe it's something she read in her guest's book today that she wants me to hear. She always wants to share something she thinks is insightful; always trying to get me to buy into that flaky stuff. Okay, I'll humor her. What else have I got to do?

He clicked 'Reply' then stopped short and drew a quick breath. He hadn't noticed a second ago. It wasn't Rose's address in the address block. It was from ermurrow@cbs.com!

Hold on a minute, he thought. *Edward R. Murrow is sending me an e-mail and asking me if I want to die? He's been dead for over thirty years, for crying out loud! Who's yanking my chain here?*

With a smile of realization, he nodded and thought, *I thought I had left all those weirdos behind when I came off the air. This has got to be some leftover bigot or some other creep who's heard me talk on the air about Murrow and some of my heroes back in the day and is doing a number on me. Idiots! You won! I'm gone, kaput. Find someone else to harass! Okay, creepo. You asked me a question. Here's your answer.*

He typed:

YOU ASKED, I'LL TELL... EVEN THOUGH, LIKE ALL YOU JERKS I HAVE KNOWN ALL MY LIFE, YOU'RE TOO COWARDLY TO SIGN YOUR NAME... YOUR REAL NAME. SO HERE'S MY ANSWER — MY FINAL ANSWER. I'D RATHER BE DEAD THAN LIVE IN A WORLD FULL OF IDIOTS LIKE YOU. NOW DON'T COME OFF YOUR MEDICINE ANYMORE. YOURS TRULY,
JOEY ROBIN

He hit the 'Send' button and off it went. A second later, he regretted he even replied. In the past, responding to these people had led to no good. *What was I thinking? I should have just let...*

"You've got mail!"

Joey was about to send the new letter to spam hell, but for some reason he hesitated. His mind told him to delete it but something he felt inside prompted him to open the new e-mail. With a feeling of *I'm going to really regret this,* he clicked 'Read'.

COWARD? IDIOT? AND I THINK I PICKED UP WEIRDO, BIGOT AND CREEP. WELL, I'VE BEEN CALLED WORSE. I AM SORRY YOU MISTOOK ME FOR SOMEONE WHO WISHES YOU HARM. THAT IS THE FURTHEST THING I WISH YOU. I ASKED YOU IF YOU WANTED TO DIE NOT IN THE SENSE THAT I WANT TO KILL YOU. I ASKED YOU IF YOU WANTED TO DIE BECAUSE I AM GETTING SIGNALS FROM THE WAY YOU ARE THINKING AND FROM THE WAY YOU ARE ACTING THAT LIFE HAS LOST ANY MEANING FOR YOU. AM I READING YOU RIGHT, YOSELEY?

Joey rested his chin on his folded hands. *This is not Rose, although it is the kind of thing Rose would say. But Rose would say it to my face. Anyway, she is too busy these days for some e-mail caper. And this is not Cris. Anyway, Cris probably doesn't have a computer; she hated computers, and hated e-mailing when she had one. So who is it? Who is this Edward R. Murrow person?*

Joey had seen so few people and talked to so few people since he came off the air that there were no apparent suspects. And those he did see and talk to got the 'Joey Robin, you're on the air, go ahead please' Joey and not the lost soul he had become.

His mind shifted. *And what's with the Yoseley bit? Only mother called me Yoseley.*

It was common for emigrant Eastern European Jews to give a Yiddish pet-name based on their children's Hebrew name. Joey's given name was Joseph, the Hebrew derivation of Yoseff, thus the pet name Yoseley. It was a loving endearment. Joey had always felt such comforting love when his mother called him Yoseley. She had passed away thirty years ago.

He looked at the latest e-mail on the screen again, and his jaw dropped. This time, the letter was sent from jpaar@nbc.com!

Joey wished there was some coffee in the house. He thought of going to Starbucks and asking for a double shot but a more compelling urge kept him seated at his computer. Whoever was perpetrating this prank knew him well enough to know — or maybe guess — that in addition to calling him a coward and an idiot in his reply, he had called the writer a weirdo, a bigot and a creep in his thoughts, not in the reply. *Is the room bugged?* he seriously wondered

He clicked 'Reply' and wrote:

WHO ARE YOU? AND HOW DID YOU KNOW THE YOSELEY NAME? AND WHY ARE YOU USING ADDRESSES OF DEAD HEROES OF MINE? AND HOW DID YOU KNOW THE NAMES I CALLED YOU IN MY THOUGHTS?

Joey clicked 'Send'.

"You've got mail."

This time Joey looked at the address box first. It was from merv@yahoo.com. Joey blew out air from his lungs. Then he read the words on the screen:

GOT YOUR ATTENTION, DIDN'T IT? I'LL ASK YOU AGAIN: DO YOU WANT TO DIE? THIS IS SERIOUS BUSINESS, YOSELEY.

Without hesitation, Joey vigorously typed:

NOW LISTEN, WHOEVER YOU ARE... HACKER,

HUCKSTER, STALKER, PRANKSTER, INMATE...
WHATEVER GAME YOU ARE PLAYING, I'D REALLY LIKE
YOU TO STOP. MY LIFE HAS NOT GONE EXACTLY
WONDERFUL LATELY. I GOT CANNED FROM THE WORK
I LOVED. NOW I AM A HAS-BEEN, TOTALLY WASHED UP.
ON TOP OF THAT, JPAAR OR JCHRIST OR WHOEVER
YOU ARE, MY WIFE OF FORTY YEARS LEFT ME. DO I
WANT TO DIE? FELLOW, I'VE BEEN THERE, DONE THAT!
NOW PLEASE GO AWAY!
JOEY... NOT YOSELEY!

He jabbed 'Send' with deliberate force, got up from the computer and started pacing the floor of his small study. *Good Lord, I need this like a hole in the head.*

He had decided to go out for a walk when "You've got mail" bellowed.

Joey looked at the computer and thought of the riff Jimmy Durante used to chant when the old comic faced a decision: *Did you ever get the feeling that you wanted to go, but then you got the feeling that you wanted to stay?*

He leaned over his chair to note the address. *Oh, my God!* This e-mail was from jdurante@mrscalabash.com!

GOTCHA! HOW'S THAT FOR REAL TIME! ABOUT YOUR
REPLY TO MY LAST LETTER, I THINK MY FRIEND
MARLON BRANDO DID THAT BIT BETTER IN "ON THE
WATERFRONT" WHEN HE MUMBLED, "I COULD HAVE
BEEN A CONTENDER... I COULD HAVE BEEN
SOMEBODY." SO WHAT DO YOU FEEL WORSE ABOUT:
NOT BEING SOMEBODY TODAY OR NOT BEING ENOUGH
OF THE SOMEBODY YOU BECAME? THINK ABOUT THAT.
YOUR ANSWER RELATES DIRECTLY TO THE QUESTION
I KEEP ASKING YOU THAT YOU KEEP AVOIDING. WE
NEED TO GET IT ANSWERED BEFORE TOO LONG,

YOSELEY. YOU ARE RUNNING OUT OF TIME. YOU NEED TO REMEMBER YOUR PROMISE BEFORE IT'S TOO LATE. HEY, WHY DON'T YOU DO WHAT YOU ALWAYS HAVE DONE WHEN YOU NEED TO WORK OUT A PROBLEM? AND DRIVE SAFELY. OH, BY THE WAY, I HAVE A FRIEND OF MINE WHO IS A SIGN MAKER. WATCH FOR HIS SIGNS ALONG THE WAY.

Joey reclined in his desk chair, propped his feet on the table, folded his hands on his chest, and looked at the ceiling. *This has got to be Rose or Cris. Only they knew I liked to take a long drive whenever I had a problem to work through. But, then, Marlon Brando isn't, or wasn't a friend of Rose... certainly not of Cris. So who is it? Who is this phantom e-mailer who knows me like a book and can even pick up my thoughts, and insists on calling me Yoseley?* After rejecting the possibility of the e-mailer being Rose or Crystal, he thought, *Mom? E-mailing? She couldn't even use a toaster?* He laughed out loud at his line.

Almost robotically, Joey went to the closet, pulled out his overnight bag, and threw in some clothes, toilet articles, his medicine and his laptop, and out the door to his car he went. And off he drove.

Chapter 4

There were many reasons why Rose Barbelo did not look forward to having lunch with Crystal Robin. She felt uneasy about the encounter even as she stepped out of her limo and signed a few autographs for the bevy of stunned lunch-hour admirers, whose mundane, cubicle-enclosed working lives were, for the moment, upgraded by such an unexpected surprise. Memphis restaurant goers were accustomed to encountering famous people, and when they did, their southern courtesy gene kicked in, allowing the celeb uninterrupted space.

Coming upon Rose Barbelo was something else, however. She had become more than a celebrity. Rose was a meteor amid a galaxy of stars. What CNN did for Atlanta; what Oprah did for Chicago, Rose Barbelo did for Memphis.

She knew the drill. Slowly and steadily press forward toward the door of the restaurant; don't stop moving forward so as not to let any person block your forward movement. Linger just a moment at the door; promise to 'have my staff look into that' to one who asks if you got her letter; 'Oh, yes, of course I remember your mom' to another. And then, as you turn to go in, the stock line, said with a big smile, 'Folks, I'd love to stay here and chat, but Elvis' been spotted inside and I want to go check it out!' On the echo of the laugh, turn and walk in smartly.

Rose had purposely picked Grisanti's on Poplar Street. It was an always trendy in-spot in the fickle world of restaurant fancy. And Rose knew she would be reportedly seen there '…having lunch with the wife of recently fired local radio and television talk show host, Joey Robin. What were those two talking about?' the article in the 'About Town' column of the *Memphis Commercial Appeal* would ask, adding, 'They looked so chummy, like mother and daughter.' Or at least that is what Rose hoped one of the outcomes of the next hour would be.

Atypically, but intentionally, Rose arrived early. She wanted to get herself seated and grounded before Crystal arrived, like a performer or speaker getting the feel of the room, a sense of union with the surroundings so as to feel comfortable. Joey had taught her that, too.

Instead of her usual spot — a back corner table — Rose had her assistant request a center table in the main dining room, its walls adorned with framed, autographed photos of local and national celebrities who have been fed and watered at Grisanti's.

"You sure you don't-a want your usual table, Ms. Barbelo?" asked Ronnie Grisanti, after greeting her at the entrance and escorting her to her table with his arm entwining hers. He was one of the two Grisanti brothers who founded the restaurant and a local celebrity himself. She loved the way he pronounced her last name, the old Italian way, with just a slight touch on the first syllable, followed by a lyrical elongation of the last two, holding the 'bel' in Barbelo, as if the sound were being sung in an ballad by Dean Martin or Al Martino or some other '50s Italian crooner.

"No thanks, Ronnie," Rose said, after brushing a kiss against his burnt umber colored cheek. "The middle of the room is perfect for today. Please give my love to your wonderful wife, Gina, and kiss the two boys for me, my dear friend."

Ronnie Grasanti beamed, bowed and said, "Gracious, my dear," as he unfurled a large white linen napkin across her lap with the flourish of a matador.

Rose sipped her club soda and lemon as her mind and spirit traded varied emotions.

This would be the first time she and Crystal had seen each other since Crystal and Joey separated a month ago. Rose felt an obligation to meet with her. She felt she owed Crystal what ever she could give to her at this time — and she hadn't a clue what that might be.

Appearing not to notice the stares from the diners seated at the neighboring tables, Rose mentally assessed the possible scenario.

She was apprehensive of engaging in a woman-to-woman chat with her mentor's wife. In the twenty years that Rose had been a part of the Robin family, she had never had a one-on-one, heart-to-heart, intimate and secret sharing talk with Crystal. Their relationship had been friendly and convivial but predicated solely on their common dedication to all things Joey. The parallel lines of their triangle were separated, both leading to Joey at the apex.

When Rose's light formed a constellation of its own and blasted out of Joey's orbit, the fickle public's excitement, interest and fascination with the new star in the Universe rendered old tales at the most apocryphal and at the least yesterday's buzz.

The cursor in Rose's mind flitted across the screen, touching scores of what-ifs. She wondered how wounded Crystal was, whether she in some way blamed Rose for what ever caused her and Joey to separate. *What if she says something catty like, 'well, you've always loved him so now you have your chance,'* Rose considered. She shuddered at the thought.

She forced her mind to get back on track. She knew her reasons for the lunch with Crystal were honorable. In their own unique way, both Joey and Crystal had enabled her to become who she became. With their lives disrupted, Rose simply wanted to be a friend to the woman who allowed her husband to be Joey Robin and subsequently Rose Barbelo's patron saint.

Rose's thoughts were suddenly interrupted by the sense that someone was standing beside her. Slowly, turning her head to the side, she locked onto the wide-eyed face of a little black girl; three, maybe four years old; holding up a piece of paper in one hand and a pencil in the other. Everyone in the vicinity of Rose's table watched to see what would happen next.

Breaking out into her patented smile, where her eyes smiled as well as her lips, Rose asked, "What's your name, darlin'?" loud enough for the folks near her table to hear.

The child held up five fingers, as if to say, 'I'm five years old,' provoking a few titters and "isn't she adorable?" from the audience.

Rose took the pencil and paper and wrote, 'To my new friend, with Love and Light, Rose Barbelo' and she handed the autograph and pencil back to the child who ran back to her beaming mother seated at a table across the room.

Treated to a show they would remember for the rest of their lives, the murmurs of warm appreciation from the lunch crowd eventually diminished to the level of the normal dining room din. Rose glanced once again at her watch. Thoughts of being stood-up crossed her mind. *No, Crystal is not the stand-you-up type, unless, of course, she believes I am responsible for...* Banishing the conclusion of her fear from her mind, she replaced the thought with a silent prayer for Crystal's safety. Then she added one for Joey, as well.

Rose began thinking of the last time she had seen Crystal. It was at the Robin's home, shortly before they separated. Rose had dropped by to give them a copy of her new book. Crystal had made an effort to be cheerful; Joey made no such effort. Rose could not help but notice that Crystal had put on some extra pounds; 'loss weight', a guest on her program once called it, meaning weight gained, especially by women, when undergoing a loss of the heart.

With that image of a heavier Crystal in mind, the tall and slender Rose chose a simple, navy blue, pullover, cashmere sweater over a white blouse — which accented her deep olive complexion and silky coal black hair — and conservative Versace charcoal gray slacks to wear this day. She had subdued her make up as well, seeking to subordinate her own appearance in deference to the woman who was now fifteen minutes late for lunch.

"Now this is a switch!" Rose heard the familiar voice say. "You early? Me late? Honey, the world's gone absolutely plum crazy!"

Rose looked up and her eyes widened in surprise. She reared back in her chair to get a better view, panning her eyes up and down the figure standing beside her. Getting up from her seat, Rose shook her head slowly as if to say I can't believe how great you look. With a warm, loving smile, she held out her arms and hugged

Crystal Robin.

"Cris, you look absolutely fabulous!" Rose exclaimed, as the two women took their seats at the table. Crystal beamed. This was the reaction she hoped for since they scheduled lunch.

"Thanks honey. I..."

"No," Rose interrupted. "You look stunning! What have you done to yourself?"

For an instant, Rose wished she hadn't said it so effusively so as not to make Crystal aware of how badly she thought she had looked the last time they saw one another. But, like she had been taught to do when she made an on-air faux pas, she just plowed through it.

"I mean, you've always looked lovely, it's just now, you're...wow! I can't believe it!"

Crystal just sat, smiled and took it all in. She knew folks were watching from the tables nearby, and she felt exhilarated with the whole scene.

Rose was not exaggerating. Crystal Robin had indeed transformed herself. At least twenty pounds lighter, and looking twenty years younger, her sandy blond hair was styled in a short perm, framing her radiant face, emitting the glow of a confident woman. Two buttons of her iron weed colored, Chanel blouse were left unbuttoned, exposing just enough cleavage to make men at a nearby table drop their eyes for just an instant as they perused who Rose Barbelo was having lunch with. The Dior designer jeans and Prada boots expressed a sense of exquisite taste with high fashion. Here was not an older woman trying to look young. Here was a woman who voided the boundaries of age and wrapped it in a package of class.

"Thank you, Rose," Crystal said, gently putting her hand on Rose's. "Coming from you, it is quite a compliment."

Rose put her other hand on Crystal's and said, "Cris, I've seen makeovers before, but yours definitely takes the cake."

"Did I look that bad before?" Crystal asked.

Instead of covering up, Rose played it Rose: real; honest; the quality that had viewers waiting for her next show, her next book, her next whatever. Rose Barbelo had become famous being Rose Barbelo.

Moving in closer and looking into Crystal's eyes, Rose said, "Last time I saw you? Yes. You looked pretty bad. Sorry."

"Well, they were hard times," Crystal said. "Just a few days before you came by, we... Joey and I decided to... you know, part ways."

The server brought Crystal some ice tea and a fresh glass for Rose. He asked if they wanted to hear the specials. They looked at each other and both said no. He looked disappointed, as if he had been denied the chance of a lifetime. Restaurant servers were always auditioning for Rose Barbelo. She and Crystal ordered salads.

After some idle chit-chat, Rose opened with, "So what happened? I talk to Joey, and he sounds like a Rodney Dangerfield impersonator. I see you and you look like you've won a role on *Sex in the City*! There are only two reasons for a woman to transform like you have, Cris: One is an affair with a younger man, and two is an affair with two younger men."

Crystal laughed. "No such luck, Rose. No younger man or younger men. It's kind of hard to explain."

"Try me," Rose said. "I do this for a living."

Crystal drew a deep breath, took a sip of tea, and started.

"Well, the bottom line is that we let life make us forget how much we wanted each other in the beginning. See, when Joey lost his job, when you two were cancelled, Joey lost himself, and I found me. I mean, when the phone stopped ringing, when people stopped calling, for the first time in, gosh, I don't know how many years; I stopped being introduced as Joey Robin's wife, or Mrs. Joey Robin. So I needed to find out who I really was because I never knew. He moaned how fate had denied him the stardom he deserved. And you know what? I felt fate denied me the personhood *I* deserved.

So he goes into a pretty bad depression, and I feel totally isolated. Life took on a familiar pattern of him lamenting his career and me sitting silent. At least he lost something he had. I never had a life except being his wife, and his despair even took that away from me. Eventually, we became strangers... no, worse than strangers, we became polite with one another."

Crystal paused for a sip of tea and a deep breath which she slowly let out with a weighty look on her face as she thought, *Whoever figured I'd be spilling my guts to my husband's closest friend... the person who makes millions listening to these stories?*

She measured Rose's intense lapis eyes and was gratified to see that she listened with as much concentration and concern in the present environment as she afforded a guest on her show. Noting this provided Crystal the assurance to continue.

"And so I left him to discover myself. And you know what, Rose? I like who I found. I found I had opinions that weren't his. I found I had self-esteem that wasn't his. I found that Crystal Robin was a person — not Joey Robin's person — but an on-her-own schedule, choosing what she wants, pleasing her own self, deciding for herself person. Does that make any sense, Rose?"

Like her mentor, Rose's first reaction was to wish Crystal had said what she just said on her show. 'Wish we had that on tape,' was what Joey and Rose always said to each other when they heard something wonderful.

Rose kept that bit of trivia to herself. This moment needed to be all about Crystal. "It makes all kind of sense to me, Cris. Sure, I understand." Actually, Rose would have difficulty comprehending any other way, having lived that way most of her life.

Crystal went on to describe classes she had enrolled in, courses she was thinking of taking, areas of interest she was thinking of pursuing. Rose listened and only added to the dialogue when filler, confirmation, or assurance was needed. She wanted to let Crystal vent; to verbally evacuate whatever emotional baggage she needed to expel. It had only been a month since Crystal and Joey had separated. Rose knew that the alone life was a new experience for them. As a single woman in her forties who devoted her life to her work, Rose was an expert on alone. This was not the time for questions about final decisions either. This was a time to show the wife of the most significant person ever to have entered her life that she cared about her well being just as much as that of her husband.

"You know, Rose," Crystal said. "I'm glad Joey had you in his life. He needed you. He has always needed someone in addition to me, someone that understood and was associated with his work. Sure, there were times I was jealous — angry even. But I got over it. And honestly, there were times I wish I had had someone like a Rose in my life; someone outside of Joey; someone I could spend time with; someone who added another dimension to *my* life, like you and Joey had; just having someone else in my life that I could say things to that I wouldn't or couldn't say to him. I never had such a person, such a friend. So I had his by proxy, sort of like a foster friend. But now, today, well, I am glad we all have you."

Rose dabbed at her eyes with her napkin. She never considered this take when going over the what-ifs before Crystal arrived. She was deeply and genuinely touched by Crystal's words.

"I have a feeling a friend will appear for you, Cris, if that is what you want."

Crystal gave Rose an odd, almost coy smile. "We'll see," she said. Rose picked up on it, but didn't pursue the meaning.

Then, changing her expression from coy to reflective, Crystal said, "Maybe if Michael had lived, things might have been different. Maybe *he* would have been my *you*. Or maybe I would have known who I was and wouldn't have to go torture myself to lose twenty pounds and spend money on some silly over-priced designer clothes after my husband loses his job. Who knows? But anyway, his death definitely changed things."

Rose didn't say anything. She was aware that Crystal and Joey had a son who died. That was *all* she knew. The subject was off limits between her and Joey. He never spoke of it and, instinctively, she never asked. It was not a part of the world she shared with him or one that he cared to share with her.

Crystal paused for a moment and stared ponderingly somewhere out into the space of the dining room. Her attention was drawn to a couple — an older attractive woman and a younger man — who seemed to be observing she and Rose in a peculiar way.

Dismissing the odd distraction with a shake of her head, as if to clear out the absurdity, she looked intently into Rose's eyes and asked, "Have you ever noticed how Joey handles the subject of death?"

Rose thought about the morning's phone conversation and Joey's shtick when she told him who was going to be on her show — the guest who would talk about premonitions of death.

"Yes. He makes light of it; he sort of deflects the subject," Rose replied. "I never really understood where he was coming from."

Crystal's eyes became watery. She reached into her purse for a tissue.

"It started with the death of Michael." Crystal said. "He was adopted, you know."

"No, I didn't know," Rose said. "Joey didn't talk to me about Michael."

Rose noticed Crystal's lips slightly smile; perceiving Crystal was pleased to hear that Joey didn't share all aspects of his life with her.

Crystal said, "Joey called him Micah for short. Only Joey called him Micah and that was only when we were at home." She paused, closed her eyes for an instant, and then softly said, "He… Michael took his own life. He was only thirteen… just thirteen."

Crystal stopped and blew her nose. Rose's eyes became misty as well. She listened as Crystal continued.

"It was totally unexpected… out of the blue. No flags, no signs. Yes there was the usual young teen stuff. I mean, a few fights at school, you know, a few teacher notes. But no real warning… no alarm bells. Pills… he swallowed pills one night. I thought he was in his room watching TV. When I didn't hear any noise I went in. He was… that was it."

Rose found herself saying, "I'm sorry" and wished she had not said anything.

Crystal continued. "At first it devastated Joey. He blamed himself; totally. He was at the studio when it happened. At that time, Joey was building a career — completely caught up in his own ambition. He and Michael always had stress between them. It used to drive me crazy. I'd be put in the middle every time they'd have one of their fights… not physical fights, verbal fights. Can you imagine, Rose, what a battle of words was like between a quick-witted talk show host and a young ten, twelve, thirteen year old kid was like? The poor child didn't have a chance! My heart cried out for him. Michael would try to fight back, but then Joey would pull the authority card, and Michael wouldn't have a chance. He'd run to his room and slam the door and turn up the radio to some acid rock music. Joey would storm off to his study.

"I tried so many times to ask Joey to lighten up on the boy, to try to overlook his hair, his music, his clothes, his whatever it was that annoyed him about the boy. It was no use. I never understood. I don't understand it to this day, what was going on between those two. They were like total strangers with one another. No bond. Nothing.

"Joey's career always came first. Maybe that was it. Maybe Michael wanted more time with his father. Maybe he… I don't know. Maybe it was about me." Crystal paused, then said, "Or maybe it was just that he wanted to die… without a rational reason behind it. I don't know. I just don't know. He didn't leave any note… not a clue. Just the ultimate cry for attention or something, I suppose."

Crystal paused and finished the last of her tea. The hovering waiter rushed over to refill, but Crystal waved him off. Again he looked crushed.

"Joey was never able to place the death of his son in the proper perspective. Whatever he was feeling about Michael's death — guilt, blame, sadness, I don't know — he'd never discuss it with me. He buried it somewhere inside of himself where no one could find it, not even himself I guess.

"The day after Michael's funeral, what does he do? He goes and gets a vasectomy! Can you imagine such... such thinking? He didn't ask me, or tell me. He just went and 'got fixed' as he said when he came home. Can you imagine what message it sent to me... the pain it inflicted on me? But I never mentioned my feelings to Joey. The show must go on. Whatever."

Crystal took a deep breath; her lips formed a brave smile.

"So, in time, he turns anything about death... something he's read, or, these days especially, with so many of our friends dying, when he hears about someone we know passing away, he goes into some shtick. He just cannot handle the subject except to turn it into a joke."

Rose smiled knowingly, and said, "Thanks for helping me understand, Cris. Frankly, it always bothered me... the death shtick he always did, I mean. I used to think, for a man as sensitive as Joey — I mean, part of his gift as an interviewer was the sensitivity he showed with his guests; it was part of his appeal! So how could this man treat death as if he was Billy Crystal in *Mr. Saturday Night*? Now, I understand."

Rose felt a change of subject was needed. "So, how about you two? Is there anything I can do for you, Cris?"

Crystal smiled warmly and said, "This lunch, I mean you reaching out and wanting to get together with me means more than you will ever know, Rose. I am so proud of you and all of your success..."

Rose interrupted saying, "If it wasn't for Joey, I..."

Crystal placed a finger to Rose's lips and said, "I know, I know, but my point is that, to me, your success isn't as great as you are as a person, Rose. I know there is a lot of stuff between the three of us that neither of us — certainly not Joey — will ever understand fully. But I want you to know that I love you."

The two women held each other's gaze for several seconds. It was broken by the low pitched roar coming from Rose's purse.

"The office," she said, resignedly. "Guess I've got to get back." She reached in to check her Blackberry, just to make sure. "Yep," she said. "Wish we could visit longer. Are you sure you're okay, Cris? I mean, you sure look like you are, but if…"

"I'm just fine, honey," Crystal cut her off. We'll see what happens. I'm not rushing into any decisions. I found a nice apartment and don't mind living alone… for now, anyway. I felt it was best if Joey stayed at the house. At least he knows where the bathroom is. He'd go crazy if he had to move somewhere and learn new things."

Rose laughed. "You are so right. He is Mr. Predictability… the furniture stays where it is put."

Crystal joined her in the laugh. Rose noticed Crystal had her teeth whitened.

"So we'll see," Crystal said.

"Do you miss him?" Rose asked.

Crystal was not prepared for the question. She pondered for several seconds, then said, "To miss him means missing who I was with him… with Joey Robin, the celebrity, that is. No, I do not miss that. And I don't miss whatever he became after he came off the air. No, I certainly do not miss that either." Crystal paused a second with a look of discovery, then said, "So I guess that's your answer, Rose. Thanks for asking, really."

Rose stood and began her exit, her arm wrapped around Crystal's. All eyes turned as the smiling star acknowledged the patron's comments with a "Thank you. I appreciate it" and one or two "Bless your hearts." Rose's car and driver were waiting by the curb.

"Can I drop you somewhere, Cris? Won't be a problem."

Crystal waved the offer off, hugged Rose, and said, "No thanks honey. I'm in the lot next door. Now you get going. We both don't have anyone to ball us out for being late anymore."

Rose's driver opened the door of her limo, and Rose slid in the back seat. Impulsively, Crystal rushed over just as the driver was about to shut the door.

"What is it, Cris?" Rose asked.

Crystal hesitated and then remembered Rose needed to go.

"I don't suppose you've heard from him, have you?" Crystal asked sheepishly.

At that point Rose wished she had gotten away without the epilogue. Obviously Joey had not left a message for Crystal as he had for her. Rose considered lying to save Crystal from more hurt. But she knew that she never lied well and always paid the price with a severe bellyache whenever she tried. Plus, the clock was ticking, and she had to get to the studio.

"He left me a voice mail this morning, Cris. He said he was going for a long drive and might be gone a few days."

Crystal faked a slight brave smile, as her eyes grew misty. Backing away from the limo, she said, as if thinking out loud, "I hope he remembered to take his medicine with him."

Chapter 5

Joey Robin's habit of taking a drive when confronted with a problem he needed to sort out began when he was a child and families took Sunday drives in the country; when two dollars filled up a gas tank; back in the day before interstate highways.

But the rides he cherished most were the drives in the summer evenings after supper. They were always spontaneous.

"It's hot," his father would say. "Let's go for a ride." Joey would race his kid brother to the '48 Plymouth Sedan and both boys would dive in the back seat, their mother warning them to be careful as she sat down in the passenger side, and his dad proudly settling in behind the wheel.

One of the reasons Joey loved those drives so well was because his dad didn't seem to be as worried or nervous when he drove as he appeared to be at home. In the car he would joke, tell stories, talk to his mother, and most of all, laugh. Oh, how Joey loved to hear his dad laugh! His dad found humor in human foible, in irony and in hypocrisy drawn either from folks they knew in their small community, or an event in the news. His dad followed current events closely and saw through the phoniness and mendacity of men in public life as if scanning their psychological X-rays.

As they'd drive through winding country roads, or to new neighborhoods to look at modern houses going up in that post World War II building boom, his father would do a monologue with insight doused in humor. His mother would laugh and offer a few ignored comments. Joey would soak up and relish those moments.

That's where Joey picked up the habit. Driving released him; helped him sort things out; allowed his spirit to fly just as driving seemed to do for his dad. That much he knew about himself.

As he set out from Memphis — his life as uncertain as his destination — he mindlessly headed his Honda Accord on to I-40 east toward Nashville. Three and a half hours later, he headed north on I-65.

Amid the congestion of Nashville's outer loop, with semi-tractor trailer trucks and other vehicles gushing past him, their lane-changing horn-blowing havoc colliding with the chaos raging in his mind, Joey thought of Crystal and Rose. Joey suffered in silence when either woman was his passenger. Neither Rose nor Crystal were as discreet.

"You drive like Mr. MaGoo," Rose used to tease. "It is a miracle you're still alive."

Joey's slow pace was in stark contrast to Rose's NASCAR style of driving; assuming NASCAR drivers applied their make-up and talked on a cell phone while speeding along to the next pit stop.

"You might try using turn signals," Crystal would advise, while involuntarily pressing her left foot on an imaginary brake pedal. "That fellow that nearly creamed us wasn't gesturing that you're number one!"

This would usually be followed by Crystal scratching around in her purse for a bottle of Tylenol, gulping two capsules with or without water.

A few miles past Hendersonville, the roaring traffic, as well as the roaring thoughts darting across the canvass of Joey's mind, became less disordered and frenzied and more uncluttered and clear. He had not yet attained that transcendental state of clarity that driving typically afforded him, but he sensed that condition was not far from the present.

Passing Gallatin, he set the cruise control on 65 miles per hour (even though the speed limit was 70), settled into the right lane and turned on the radio. He thought he might pick up Bernie Frank's program. Bernie was to Nashville what Joey had been to Memphis: a local broadcasting institution.

However, instead of Bernie Frank's local show, Joey was surprised — then not surprised — to hear Sean Hannity warn against universal health care.

They got Bernie, too, Joey sadly mused as he jabbed another button. Out poured the unmistakable voice of Rush Limbaugh, warning how the country would suffer with a democrat in the White House.

Joey poked another button. Bill O'Reilly railed against the ACLU.

He stabbed the next button on his radio consol. G. Gordon Liddy was cautioning that the democrats wanted to take away your guns.

The last button was set on NPR, where a guest was telling the moderator "many sociological, biological, and environmental secrets are being unveiled through our research into the sexual behavior of the fruit fly."

As a repeated mantra clears the mind of clutter and opens it to clarity, so the rhythmic drone of the engine released flickering sparks of thoughts darting across the monitor of Joey's mind, like stars in the vast Universe on a clear dark night, seemingly random but with a mysterious sense of order.

Finish your fish, Yoseley. It's brain food.

And for the fifth straight year, the winner of the best talk show host award in Memphis is Joey Robin!

Do you want to die?

I've got an idea I'd like to talk with you about.

What's happened to my life?

Oh Cris, I miss you so much.

You need to pick up your pace, bro. I mean, like, you know, move it along. Like, try to get them mad at somebody. I mean, this ain't the BBC, man. Make 'em mad, dude. I mean, like cardiac arrest mad.

I asked you if you wanted to die, not in the sense that I want to kill you. I asked you if you wanted to die because I am getting signals from the way you are thinking and from the way you are acting that life has lost any meaning for you now. Am I right, Yoseley?

I have a friend who is a sign maker. Watch for his signs along the way.

Joey, come home quick! It's Michael. Oh my God! He's...

Joey blinked his eyes several times, sending a signal to his brain to turn off the monitor in his mind. He didn't like the direction in which his thoughts were heading.

At that moment, he noticed a cluster sign advertising fast food restaurants at the next exit, outside of Bowling Green, Kentucky. Included with McDonalds, Wendy's, Taco Bell, and Cracker Barrel was one advertising Clara Ann's Country Cooking. When he and Crystal were on a trip, they would always try to find a local café that served home cooking. Joey pulled his Honda into a parking space in front of Clara's. His car was one of only two Sedans in a row of pick-up trucks. *Cris would have said 'Our kind of place, honey'*, he thought.

After checking to see if there was any change in the coin return slot, Joey inserted three quarters, pulled out a *USA Today* and walked in to Clara Ann's.

"Welcome to Clara Ann's," chimed a woman's voice from behind the counter. "Grab a seat wherever you can find one. Dixie'll be servin' you in a minute, hon."

At first, Joey considered taking a seat at the counter; instead he decided on the only vacant booth. It was the kind of booth one would expect at Clara Ann's Country Cooking; the kind he had sat in hundreds of times since coming south nearly fifty years ago. The stuffing in the seats had compressed so that even adults needed booster chairs to raise them up to a comfortable height at the table.

Not only were the seats low, the old red vinyl covering had split in several places, providing a sharp hazard if you accidentally rubbed your hand across edge of the slash. The tables had cigarette burn marks and initials scrapped in the Formica.

An out of service, miniature jukebox — the kind where you flipped the pages listing the selections — hung from the wall beside each booth. Joey scanned some of the titles and thought, *They read like the story of my life*: *Oh Lonesome Me* by Don Gibson, *I'm Sorry* by Brenda Lee, Farron Young's *Hello Walls*, *Who's Sorry Now* by Connie Frances, and *Make the World Go Away* by Eddy Arnold.

He had personally known and interviewed each of those artists, which gave him some idea of the box's vintage as well as his own.

Under the silver juke box was an assortment of roadside café required condiments: plastic squeeze bottles of ketchup and mustard, bottles of vinegar with hot green chili peppers, bottles of picante, Tabasco and one labeled "Clara Ann's own kick-ass hot sauce," plus packets of sugar and Sweet & Low were in a small straw basket. Glass salt and peppershakers filled out the ensemble.

"Hi, honey," the plump, smiling woman said. "You eatin' alone?"

Joey looked up and noted 'Dixie' printed on her name tag.

"Yes ma'am. It'll be just me."

"That'll be just fine. No problem," Dixie said, which Joey took to mean, behind the southern smile, *I'll only be getting a dollar, two at the most for a tip.*

"Thank you, ma'am. I'm glad it is no problem."

Dixie's smile slightly evaporated as she tried to figure out if this old guy was simply stupid or just being a jerk.

"Special's chicken 'n dumplins," Dixie said. "How's that sound?"

Joey smiled and thought *Cris would be thrilled*. That was one of her favorite road dishes.

"Do you mind just fixing me some scrambled eggs, wheat toast and black coffee, please?"

"No meat?" Dixie asked, with a slight pout to her lips.

Actually, Joey craved an order of the sausage he saw on a trucker's platter as he walked in. But he reckoned that his 10 milligrams of Lipitor would probably lose out in the battle raging in his arteries with the saturated fat of the sausage, even if his arteries were aided by his Omega 3 fish oil capsule, resulting in an elevation of his cholesterol. Plus, his Liprinosil would be no match against the fatty sausage either, resulting in his blood pressure zooming. Such was the mind of Joey Robin when it came to each and every decision outside of how to handle a talk show.

"Nope, no meat," he said with a smile of quiet confidence.

Dixie turned and walked behind the counter, to the register, to program in Joey's order. A rather large, middle-age woman with rosy cheeks, wearing an unusually clean, crisp white uniform — like that of a hospital head nurse — and holding a spatula, came out from the kitchen and whispered something in Dixie's ear. Joey opened his newspaper and immediately turned to the Lifestyles section and read headline:

"The Factor with Bill O'Reilly Tops Cable News Ratings."

Why? Joey asked himself, and then quickly turned to the sports section. He noticed that Dixie and the other woman were looking at him in a kind of goofy way. Noticing that he noticed them, the older woman shook her finger at him as if to say *I know you* and yelled, "Hey, didn't you used to be someone?"

I'm two for two this morning, Joey thought. *First O'Reilly and now this. Am I supposed to yell back who I am…was*? he wondered.

Fortunately, that issue was solved when Dixie ambled over holding a thick cup of hot steaming coffee and set it down in front of him.

"Clara Ann — that's her over there," she pointed. "Says she used to have a place in Nashville and recognized you. Were you someone?"

It was as if he had been stabbed again in the same wound. But instead of showing his hurt, Joey smiled and said, "Yes, I used to be Bill Cosby."

By this time, all the truckers at the counter had turned around and were discussing between themselves whether the gray haired, older guy in the booth is, was, or had been somebody and who he is, was, or might have been.

With a straight face, Dixie turned toward the register and yelled, "He said he used to be Bill Cosby." The place broke into wild laughter. A few truckers raised their coffee mugs and ice tea glasses to Joey in tribute to a beautiful put-on. Dixie looked puzzled. The older woman returned to the kitchen and Clara Ann's

Country Cooking returned to normal.

Joey finished his breakfast, left two dollars on the table, and walked out the door to his car, accompanied by a leer from Dixie, who, by this time, had been told she had been had. He filled his tank with gas, got back behind the wheel, and continued heading north.

After a few miles he decided to try the radio again and lucked out on his first try. An oldies station; real oldies; big bands and crooners from the '40s and '50s; his kind of stuff. *Love Somebody* with Buddy Clark and Doris Day was just ending. Then a dulcet voice announcer introduced the next record. Joey imagined him holding one hand to his ear like Don Pardo used to parody on *Laugh In*. "Now here's Nancy Wilson with her inimitable rendition of the classic bistro ballad written by the great jazz composer, Matt Dennis. Here's *Guess Who I Saw Today?*"

Joey recalled when Nancy Wilson appeared on his show. Interview moments with some guests are easily forgotten. Some linger forever. *Such class* he remembered. *Where has it gone?*

Joey's mind wrapped around Nancy Wilson's coy, sophisticated reading of the lyric about a lady who stops into a cocktail lounge before going home and sees the man, she assumed was in love with her, amorously having a drink with another woman. The song ends, 'Guess who I saw today? I saw you!'

For some reason, or combination of reasons, Joey was overcome with melancholy. Melancholy was not a newly acquired companion. It was an old friend from his youth who appeared out of nowhere, even when things in his life were going well. He flipped off the radio and drove on with his mind and his emotions engulfed in a cloudy collage of memories. *My God, I've done so much,* he thought. *I tried so hard to be good at it. I was good at it. For what? What was it all for?*

By late afternoon, he began to feel tired. He had never intended to drive this far, but he had never intended not to either. He decided to stop and spend the night at a Residence Inn — the one where he and Crystal used to stay when they'd drive up to Louisville for the races.

Joey loved going to the races. It wasn't about having a good time — Joey didn't know how to have a good time outside of being on the air. Going to the races was one of several vicarious connections with stardom that he employed during his life. When he was growing up and dreaming of success, he'd see movie newsreels and magazine photographs of Jimmy Durante, Bob Hope, Bing Crosby and other celebrities at Santa Anita race track in Hollywood. *Imagine having the time and money to do that!... and in the daytime!* he'd dream. *That's how a star lives.* Years later, going to the races was less about wagering and more about self-valuation.

He checked in and slowly drove around the complex to find his room on the back side. True to his habit, he scanned the license plates of the cars. "I just like to see how far away some folks have traveled," he once told Crystal. But she knew he was hoping to see a Shelby County, Tennessee plate so someone might spot him and marvel 'Say, aren't you Joey Robin! I love your show!'

And sure enough there was a 2006, dark blue, Mazda Tribute with a Tennessee license plate beginning with a 3 for Shelby County — Memphis' county. Spotting it made Joey do a double-take and slam on his brakes. He got out of his Honda and peered in the driver's side window just to make sure. There was no doubt. He felt blood rushing to his head. The back of his neck was suddenly wet from perspiration.

It was Crystal's car!

Tires screeching, Joey swirled his car around the parking lot and headed back to the office and, leaving the motor running, raced up to the front desk. The clerk was checking in a Hispanic family with five children, each holding something to eat. The woman was holding an infant in her arms. There seemed to be some issue between the man and the desk clerk regarding the accommodations. Joey paced back and forth, picked up a newspaper, laid it down then leafed through an *Around the City* magazine and threw it on to a lobby chair. *Begin and Sadat at Camp David didn't take this long,* he thought.

After what seemed to Joey like an hour, the man said something rather loud in Spanish and motioned to his wife and children to follow him to the car. They piled in and drove off. The desk clerk reached under the counter for a bottle of water, wiped his brow with his handkerchief, blew out some air, blinked his eyes a few times, and with a look of *why did I ever enroll in hotel management* looked at Joey and said, "Can I help you, Mr…"

"Where's my wife?" Joey interrupted. His voice was Eastwood — low pitched but intense.

"I beg your pardon," the clerk said, his eyes saying, *I don't believe this day.*

"My wife; you have her. Where is she?" Joey bored in, more De Niro now.

"Sir, please calm down and tell me what the problem is."

Joey drew in a deep breath. He felt his heart racing. This was not good. He was glad he didn't order the sausage. He eyed the desk clerk's name tag. Homer, it said in black letters. Gathering his thoughts and emotions, he said, calmly, "I'm sorry, Homer. It's just that… you see that car out… no, you can't, it's on the other side. Anyway, Homer, it's my wife's car, and we… that is, I didn't expect to see it… *her* here. So I was wondering if you could kindly tell me if she checked in and, if she has, what room she is in, and whether she is… you know, whether she is…"

"Alone?" Homer offered sympathetically.

Joey nodded. "Yes. Alone," he said, sotto voce.

"Sir, you…"

"Call me Joey," Joey offered, trying his best to be civil.

"Thank you, Mr… a… Joey. But you see; our policy is to not identify the names of our guests nor to…"

Joey broke in holding up one finger like a prosecuting attorney to a witness. "Ah ha! So she *is* here. You just won't confirm it. Do you deny that?" His voice rose. He was now Pacino.

Homer wiped his brow with his handkerchief. It needed it. He started to reply but just then a car screeched to a halt in front of the lobby and out poured the Hispanic man, his five children — each with an ice cream cone — and his wife holding the infant, plus a very large Hispanic man, his bare arms covered with slithering, black serpent tattoos, his black hair stretched in a pony tail, and sporting a large, black mustache, the points of which curled down to his jaw bone. He looked like seething fury.

Homer saw them and his, suddenly colorless, face took on the look of stark fear. He grabbed the telephone and punched three keys. A door off the lobby opened and a huge African American man appeared and lumbered up to the desk.

"I'll handle it," he said in a low, gravely voice.

Joey had had enough. He had driven over two hundred miles for the purpose of sorting out his toppled life, only to spot his wife's car in the parking lot of a motel where he and she had wonderful times, not knowing if she was alone or with someone else. And the last thing he needed was to be in the middle of an ethnic race war. So he eased out the door, got into his car, and slowly drove back to his, and his wife's, side of the motel.

When he reached the space where he had spotted her car, it was gone! *Had she seen him?* he wondered. *How must she have felt if she did? Could it be that, like him, she had driven unconsciously to a familiar place to sort things out?* He played with the possibility in his head. *No, that wasn't Cris' thing,* he concluded. *Then if she didn't come here by herself, could it be that she... that she was with someone? Another man? Cris? With another man? Impossible. But then, who'd ever believe she would walk out on me in the first place? Oh, honey,* Joey wept. *Oh honey.*

Joey opened the door to his room, threw his overnight bag on the stand, and plopped down on the bed. His mind raced. He considered hundreds of possibilities. Oddly, he wondered if Homer had survived the race war in the lobby.

Chapter 6

It was nearly seven in the evening when he suddenly woke up to the sound of a car door slamming. Bolting out of bed, Joey raced to the window and pulled the drawstring. There she was, his wife, standing close to another man. He was holding both her hands, and she looked so happy. They were talking. He had just made her laugh. She threw her head back laughing; as Joey loved to see her do when he used to make her laugh.

In spite of his shock, Joey marveled at how good she looked. *Apparently she hasn't spotted my car,* he thought. *By the way she's looking at him she's not seeing anything else. Who is this guy?* Joey pondered.

Joey considered his options: A - Go back to bed. B - Stay by the window and keep watching to see where they go. C - Confront them. Without much deliberation, he opted for C. It was more theatrical, more showbiz; it played better.

He opened the door and stood in the doorway, knowing the backlight from his room would create a dramatic silhouette. The staging was perfect. For some idiosyncratic reason, down deep, Joey was enjoying the moment, one that would crush the heart of most other people in a similar situation. *Always find a way to do a good show no matter the circumstances.* Such was Joey Robin's inner compass. He stood there until, finally, Crystal looked his way.

She gasped, throwing both hands to her mouth as her wide eyes fixed on him in disbelief.

"Joey?" she half screamed, half asked. Her friend just stood, seemingly unfazed. Joey noticed that the man didn't appear to behave as if he'd been caught doing anything wrong.

"Hi Cris," Joey acknowledged calmly, having learned long ago to never lose control of a show regardless of inner turmoil.

She ran over to him and started to give him a hug, but then she hesitated and drew herself away. Joey knew she was nonplussed, while continuing to observe how cool her friend seemed.

"What in the world are you doing here?" Crystal asked.

"Waiting for post time," Joey replied with a smile.

Crystal's eyes and lips formed an evocative smile. "Really, Joey. What brings you here, of all places?"

Joey wanted to answer 'my Honda Accord' but figured they needed to get down to who's doing what with whom and forego the shtick.

"You know me, Cris. I love a drive. This one just got longer than most. It's not like I don't have the time these days."

Joey's sullen commentary, oozing with self-pity, jolted Crystal back to their current status, and reminded her why she and the man in the doorway had separated after so many years together.

At that moment, sensing the right time to make an entrance, Crystal's friend walked over to her. He was tall and lanky, but his body ambled with the grace and ease of motion of a yoga instructor. His hair was wavy blond, nearly down to his shoulders. He was wearing designer jeans and sandals on his feet. His shirt was a white linen brocade with Native American symbols embroidered around the border of the collar and full long sleeves, which he rolled up twice, exposing tan muscular forearms. The right one had a tattoo of the sun with small astrological symbols around it. He wore a silver necklace with a turquoise amulet of a wolf, a large turquoise ring on his right hand, and a bracelet of turquoise beads on his left hand. He had the poise of a man comfortable in his own sun-tanned hide.

To Joey, the man looked like an aging rock star; a sixty-something trying to look forty. But it was his eyes that Joey honed in on. They were like blue ice, almost translucent, magnetic. They locked in on Joey as if the man was deciphering a code. After several seconds, the man released his gaze, and returned his focus toward Crystal with a tender ambiance.

Who is this Mr. Malibu? Joey joked to himself. *What has gotten into Crystal?* Then he chided himself for the double entendre.

"Joey," Crystal said, taking the man by his arm. "I want you to meet David Malak." The name went right by Joey. "David, this is my husband, Joey Robin."

The two men shook hands and exchanged some 'nice to meet you' type comments to one another. Always poised on his show, never thrown by anything unexpected, Joey became aware of feeling a bit flummoxed — a peculiar, novel sensation

Crystal broke the awkward mood. "Boys, this lady is feeling a little chilly. How about we all go to the restaurant next door and warm ourselves up with something? David, when does your plane leave?"

"I'm cool. The red eye special doesn't depart until eleven. As long as I get the rental back by ten, I'll have plenty time to check in. Will you be staying over or are you driving back?"

Crystal glanced at her husband and then said, without reservation, "I'll be driving back home after you leave,"

Joey tried his best to process the information. *Red eye means he's from the west coast. Does the rental mean he flew here to meet Cris, or was he here doing something? How does she know him? What is this guy doing in my wife's life? Crystal made it a point of letting me know she's not staying. What does that mean about how she feels about us? And the way she looks! I can't believe it! She looks incredible! Radiant! One month away from me and she loses twenty pounds and twenty years! Is it for him? Is it being away from me? My God, what in the world is going on here? What's happening to my life?*

They seated themselves at a table and ordered drinks. Crystal ordered a white wine. Malak said, "I'll have the same."

I could have placed a bet on that, Joey thought as he faked a smile and ordered a George Dickle on the rocks. *They seem so relaxed, so natural*. Joey felt sweaty and on-edge.

"So," Joey began, trying his best to appear nonchalant. "How'd you two meet?"

Crystal looked at Malak and he returned her glance. They both smiled, which oozed more perspiration to the back of Joey's neck.

"Through Rose, actually," Crystal began. "David was a guest on her show and said some things which, you know, at the time, just seemed to speak to me at a level that is hard for me to describe. So I called Rose's office and asked if there was any way I could get in touch with him. Rose had them give me his number, which I called and... we... became friends. Right David?" Crystal looked at him for assurance.

It was then Malak's name registered with Joey as the person Rose told him would be her guest on her show that day. *The premonitions of death man*, Joey mentally reminded himself.

Malak smiled reassuringly at Crystal, drew in a breath, then looked squarely at Joey, and said, "When two people share many years of experiences, they often assume that their reaction to transitions will be almost identical; that change will affect both of them the same. Sometimes it does. Most often — especially in these more liberal, less orthodox times — it does not."

Joey listened intently without indicating approval or agreement. He was back on the air.

"So when you lost your show," Malak said straightforwardly. "When the transition occurred in your career, so to speak, the effect it had on you and the effect it had on Crystal were not the same. When she heard me talk about change on *Pathways,* she reached out to me for counsel. It happens all the time."

Joey wanted to ask what was the arrangement between he and his wife for his counsel, but he decided not to ask that. Instead, he settled for, "So exactly what is it that you do, David?"

Again, he and Crystal exchanged looks that said 'which one of us should tell him'?

"David is an intuitive healer and hypnotherapist, Joey," Crystal said. "He does past life regressions and he..." she glanced at Malak for assistance and he took it from there.

"I take people to the source of their pain," Malak said. "Years ago, I discovered that much of our pain, our fear, or problems lie in an experience we had in a past life that we've brought forward to

43

the present. I take people back to that place, help them confront it and help them move past it." He paused, smiled and added, "Runs in the family, I suppose. My dad was a physician, the old style. Did everything from deliver babies to setting broken bones. He tried to heal the body. I work on another part of the person."

This concept was not foreign to Joey. Over the course of his broadcasting career, he had interviewed hundreds of psychics, mediums, channelers and other New Age spokespersons and authors, most of who talked about reincarnation. He liked having these folks on his show. They always got the phones ringing and the ratings rising.

But his enthusiasm for the topic ended there. Personally, he thought the whole New Age field was populated by a combination of kooks and con artists. When she worked with Joey, Rose would beg him to treat them with the same respect he treated some politician or entertainer. "I'm telling you, Joey, this is important stuff," she would plead. "People need to hear what they have to say. For goodness sake, stop treating them as if they had two heads!" Joey would hum the theme to the *Twilight Zone*, which would make her furious.

After Joey was fired, Rose distilled, refined and filtered the metaphysical and paranormal field, weeding out the kooks and con artists and, on that rock, she built her show: *Pathways with Rose Barbelo*. It offered new ways — alternative ways — to think about one's life and one's death. Much of its success was due to the audience sensing Rose's receptivity and sensitivity; that she walked the walk and talked the talk.

Crystal was aware of Joey's view on the subject. She had often wanted to discuss experiences that she had encountered; intuitions and feelings that were beyond the norm, especially after Michael died. But when she broached those subjects with him, Joey would roll his eyes, and she would feel hurt and terrible alone. Perhaps sharing her feelings with Rose had crossed her mind several times. While having a kindred spirit such as Rose Barbelo to share her inner feelings with would have been a comfort, Crystal knew that Rose was Joey's province. And she had learned early on not to cross over into 'Joey land'. And so she contained and sheltered the promptings of her soul in a secret place deep within her heart — until she met David Malak.

Crystal said, "Joey, you must be exhausted. Why don't you turn in? David, you need to get the car back to the airport and get checked in for your flight."

David glanced at his watch and nodded. Joey noticed the turquoise band.

Joey leaned closer to Crystal and asked, "And what about you, Cris? Will you be staying over?"

A shrewd smile crossed his wife's lips. "I'm heading back home," she said resolutely.

Home is with me, Joey thought. Instead, he said, "Cris, it's getting late. Why don't you stay here at the hotel? I hate to see you drive back this late. Look, I'll get you a room for yourself, whatever. Just stay. Don't go."

For an instant, Crystal wavered. He looked so pitiful to her. He seemed to her to have aged five years in the month they'd been separated. She wondered if he had been eating well. She looked intently at his face as if her answer lay behind his eyes. His eyebrows were slightly lifted as if to say 'please'. He waited for her answer, like a puppy waiting for his treat.

Finally, with a tone of 'case closed', Crystal said, "No, Joey. You stay. I'm heading back. I'll be fine. Don't worry."

She stood, gathered her purse, and said, "I need to stop at the restroom. I'll meet you boys in the front."

Joey followed his wife's graceful movement, as she walked, with his eyes. "God, she looks good," he said to himself.

With passive but keen observation, like an audience at a chess match, Malak had watched the scene played out between Crystal and Joey. After Joey paid the check, he pushed his lanky frame away from the table and said, "California, here I come."

Joey looked at him and faked a smile. *Is that the best exit line you can come up with*? Joey thought.

To his utter amazement, Malak took Joey's arm, smiled at him, and said, "I know it's corny, but it is the best line I can come up with. Just needed something to break the ice, Joey. I'm usually more original than that. Guess I'm tired."

Joey's face turned red. *Had Mr. Malibu read my mind*? he wondered. *Or was it just a coincidence*? Actual or coincidence, Joey was slightly rattled. "What a day!" he said to himself.

Crystal was waiting as the two men walked toward her. She leaned in to kiss Joey on the cheek.

"Sure I can't convince you to…"

"No, Joey. Don't make things… I'm driving back."

She turned to Malak. "David, I'll walk you to your car."

"Cool," Malak responded. Joey rolled his eyes with his head turned away from Malak, then wondered if Malak had somehow picked that up, too.

Malak said, "Joey, it was good to meet you. The vibes I'm picking up are of a confused and, please don't be offended by this, frightened man. Well, the confusion I can understand — running into Crystal and me here and all. You'll probably disagree with what I'm going to tell you, but the truth is that nothing happens by accident. The three of us were supposed to meet here, at this place, at this time. Let me put your mind at rest about that. Your wife needed me to help with some issues in her life. That's what this is all about. Again, nothing by accident, my friend."

Malak turned to Crystal. "Crystal, have you ever tried to reach out to any other person on Joey's show or Rose's show or anyone else's?"

"Not that I can recall," Crystal said, a bit confused by the question.

"See what I mean?" Malak said, turning back to Joey. "Nothing by accident. She needed someone to guide her through some things; I turn up on Rose's show; Crystal has a link with Rose, through you and she gets a hold of me; I'm scheduled to do a seminar in Louisville and I agree to meet her here. Then, there's you; you need to take a drive to air out some problems. Where do you unconsciously drive? To the very spot your wife and I are meeting!"

Joey thought of trying to do Bogart saying, 'Of all the gin joints in all the world, you have to walk into mine,' but he dismissed the urge and just listened to the rest of what Malak had to say.

"I mean, come on, Joey," Malak said, holding his arms out. "Even a skeptic like you would have to say all this is too coincidental."

Joey did a thing with his head, as if to say 'maybe' but didn't say anything.

Malak looked at his watch. "Wow! I gotta split. But I just have to say this…"

Malak moved his body only inches away from Joey's. Putting his hands on Joey's shoulders, he peered into his eyes and said, "You are going through the most spiritually profound period of your present life. I know you think your life was important when you were doing your show. You're wrong. It's now! You are at a critical crossroad. The Universe is sending you signs and signals, my friend. Pay attention. Listen. Learn. You are protected beyond your wildest imagination. I sense there has already been some contact made."

The e-mails! Joey immediately thought. *It's him! Sure, it all makes sense. Cris told him what I'm going through, even about some of my heroes: Arthur Godfrey, Jack Paar, Edward R. Murrow. But how did he pull of the Jimmy Durante bit? I thought of Durante and immediately he sends me an e-mail. But then, he picked up my 'California here I come' thought. Or did he?*

"If not, you *will* be contacted — perhaps in ways you never dreamed possible. You may have thought your life ended when you lost your show. My friend, it is only beginning — unless you want it to end. It's really up to you. Your protectors are here, all

47

around you, waiting for your decision. Either way you decide, whatever you want to do, they'll take good care of you. My spirit guide is telling me now that you completely missed a sign today. Did you?

Joey thought, *Should I tell him I'm on to his Karnack bit. Do I go into my act?*

"Well," Joey began, creasing his brow as if in deep reflection, "There was one sign I missed that I remember... it was a sign pointing to a turn off to a rest area when I really had to take a leak," he said in mock seriousness.

Crystal looked at Joey with disgust, and said in a low voice, "See David? See what I told you? It's all a game to him, a show. He refuses to get real."

Malak loosened his grip on Joey's shoulders, stepped back, shook his head and took his car keys out of his jeans.

Crystal took a few steps close to Joey and said, "This man," pointing to Malak. "Is giving you pearls. Pearls! And you are giving him Don Rickles! He's trying to help you, Joey!" Tears streamed down her cheeks.

Joey wanted to say 'this man is sending me e-mails from dead talk show hosts, thanks to you, dear'.

Instead, Joey stood and watched Malak and his wife walk slowly to Malak's car. He watched his wife kiss Malak goodbye on the cheek. As Malak drove off, Joey turned and walked toward his room. Seconds later, he heard his wife's car drive away. He unlocked his door; the light from the parking lot illuminated the interior enough for him to take the few steps toward the bed, where he collapsed into a deep sleep.

Chapter 7

After a few bars of *Seems Like Old Times*, the music faded and a mellifluous voice announced, "It's Arthur Godfrey Time, today featuring the McGuire Sisters, Julius La Rosa, special guest Patsy Cline, and Archie Bleyer and his orchestra. I'm Tony Marvin, and now, here's the ol' boy himself — Arthur Godfrey!" (Applause! Applause! Applause!) A few strums on the ukulele, and the deep, nasally resonant voice sings 'In the blue ridge mountains of Virginia, 'neath the trail of the lonesome pine'. He kept strumming as he uttered his trademark greeting with a lilt in his unmistakable voice: "How-warr-ya? How-warr-ya? How-warr-ya? This is Arthur Godfrey and welcome to our show."

That's the way eleven-year-old Joseph Rabinowitz heard it in his head, as he mimicked the most popular radio personality of the '50's; the man the little boy dreamed of becoming. Today his routine was the same as it had been every day since Godfrey's voice on the radio touched something inside his own soul. He took his seat at the dining room table and set Julius La Rosa and the McGuire Sisters — represented by the salt shaker and the pepper shaker — in front of Archie Bleyer's orchestra — represented by the fruit bowl. Off to the other side was Tony Marvin —played by a candlestick holder. Joseph — holding a ukulele his mother bought for him — was Godfrey. His mike was a small silver vase.

The day that Godfrey fired Julius La Rosa on the air — an incident that rocked the country back in the day — Joseph got rid of the saltshaker.

"Yoseley?" his momma asked that day while setting the table for supper. "Have you seen the salt shaker?"

Joseph looked up at his momma, and said, "I fired it!"

So went the childhood fantasy life of Joseph Rabinowitz. There would be other heroes and role models, but Godfrey, and the Universe of possibilities he instilled in little Joseph Rabinowitz, was his first and most profound influence.

Joseph did more than simply admire his heroes; he studied them — their habits, their lives, their tendencies, and their craft — as assiduously as an astronomer peering through a powerful telescope studies a distant new star. However, to Joseph, his stars were not distant and remote; they were each an aspect of his self. They were the self he grew to know and understand and feel comfortable with. By absorbing the light of his stars, he lost his own.

Joey woke several times during the night, once to get out of his clothes, another time to use the bathroom. Each time he'd return to the bed and fall, once again, into a deep sleep and a dreamed return to his childhood days, as Arthur Godfrey, sixty years ago.

The knock on the door startled him.

"Maid service!"

"Go away!"

Joey heard the cart roll down the concrete walk to the next room. He yawned, stretched, and rolled out of the bed.

"Coffee, I need coffee," he said to himself, as he mindlessly walked from the bedroom to the living room portion of his Residence Inn suite. The first thing he spotted was the percolator on the small kitchen counter. Moving toward it, his head did a double-take. His eyes opened wide. He felt his heart race. He starred in disbelief.

Arranged on the small round dining table was a fruit bowl with a salt and pepper shaker in front, a candle stick holder to the other side; on the edge of the table in front of the chair was a small silver vase. And resting on the chair was a ukulele!

How could this be? What is going on here? Am I going mad? Joey thought. But it was real; it was all there, just as he used to set it up in his parents' home when he was a young child, when he dreamed of becoming what he became.

Joey looked away from the table and took a deep breath. "Maybe it will disappear if I look away, if I ignore it for a few moments," he said to himself.

He fixed a pot of coffee, taking precautions not to look at the table. When it finished perking, he poured himself a cup, and slowly peeked over at the table. The mock set of *The Godfrey Show* was gone! So was the uke'. Just a tiny wicker basket with packages of fake cream, fake sugar, some plastic stirrers plus a few other items with a Residence Inn label sat coldly in the middle. Joey blinked; still gone.

He sat and drank his coffee. His pulse had returned to normal. In fact, he had an almost serene feeling throughout his body. Seeing the exact replica of his childhood fantasy world brought back a feeling within him that he had not felt for many years. He could feel how much he wanted to become what he became. He could feel the dream he used to have, the dream he followed. He could feel the indescribable wave of exultation when one's reality is the one once visualized. A feeling of bliss overtook Joseph Rabinowitz aged seventy. He felt the bliss of childhood anticipation.

"If David Malak pulled this one off, he's far better than I thought," Joey said to himself. "Could have he somehow done it? Or do I have the wrong suspect?"

Still maintaining the odd sense of euphoria, Joey walked into the bedroom with his second cup of coffee, thinking he'd lie down for a while before he headed back to Memphis.

His euphoria vanished faster than the speed of sound when he glanced at the cover of *TV Guide*. The headline said, 'This Man Has Really Beat the Odds! Twenty Five Years and Still Number One!'

Underneath the headline, was the photograph of the smiling face of his brother.

Chapter 8

Joseph and his younger brother Benjamin were the sons of Jacob and Rachel Rabinowitz. Jacob Rabinowitz had immigrated to America from Lithuania in 1913, at the age of seventeen, with twenty-two dollars to his name. He lived with his older brother, Morris, in Johnstown, Pennsylvania. Morris charged his brother twenty dollars a month for room and board. To pay for his upkeep, Jacob peddled rags and novelty items around the small neighboring towns. While attending night school to learn to speak and write English, so he could become an American citizen, he met, courted and fell in love with Rachel Lowenstein, who had immigrated to America three years later from Poland.

A daughter, Iris, was their first-born child. When she was five, she contracted diphtheria and died. Joseph was born three years later and Benjamin came along four years after Joseph. After Benjamin was born, Jacob and Rachel slept in separate bedrooms, the most effective birth control method prior to the pill.

Benjamin worshiped his older brother, sticking to him like glue wherever Joseph went, relying on him for answers, looking up to him as a god who could take care of practically anything. Their mother enabled the brotherly bond by encouraging, no, *demanding* that "Joseph, take Benny with you," or "Joseph, stay with Benny while we're gone."

By the time Benjamin came along, her husband, Jacob, was too worn out from trying to make a living for his family to do the dad things with his youngest and very energetic son. So he also facili-tated the attachment between the brothers Rabinowitz: "Joseph, here's fifty cents, take Benjamin to the movies." Or, "Joseph, help Benjamin with his Hebrew studies." Or, "Joseph, go out and play ball with Benjamin."

Joseph accepted the responsibility for, what amounted to, practi-cally raising his younger brother without the slightest resentment or resistance. In some peculiar way inside of himself, it gave young Joseph Rabinowitz a feeling of being needed as a role model. And that feeling pleased him. Being looked up to satisfied something inside the youngster's spirit.

But while Joey would devour radio and television magazines for stories about the media, and honor broadcasting's customs, traditions and craft, and esteem its pioneers and legends, his younger brother was totally devoid of any such interest or sense of value of Joey's Universe.

As Joey Robin stared at the cover of *TV Guide*, with his brother's color photo staring at him from the top of the television set in his motel room, Joey's thoughts traveled back to a warm summer day in 1949. His father had given Joey twenty dollars to go to the ball game. "And take Benjamin with you." The Pittsburgh Pirates were playing the Brooklyn Dodgers at Forbes Field in Pittsburgh.

"Wow, Dad!" Joseph exclaimed. "Thanks!"

"Yeah, yeah," Jacob Rabinowitz muttered. "I know how much time you boys waste listening to the ball games on the radio. So I figured maybe you could go see a game and get such foolishness out of your system. I'd take you myself, but, in the first place, I don't know a thing about baseball and, in the second place, I'm tired. So go! Enjoy! And come back safe. Oh, and Joseph, make sure you go into the bathroom with Benjamin when he has to go; and remember to put paper on the seat like I showed you. Understand?"

Their father was right. Joseph did spend most summer days listening to the broadcasts of the Pirates games. He collected the baseball cards of all the players and kept them in a King Edward cigar box. As each player came up to bat, he would read out loud the blurb about the player on the back of the card. Each card came in a colorful wrapping and inside, along with the card, was a pink sheet of Fleer's Double Bubblegum. Chewing the gum, blowing and popping bubbles, and drinking A&W root beer were all a part of the hot summer ritual for Joseph Rabinowitz, his kid brother alongside him on the front porch.

But for Joseph, the ball game was only half the excitement. The other half was the announcer: Rosie Rosewell and his color commentator, Bob Prince. Rosie Rosewell was a god to Joseph. He was one of those radio play-by-play announcers who made the game better than it was because of his style, personality, and showmanship. Rosie was an artist who painted pictures through his microphone. When Ralph Kiner or Hank Greenberg hit a homerun, it wasn't just a homerun to the radio audience. Rosie would exclaim, "Open the door, Aunt Minnie... She's comin' home!" Or, when Rip Sewell struck out an opposing player, it was more than a strike out to the Pirate radio audience. Rosie Rosewell would loudly intone, "And it's the old dipsy-doodle!"

By the time he was pretending to be Godfrey at the dining room table, Joseph had picked up on the nuances in Rosewell's performance. How he kidded when necessary, moaned when required, and hollered when demanded.

The twenty dollars paid for two round-trip tickets on the Greyhound Bus for Joseph and Benjamin and two bleacher seats at the game. The two youngsters arrived forty-five minutes early, during batting practice. As soon as Joseph found their seats, he looked up and around. Finally, high above the stadium, he spotted what he was looking for — a booth with two men sitting behind microphones. Joseph gulped.

"It's Rosie Rosewell," Joseph blurted. He was awestruck. Even from his low vantage point, he could make out the engineer behind the two announcers, the equipment, someone else holding some papers. He ardently wanted to be up there with them.

Joseph bought a bag of peanuts for he and his kid brother and they eagerly opened the brown bag and started cracking open the nuts.

"What's that?" Benjamin asked, pointing to a box, a level below the announcer's booth.

Joseph looked to where his brother was pointing and answered, "That's Mr. Galbreath's box. He's the man that owns the team. He gets all the money."

Benjamin and Joseph ate a few more nuts. Then Benjamin asked, "What's that?"

Joseph looked down. "That's the dugout. That's where the players sit until they come up to bat or go out on the field."

A few more nuts, then, "What's that?"

Joseph knew exactly where his kid brother was pointing because he hadn't taken his eyes off the site since taking his seat.

"That's where Rosie Rosewell and Bob Prince announce the game. It's called the broadcasting booth. It's part of what they call the press box. And that's what I'm going to be doing some day! I just know it! You're going to do that, too. Right, Benny?"

Benjamin's small head slowly moved from one side to the other, meaning no. Then he giggled, jumped up and down in his seat and pointed his small finger to the owner's box. "That's where Benny's going to be!"

Joey remembered the incident as if it had been yesterday. He looked again at his brother's face on the cover of *TV Guide*. *Not bad, Benny*, he thought. *Probably the best eye job I've ever seen and you'd never notice the chin tuck unless you saw Dad's and mine and realized what yours would have been without it. The nose job? Well, I always thought it was too straight. But hey, it's worked for you. Got you where you are today, brother.*

Joey sat down in the easy chair that's supposed to make you feel at home in a motel, and laid his head back on the cushy backrest. There he sat in silence, his tired eyes closed; the embodiment of the words of the poet, Dante Gabriel Rossetti: "Look in my face; my name is Might-have-been. I am also called No-more, Too-late, Farewell."

In his emotional anguish, he thought, *Twenty-five years and still going strong, it says on the cover. Me? Seventy and going nowhere. What good does it do to perfect your craft, to love what you do, to honor a profession? To you, Benny, it means nothing. And you're still going strong.*

When he was a junior in high school, Joseph Rabinowitz got a weekend disk-jockey gig with a radio station a few miles from Johnstown and worked under the name of Joey Robin. After graduation, he accepted a daily afternoon slot in Bedford; from there to Harrisburg; from Harrisburg to Ashville; and then on to Memphis, where he stayed until he got fired.

In the beginning of Joey's professional career, Benjamin sometimes went along with his older brother to the station. But he got bored just watching Joey introducing and spinning records. When he'd visit with his brother after Joey got a full time job, Benjamin became engrossed with the sales staff; how they pitched advertising to prospective sponsors over the phone and rung a bell when they scored a sale; the way they would berate the competition and make lewd, raucous jokes aimed at the few women in the office. The culture of sales, advertising and promotion turned him on.

After graduating from high school, Benjamin Rabinowitz moved to Philadelphia, changed his name to Benny Rich and got a job selling ads for the Yellow Pages by day and used cars at night.

Following a succession of jobs — including a song plugger for a music publishing company, an agent for a talent agency, an events coordinator, an independent record promoter — he changed his name again — this time to Liberty Fortune — and opened Fortune Media, a small advertising and public relations agency. When Joey learned about his brother's new name he sarcastically said, "Remember, Benny: The statue's not about you."

Benny, now Liberty, smiled obligingly, looked at his older brother, and said, "It's all about selling, brother. No sales? No job for Joey Robin, no matter how talented he is. If they buy the salesman they'll buy his product. But first they've got to remember his name."

And Liberty Fortune knew how to sell, how to meet people, how to do favors, how to network and how to collect IOUs. He had learned the secret of selling the sizzle not the steak. The total opposite of his older brother — whose demeanor evoked the intensity of a tightly wound coil — Liberty Fortune exhibited the glad-handing, jaunty strut of Professor Harold Hill selling musical instruments to the town of River City so they could have a boy's band in *The Music Man*.

One of the many people Liberty had met and helped in a big way was Ken White — at the time a rather innocuous midday disc-jockey on a Philly radio station. When the payola scandal hit the broadcasting world — whereby an investigation of high profile local disk-jockeys in major markets disclosed that several had accepted bribes to play certain recordings — the jock who hosted a popular afternoon sock-hop on television, called *Afternoon Dance Party*, was caught up in the mess and fired. The management needed to replace him quickly with someone who looked, acted and *was* squeaky clean primarily because the Westinghouse Television Network had been searching for a teen dance show to televise nationally and had selected *Afternoon Dance Party* from Philadelphia if they had an acceptable host.

They did. His name was Ken White — as all-American, unvarnished, squeaky clean as Ivory Soap.

And who zealously advocated, touted, and went to bat for Ken White — untried and unknown — for this humongous opportunity? The person who sold Ken White to Westinghouse to host *Afternoon Dance Party* was none other than Liberty Fortune.

Several years later, when Ken White Productions was posting record profits and record ratings with the shows it created and produced, the founder of the company received a telephone call.

"Ken," the voice on the other line sang, with the exuberance its owner had learned to employ when he was going to pitch something. "Liberty Fortune!"

No matter where he was, or how busy he was, Ken White always took Liberty Fortune's call. Liberty, knowing the art of the deal, didn't call often.

After the usual 'how are yous?' and 'how's the families?' Liberty got to the point.

"Ken, I have an idea for a show: A game show. Your company is the perfect company to produce it. Can I come over?"

"Sure, Liberty. You know you're always welcome. But 'over' is the Claridges Hotel in London. That's where I'm at. They patched you through. We're doing a thing with the Stones. I'll be back in the states next..."

"How about dinner tomorrow night? Your hotel?" Liberty asked.

White laughed. "I'll be looking for you, Liberty," and hung up.

At seven o'clock the next evening, Liberty Fortune sat alone with Ken White at a back table at the Claridges Hotel dining room in London, England. Two hours later, the two men signed their names on a napkin under the sentence, 'Ken White Productions agrees to produce a TV program created by Liberty Fortune. Details to be worked out within two weeks.'

What was not on the napkin was a verbal understanding White and Fortune had made near the end of their dinner meeting.

"Who'll we get to host it? White asked.

"We'll hold auditions. We'll know the person when we see him," Liberty replied.

White rubbed his chin with his hand, and said, "I've already seen him."

Liberty smiled, and asked, "Oh yeah? Who is it?"

White paused. Good broadcasters know how to milk a punch-line.

"You," he said.

Liberty was genuinely taken aback. He had invested his time and energy into creating the program and pitching it. He had given no thought to the host. He argued every reason he could think of for the choice of the host to be someone other then himself. But White stood his ground.

"The show is about deal making, risk taking, knowing the ropes of buying and selling, Liberty. It's about you… what you are, who you are, what you know. No. You're the host or we don't do the deal."

Those were the magic words for Liberty. He accepted the hosting role; not because he wanted to be a television star like his brother craved; not because he loved the art, the craft, the tradition, the energy of broadcasting, like his brother. Liberty Fortune accepted the job of hosting *Playing the Odds* because without him accepting the job, there would be no deal. It was strictly business for Liberty.

And so *Playing the Odds* hit the airwaves and became an instant hit. Liberty Fortune became a national overnight sensation. Ken White was right — Liberty was the perfect host for this program. He played himself. And he sold himself all the way to the top.

And, in accordance with the terms of the deal, that was worked out by the lawyers five years after Ken White and Liberty Fortune signed their names on the Claridges Hotel napkin, Fortune Media purchased the ownership rights to *Playing the Odds* as well as the rights to license the name from Ken White Productions. *Playing the Odds* became as valuable a proprietary entity as it was a television program; *Playing the Odds* board games, video games, gifts, calendars, greeting cards, foreign versions, and more proliferated the marketplace.

In the intervening years, Liberty Fortune had gone on to create other television programs as well as becoming an entrepreneur of worldwide proportions, with businesses ranging from radio station ownership to mineral mining. Last year, Forbes listed Liberty Fortune's net worth at 1.5 billion dollars.

Oh, and yes, his childhood prediction came true — He purchased controlling interest in a major league professional baseball team.

And with every step up the ladder of Liberty's success, Joey's relationship with his brother deteriorated. Liberty tried to stay close to his brother, even offering to pitch him to ABC Television for a network show, an executive job with his company, or a better gig at one of his stations.

"I don't need your help, Benny," Joey would respond. "I'm doing fine."

Joey was more than sibling rivalry jealous. He felt Liberty didn't disserve his success, that he was an interloper, an imposter in his beautiful world. Beyond that, he could not reconcile that fame came to someone with such seeming ease, the fame that he so desperately wanted, believed he had earned and had been unmercifully denied; that finesse, taste and nuance were trumped by moxie, grit and chutzpah.

Joey eased from the motel room bed and drew open the drape of the window and stared out into the light. Cars were pulling in and out of the parking lot, but he saw none of it. His mind took him to a scene played by him and his brother. It was the last time they spoke to one another, at their father's funeral five years ago.

As Joey recited the mourner's prayer at the graveside and threw the ritual shovel of dirt on to the lowering casket, Liberty hunkered several yards back behind the gravesite. Years earlier, his father had ordered him not to come near his grave at his funeral. "You're a disgrace to the faith and to the family," his father had said at the time.

Afterward, the two sons walked slowly to their cars. Crystal and Liberty's fourth wife, Tracy, a former Penthouse Pet, walked ahead of them.

Even considering the cosmetic procedures performed and applied to Liberty above the shoulders, the brothers shared none of the same physical characteristics. It was as if Jacob and Rachel Rabinowitz had ordered up sons from separate suppliers.

Joey was around five feet eight inches tall. His unruly head of dark hair — that defied discipline no matter how much Vitalis or Brylcreem he'd coax it with — quickly turned silver when he turned sixty-five, as if his mind had sent a memo to his head saying, 'Today you became old. Turn gray.' Since he was kid, he nervously gnawed and picked at the nails on his stubby fingers. His brown eyes were sad, even when he laughed his eyes were sad, as if he were always off to someplace other than the present. Joey could be invisible in a crowded room.

Conversely his younger brother lit up every room he entered. At a strapping six foot one, one hundred ninety-five pounds, he moved about with the grace of an antelope, his gray eyes darting, calculating, remembering and his killer smile attracting. With his manicured nails complimenting his slender tapered fingers, he had an appeal that captivated both sexes. His energy was magnetic, his attitude jovial, his mind linear and in the moment.

Liberty spoke first:

"Joey, I'd say let's bury the hatchet if I knew why there is a hatchet. This is the time and place, our father's burial, to put whatever it is that kept us apart behind us." He draped his huge arm around Joey's shoulder.

Joey scoffed and said, "Good timing, Benny. It will make a good photo op for those photographers up ahead. 'Super star Liberty Fortune consoles his brother, a Memphis talk show host, at their father's funeral. It ought to make the wires by this afternoon."

Liberty pulled his arm away and spun Joey around to face him. "Look, Joey, I don't know what it is that has turned you against me. Honestly, I have no idea. If my becoming rich and famous offends you, if what I have accomplished in my life annoys you, I'm sorry for you but I have no apology. If you're jealous of my success, it's not my problem. It's yours. Get over it."

The remark cut through to Joey's heart, reopening an old deep wound with the jagged edge of a red-hot knife. He tried to walk away but Liberty stepped in front of him. Putting his hands on Joey's arms to prevent him from moving and bringing his face inches from his brothers, Liberty produced a smile so the on-lookers would think the two brothers were sharing a warm family story, Liberty spoke sotto voce:

"I tried to be to you, as an adult, what you were to me as a kid, Joey. I tried to take care of you like you took care of me. And what do I get? I'll tell you what I get; resentment, hostility, and condemnation. Now I am offering my friendship here, at dad's funeral, Joey. Let's cut this crap and be brothers, okay? "

Liberty waited for Joey to react. He could see tears well in his older brother's eyes. Joey wanted to throw his arms around his kid brother; he wanted to tell him how proud he was of him; his heart ached to tell him he loved him.

Instead, he stepped back from Liberty's grasp, and said, "Mustn't keep your limo waiting, Ben. I'm out of here." And he walked quickly toward his car, where Crystal was waiting.

Liberty kept pace behind him, talking softly but with force, directly into his brother's ear. Joey tried to shield Liberty's voice with his hand, but it penetrated, like words delivered by laser beam.

"You understand what you're doing, don't you, Joey? I offered you my help. You threw it back in my face. I don't want to ever talk to you again. I don't want your name mentioned. To me, you are what you are in life — a loser. That's what you are, Joey — a jealous, small time, loser. And that's the last I want to see or hear of you."

Liberty's diatribe echoed in Joey's brain as he finally reached his car, got in and slammed the door.

As he drove off, Liberty waved and posed for a few pictures before stepping into his limo.

For the first fifty miles of the trip back to Memphis, they didn't say a word. Finally, Joey told Crystal what had occurred. Crystal just listened. She knew better than to verbally react. She let Joey talk and rant.

"Things just come to him, Cris. It's like with him it's no effort. That's what gets me, or part of what gets me. I mean this business, broadcasting, it's my life. I love it so much. Him? It's a business. He gets as much pleasure from his car dealerships as he does from being on the air! And he's a huge star! Why? Why does one person, whose heart and soul is devoted and dedicated, be kept down in the minor leagues and another person, who has no emotional attachment to the sport, get to play in the majors?

Crystal starred out her window. This was not a new routine. She had heard it before... many times before. She knew what was coming next — the story of Jacob and Morris, Joey's father and uncle.

"Did I ever tell you about my dad and Uncle Morris? No wonder I am hung up on this question of who gets what and why. I had heard it argued since I was a kid. Did I ever tell you about this, Cris? Maybe not."

When she heard the intro, she tuned him out and what she needed at the grocery store, when they got back to Memphis, in.

"Every other Sunday afternoon my father's brother, my Uncle Morris, would come by to visit. My father would go to Morris' home on alternating Sundays and play the same scene there.

"Morris was the older brother, an austere man, with the dark presence of a prosecutor for a Russian Czar. He made a fortune running his haberdashery store.

"My father, a sensitive man, a Tevya-like man — philosophic, gentle — barely eked out a living running his store.

"Morris' wife and children feared and loathed him. Today his family would be called dysfunctional.

"My mother adored my father all her life, and Benny and I loved and respected him, at least I did; I'm not sure about Benny. Men in town would come to my father to unload their emotional burdens, to seek advice on personal matters. He was a terrific listener. That's the key to doing a talk show, you know — Listening.

"Anyway, men went to Uncle Morris for a loan when they couldn't get it anywhere else. They paid him back dearly, with exorbitant interest, and on time, or else! I'm sure they called him

Shylock behind his back.

"Well, during these Sunday visits, the subject would invariably turn to success. By worldly standards, Uncle Morris had it, and Dad did not. By universal standards, Dad should have had it and Morris should have not. Now I'm sounding like Rose!

"Now, Uncle Morris used to claim that success was due to ability. Dad would argue that success was due to mahzel, you know — to luck. The argument would get heated, often mean and loud. I would silently serve tea and cookies that mom had prepared. I'd then take a seat in the corner. A few slurps, a couple of bites, then the action began. It would go like this..."

Crystal tuned him back in. She liked this part. Anyway, she had already made her grocery list. Joey had the car and his story in cruise control.

"Uncle Morris would surgically clip the tip off his one dollar Monte Cristo cigar, with an implement housed in his vest pocket, light it with his gold lighter, and slowly say to the gray whiff of smoke, 'Jake, you are a failure, and you blame it on bad luck.'

"Uncle Morris would pause then say, 'I, on the other hand, am a success. I have business ability. Luck has nothing to do with it.'

"Uncle Morris would wait for a response, his chin raised in anticipation.

"My father would bite the tip of his five cent King Edward, take the soggy sliver of tobacco off his tongue with his fingers and shout back, 'As far as your ability is concerned, you have a lucky location. It is my bad mahzel to have a terrible location.'

A slight pause, then he would add, 'But at least my wife and children talk to me!'

Uncle Morris would leer daggers at his younger brother then counter even louder, 'At least I can pay my rent!'

"After several more rounds, Dad would then call Uncle Morris an offensive name in Yiddish and Uncle Morris would bolt from the chair, turn, and exit in a rage, vowing that he'll never 'set foot inside your cheap, run-down, old house again!'

"Dad would pace for an hour afterward, biting his finger nails. Yet, the following Sunday, they would resume the ritual and continue the mete. This went on most every Sunday when I was growing up until Uncle Morris died. I'll bet today, in heaven, Dad asked God why so many fools get rich and famous.

"I inherited his frustration with the enigma. The system under which fame and fortune is awarded appears ungracious, if not cruel."

Crystal put her hand on her husbands arm, and said, "I wish your dad could tell you what he found out, my darling."

And they drove on in silence through the night, listening to CDs of Barbra Streisand.

The mid-morning sun reflected off the automobiles parked in the lot outside his door, making Joey squint, as his mind returned to present time. Just as he put his hand on the cord to pull the window curtain closed, his eyes were drawn to something off in the distance, above the roof of the adjoining building. It was darker than a storm cloud, about the size of a giant human being and yet it was without specific form.

Joey watched as it floated down from the rooftop and, as if propelled by some form of its own energy, slowly moved across the parking lot, seemingly immune to the penetrating light of the sun. It was headed for Joey's doorway. With his eyes wide with terror, and his heart pounding as if ready to explode in his chest, he watched the ominous thing seem to pulsate; a diabolical glob of evil beckoning to him

With a strong tug that almost tore the valance from the wall, Joey yanked the window curtain shut. He slammed the deadbolt lock on the door and fastened the chain safety latch. He felt the cold numbness of stark fear throughout his body.

"Dear God. Please protect me. Keep it away from me!" he pleaded, while noticing his hands trembling uncontrollably.

Forcing his eyes to stare through the peephole in the door, he scanned the perimeter. The thing was gone! The air rushed out of his lungs. He couldn't seem to replenish it. His chest hurt. Finally, he sucked in a short breath. Quickly he gasped another and then another; this one deeper, which he held for several seconds before allowing the air to slowly evacuate his lungs.

He walked quickly to the bathroom and splashed his face with cold water. He looked in the mirror and saw the face of fear. He doused more water on his face, hoping it would wash away that terrible look. He began to feel a little better. He moved to the kitchen area.

After swigging down a gulp of cold coffee, he breathed deeply several times. Impulsively, he went to his overnight bag and pulled out his laptop computer. It was an involuntary act. He didn't think about doing it, the thought just seemed to occur to him, and he did it.

He noticed himself beginning to settle down. His hands had stopped shaking. The thumping in his chest stopped. Placing his laptop on the dining room table, he fired it up and logged on to the internet.

"You've got mail!"

Chapter 9

Joey deleted the e-mail with 'Sexy Russian girl looking for older man' in the subject line, plus the advertisements for Viagra and other sexual enhancement products that got through his spam filter, and opened one from Rose.

HI SWEETIE,
JUST MAKING SURE MY BEST FRIEND IN ALL THE WORLD IS OKAY. TRIED CALLING YOUR PLACE BUT NO ONE ANSWERED. YOU'VE GOT TO CHANGE THE MESSAGE ON YOUR ANSWERING MACHINE. IT STILL TELLS FOLKS TO CALL YOU AT THE STUDIO IF THEY MISS YOU AT HOME. YOU MIGHT WANT TO GIVE YOUR CELL AS A FORWARDING NUMBER. JUST A SUGGESTION. GOT A NOTE FROM DAVID MALAK. SAID HE MET YOU. HE SAID YOU SEEM UNDER GREAT STRESS. DROP ME A NOTE OR CALL AND LET ME KNOW YOU'RE OKAY. I WORRY ABOUT YOU.
LOVE,
ROSE.
PS. PICK UP A COPY OF TV GUIDE. THERE'S A GREAT COVER STORY ON YOUR BROTHER.

HEY KID,
I'M FINE. I DROVE FURTHER THAN I THOUGHT I WOULD AND I WOUND UP AT THE MOTEL IN ELIZABETHTOWN, KENTUCKY WHERE CRYSTAL AND I USED TO STAY WHEN WE WENT TO THE RACES. SO WHO DO I RUN INTO? CRYSTAL! NO, NOT JUST CRYSTAL, BUT CRYSTAL WITH ANOTHER MAN, AT OUR HOTEL! SHE SAYS HE'S HER TEACHER. I DON'T WANT TO IMAGINE WHAT SHE'S LEARNING. SHE SAYS SHE

MET HIM VIA YOUR SHOW. NONE OTHER THAN YOUR PREMONITIONS OF DEATH MAN, DAVID MALAK. DIDN'T I TEACH YOU TO NEVER GIVE OUT PHONE NUMBERS OF GUESTS, EVEN IF THE POPE IS CALLING! REMEMBER? SO THERE IS MY WIFE WITH THIS TALL LANKY MAN WITH ORANGE SKIN AND LONG BLOND HAIR AND TURQUOISE ALL OVER HIM. ARE THEY EMBARRASSED? NERVOUS? DO THEY PRATTLE OFF EXCUSES? NOTHING! IN FACT, HE SEEMED ABSOLUTELY COMFORTABLE... COOL, AS HE WOULD SAY AND SAID OVER AND OVER. AND HE WRITES TO YOU AND SAYS I SEEM STRESSED! ANGELICA ROSE, I WASN'T STRESSED — I WAS INTENSIVE CARE TRAUMA UNIT CPR STRESSED! OH, BY THE WAY, CRIS LOOKS BETTER THAN I'VE SEEM HER LOOK IN YEARS. WE'LL TALK SOON. HAVE A GOOD SHOW.

JOEY

PS. I SAW THE TV GUIDE STORY ON MY BROTHER. IT'S HERE WITH ME IN THE ROOM. HE NEEDS A BOTOX RETREAD.

Just as he clicked 'Send', he heard, "You've Got Mail."

The sender was dixie@claraanns.com.

Joey smiled perceptively. *Even mom and pop shops have learned e-mail marketing. But how'd they get my address? Oh yeah. They recognized me, Googled me, and now they're pitching their jams and jellies. Okay, I'm game.* He opened the e-mail.

GOTCHA! it began. Joey's shoulders quivered. *He's back.*

He took a deep breath and read:

WOW! WHAT A DAY YOU'VE HAD! TELL YOU WHAT: WE NEED TO TALK IN REAL TIME, OR FOR YOU REAL TIME. I'M GOING TO SEND YOU AN INSTANT MESSAGE. GET BACK TO ME. IT'S IMPORTANT. HERE I GO I.M.ING YOU.

The instant message box on Joey's computer opened with a chime and a message appeared saying:

AGAIN, IT'S IMPORTANT WE TALK. PLEASE REPLY.

Joey's rational mind told him to log off. Something else told him to respond. The war in his mind raged several seconds. Responding won.

ALL RIGHT, I'M HERE ALREADY. SHOOT. WHAT'S SO IMPORTANT, DAVID! AH HA! SEE? I KNOW WHO YOU ARE! HOW'S MY WIFE?

YOUR WIFE IS FINE. BETTER THAN EVER, ACTUALLY. MUCH BETTER THAN YOU, REALLY. BUT YOSELEY, IF I AM DAVID, HOW DID I KNOW YOU STOPPED AT CLARA ANN'S COUNTRY COOKING?

Joey's face reflected his reaction. *I must have told him at the restaurant,* he figured.

I MUST HAVE TOLD YOU AT THE RESTAURANT.

NO, YOU DID NOT. BUT THAT'S OKAY. REALLY, WHY DON'T YOU STOP TRYING TO DISCOVER WHO I AM AND START FOCUSING ON WHAT I HAVE TO SAY TO YOU?

BY THE WAY, DAVID. PRETTY NEAT TRICK WITH THE GODFREY BIT. I'VE GOT TO HAND IT TO YOU, I'VE SEEN THE BEST AND MARVELED AT MANY OF THEM. BUT YOU? YOU? YOU PICK UP ON THOUGHTS BETTER THAN ANYONE. NO WONDER ROSE HAS YOU ON HER SHOW.

YEAH, I'M PRETTY GOOD. BUT HOW'D I DO THE UKULELE BIT?

Joey thought for a second then replied:

YOU DID A YURI GELLER.

YOU MEAN I BENT IT? DIDN'T MEAN TO DO THAT!

NO, YOU MENTALLY... YOU. I SAW A FILM ON THE RUSSIANS EXPERIMENTING WITH MOVING OBJECTS WITH THE MIND. WHAT DO YOU CALL IT?

TELEKINESIS.

YES! TELEKINESIS! THAT'S IT. THAT'S WHAT YOU DID.

SO... IF I MOVED IT, WHERE IS IT? I MEAN, THERE HAVE BEEN SUCCESSFUL EXPERIMENTS OF MOVING OBJECTS ACROSS A TABLE USING THE POWER OF THE MIND. BUT THE OBJECT STAYS ON THE TABLE. IT DOESN'T DISAPPEAR. SO WHERE IS THE UKULELE? LOOK AROUND THE ROOM. WHERE DID I HIDE THE UKE?

Joey thought for a moment. Then he got up and looked around the room, in and above the closet. Then he went into the other room and searched. No uke'. Actually, there weren't too many places to hide anything in modern motel rooms. He shrugged his shoulders and sat back down at the computer.

LOOK. I SAID YOU WERE THE BEST. I DON'T KNOW HOW YOU DID IT, BUT YOU DID IT.

ACTUALLY, I MAY HAVE BEEN TOO CUTE GETTING YOU

TO STOP AT CLARA ANN'S. BUT I DID TELL YOU TO WATCH FOR THE SIGNS. AND ABOUT MY FRIEND WHO IS A SIGN MAKER. CLARA ANN'S WAS TOO SUBTLE. LATER ON YOU WOULD HAVE PICKED UP ON IT. ROSE WOULD HAVE PICKED UP ON IT.

ON WHAT? WHAT ARE YOU TALKING ABOUT?

CLARA ANN'S. WHO WAS THE ANGEL THAT HELPED JIMMY STEWART APPRECIATE LIFE?

YOU MEAN IN "IT'S A WONDERFUL LIFE?"

YES.

Joey, along with everyone else on the planet had seen the movie at least once a year since 1947.

CLARENCE, Joey wrote.

RIGHT. CLARENCE. CLAR-ANS. CLARA ANN'S. GET IT?

ALL RIGHT. I GET IT. WHAT DID I GET?

IT'S ALL ABOUT SIGNS, YOSELEY. WHEN A PERSON FEELS HELPLESS, SIGNS APPEAR TO EITHER ASSIST THEM OR ASSURE THEM THAT THEY ARE NOT ALONE. I TOLD YOU TO WATCH FOR THEM. I PROBABLY SHOULD HAVE USED LESS NUANCE TO BEGIN WITH.

Seeing the word nuance, Joey's eyes opened wide for a second. Nuance was one of his favorite words. To him it signified artistic excellence, taste, and class.

Before he could respond, he received:

YOU LOVE THE WORD AND ALL IT IMPLIES, DON'T YOU YOSELEY?

Joey leaned back in his chair for a moment of reflection. Then he wrote:

AND DID CRYSTAL TELL YOU WHAT COLOR UNDERWEAR I WEAR TOO, DAVID?

WHITE. Came the reply. JOCKEY SHORTS. FRUIT OF THE LOOM.

OKAY, DAVID. WHAT OTHER SIGNS HAVE I MISSED?

WELL, THE NANCY WILSON SONG WASN'T EXACTLY NUANCE. IT WAS SLAM BANG, FLAT OUT IN YOUR FACE. I MEAN, ONE OF YOUR FAVORITE SINGERS SINGS ONE OF YOUR FAVORITE SONGS, "GUESS WHO I SAW TODAY" AND YOU SEE YOUR WIFE WITH ANOTHER MAN? COME ON, YOSELEY, EVEN HOMER THE MOTEL DESK CLERK WOULD HAVE GOTTEN A STIR OUT OF THAT! EVERYONE HERE LOVED IT. BUT YOU? WELL, IT JUST WENT RIGHT BY YOU. SEE WHAT I MEAN?

Joey reflected on the incident. His head nodded affirmatively as he rubbed his fingers across his chin like he did when he learned something new.

As if on cue, he received:

I'M TRYING TO CONVINCE YOU THAT YOU HAVE HELP. DAVID TOLD YOU THAT YOU ARE PROTECTED. YOU ARE. ESPECIALLY NOW SINCE YOU ARE SO VULNERABLE.

VULNERABLE?

YES, WE'LL GET TO THAT IN A MINUTE. YOU WANT TO KNOW WHAT OTHER SIGNS YOU MISSED. WELL, LET'S TAKE DAVID, FOR EXAMPLE.

PLEASE! Joey replied.

FUNNY! YOU'VE STILL GOT THE QUICK COME BACK, came the instant reply.

Joey was beginning to enjoy this. *David is not only a heck of a mind reader, he appreciates my stuff,* he thought.

YOU DRIVE TO THE VERY PLACE WHERE YOU AND YOUR WIFE USED TO HAVE GREAT TIMES AND, LO AND BEHOLD, THERE IS YOUR WIFE WITH A STRANGER NAMED DAVID MALAK. AM I RIGHT SO FAR?

YOU KNOW YOU ARE. YOU WERE THERE.

YOU ARE SHOCKED, SURPRISED, ON EDGE, ANXIOUS, UNCERTAIN, SUSPICIOUS, ALL THOSE THINGS. RIGHT?

ALL THOSE THINGS YOU SAW. YES. SO?

SO DAVID TELLS YOU THINGS, THINGS YOU NEED TO HEAR. ALL THE REST, THE SUSPICION, THE FEAR, THE UNCERTAINTY, THAT'S ALL IN YOUR HEAD. WHAT DAVID SAYS TO YOU IS WHAT YOU NEED TO KNOW.

AGAIN I ASK: SO?

GOOGLE MALAK.

WHAT?
SEARCH 'MEANING OF MALAK?' IF YOU JUST GOOGLE

DAVID MALAK, YOU'LL GET PAGES OF ARCHIVAL MATERIAL REGARDING HIM AND HIS WORK. THAT'S NOT WHAT YOU NEED TO KNOW. YOU NEED TO SPECIFICALLY SEARCH 'MEANING OF MALAK'.

OKAY. I'M GAME. I'LL BE RIGHT WITH YOU.

Joey logged on to Google.com and typed the question, just as he was advised. The answer came up instantly. Joey starred at it for several moments. After an initial reaction of disbelief, his emotions transformed into an odd sense of comfort. Involuntarily his lips smiled a most gentle smile.

His instant message chimed.

SEE? the message read.

YES. was all Joey replied.

I'M GLAD YOU ARE BEGINNING TO GET IT, YOSELEY. THE MORE YOU LOOK AT THINGS THIS WAY, ESPECIALLY IN TIMES OF DURESS, THE BETTER YOU WILL FEEL. LIKE HOW YOU FEEL NOW.

Joey typed, WHAT WAS THAT AWFUL DARK THING, THAT CLOUD OR SOMETHING OUTSIDE THE DOOR A FEW MINUTES AGO?

After sending the question, Joey thought to himself, *What am I doing? Now I'm asking this person questions like he's here with me! This is nuts!*

A chime and then an instant message appeared.

NO. IT'S NOT NUTS. YOU'RE GETTING WITH IT AND YOU DON'T REALIZE IT. YOU ARE BEGINNING TO OPEN UP TO POSSIBILITIES BEYOND YOUR OWN REASONING. RELAX. ENJOY THE JOURNEY. NOW, ABOUT THE THING OUTSIDE. YOU'RE NOT QUITE READY FOR THIS YET.

YOU WILL BE LATER, BUT RIGHT NOW I'LL JUST TELL YOU THAT JUST AS THERE IS PROTECTION AVAILABLE TO VULNERABLE PEOPLE — PEOPLE, LIKE YOU, UNDER EMOTIONAL DURESS — WHICH EMANATES FROM ANOTHER PLANE, THERE CAN BE HARM TO THE VULNERABLE PERSON AS WELL THAT EMANATES FROM A DARK PLANE OF EXISTENCE. IT'S SERIOUS BUSINESS. IT COULD HAVE HURT YOU, HURT YOU BADLY. BUT YOU SAVED YOURSELF.

HOW DID I DO THAT?

WHEN YOU PRAYED AND SAID, 'GOD, PLEASE PROTECT ME. KEEP IT AWAY FROM ME.' GOD ANSWERED YOUR PRAYER. LOCKING THE DOOR DIDN'T SAVE YOU, YOSELEY. GOD DID.

As Joey cogitated, his instant message box chimed again.

SO, HAVE YOU COME TO A DECISION ABOUT MY QUESTION?

Joey responded, QUESTION? DID I MISS SOMETHING? SEND AGAIN IF I DID, PLEASE.

NEVER MIND. I KNOW YOU HAVE NOT ANSWERED THE QUESTION YET. YOU'RE GETTING CLOSER TO FINDING THE ANSWER, BUT YOU'RE STILL IN A STATE OF LIMBO. YOU STILL CAN'T COME TO TERMS WITH NOT BECOMING A STAR, LOSING YOUR SHOW, EVEN WITH YOUR WIFE'S NEW-FOUND HAPPINESS, NOT TO MENTION YOUR BROTHER'S SUCCESS — AND BY THE WAY, ISN'T IT ABOUT TIME YOU BROKE DOWN AND CALLED HIM BY HIS NAME? SAY IT. LIBERTY. LIBERTY

FORTUNE. I MEAN, JOEY ROBIN AIN'T EXACTLY JOSEPH RABINOWITZ, YOU KNOW! YOU'RE STILL VULNERABLE, YOSELEY. STILL NOT HERE AND NOT THERE, AND I'M TRYING MY BEST TO HELP YOU. LISTEN: YOU NEED TO KEEP GOING, KEEP DRIVING. AT LEAST YOU UNDERSTAND NOW TO WATCH FOR THE SIGNS, TO UNDERSTAND THAT PROTECTION IS THERE FOR YOU. THERE IS MORE FOR YOU TO LEARN, YOSELEY. MAYBE YOU'LL GET IT. MAYBE NOT. WE'LL SEE. BUT IT'S GOING TO BE QUITE A TRIP. I'VE GOT TO GO NOW. TALK TO YOU LATER.

Before Joey logged off the internet, he went to Ask.com. *I want a second psychic opinion*, he joked to himself. He typed, 'meaning of Malak?'

In a second, up popped the response, the same as it had been earlier from Google.

Malak. Hebrew word for angel.

Chapter 10

"Mr. Fortune, Rose Barbelo is calling," the soft, sultry voice announced.

Liberty Fortune was seated at his massive desk going over financial statements from his automobile dealerships. He had a frown on his face. Sales were down three percent this quarter.

He slowly reclined in his custom-made, black leather chair, propped his feet on the pull out panel on the right side of his desk and said to the air, "Put her through, Casey. Oh, and Casey, get a hold of Sam Saltsman and tell him to drop by before lunch." Saltsman was chief financial officer of Fortune Holdings, the investment arm of Fortune Enterprises.

"Rose! How in the world are you?" Liberty bellowed exuberantly.

"I'm good, Liberty. And how is the prince of the city?"

Liberty smiled. He liked the sound of that title, especially from one familiar with the highest echelons of famedom. But in an instant his smile abruptly broke as his, always suspicious, mind considered if his brother's other self was being facetious.

"Top of my game, darlin'." It was Liberty's stock reply. "To what do I owe this pleasure?" Liberty raised his internal antenna so that he could pick up the signal of the purpose behind her call. One shared gift possessed by both he and his brother was a trustworthy gut that they each relied upon to make them who they were: Joey — the artful, local talk show host; Liberty — the pragmatic, famous billionaire.

"Liberty, I'm up here on business and was wondering if you'd have any time to drop by my suite at the Waldorf for a little chat. I'd come to you but it never fails, when I come up here, that I don't come down with some kind of cold or sinus or something. Must be the dust or… I don't know, but it's as sure to happen as rain on a washed car. Anyway, you don't need to know all that, but it would help me if you'd come by here."

Liberty's antenna rose higher. *Why does she want to see me? She had never called before.* They had only seen one another at broadcasting conventions and those were only quick 'How's the show going?' 'You look great,' 'Call me sometime,' showbiz, phony moments. *So why now? And what's this sinus baloney? She wants me on her home turf for leverage for something. Does she think I was born yesterday? I'm still more popular than Rose Barbelo ever will be, and I can buy and sell her three times over.*

"Rose, darlin', this is an invitation I've been waiting for all my life," he cowed. "You name the time, and I'll be there." While he talked, his mind kept circling around *why*.

"Terrific!" Rose said. "You've probably got a full plate for today, but is there any chance at all you could come by around five? I could order up some food and drinks and we could just relax and chat. Any chance for today, Liberty?"

Liberty fiddled with his Blackberry. He had a cocktail party at five scheduled with several prospective donors to his charitable foundation, dinner at 6:30 with two Saudis interested in a couple of his thoroughbred race horses, and later, tickets to the premier of a new Andrew Lloyd Webber musical, followed by a late dinner with the composer himself.

"I'll be there," Liberty said, his chipper tone disguising his misgivings.

"You are a doll," Rose said. "Thank you. I know you're putting yourself out to do this, and I appreciate it more than you know. See you in a few?" she confirmed.

"No problem, darlin'. As you said, I'll see you in a few."

Several hours later, Liberty was receiving a four-handed massage in his private gym, a floor above his offices from his Swedish personal trainer and his assistant, whom he referred to as Hansel and Gretel, when his cell phone rang.

"Hand me that thing will you, darlin'?"

The young woman reached over to the table and picked up Liberty's phone and placed it in his hand. Liberty looked at the incoming number, smiled and flipped the lid.

"Yeah, Mousy. What'd you find out?"

Mousy Powell was a former prizefighter who Liberty met when he purchased an interest in a promising heavyweight years ago. Mousy used to hang around the gym where Liberty's fighter trained. Before long he became one of Liberty's gofers. Soon Liberty learned Mousy had access to the dirt on well-known people that had been swept under the rug — information not available through conventional resources. Mousy was Liberty's personal search engine. Liberty rarely met with anyone with whom he was unfamiliar without first calling Mousy Powell. This call would provide Liberty information on the subject of his most recent curiosity.

"She's clean as a whistle, boss. Nothing there. What you see is what I got."

Liberty sat up, and barked to the bronze statues standing at the foot of the massage table,

"One of you, throw me a robe. Now!"

Hansel grabbed a white terry cloth robe off the hook and handed it to the, now pacing, naked man, who looked as if he was eating his telephone.

"What do you mean she's clean? How deep did you go?"

Mousy replied, "As deep as the deep blue sea, boss. I looked at places she's never been looked at before. I'm telling you, except for a couple of speeding tickets and a failing grade in geometry in high school, she's so clean she squeaks."

"The stuff about her and my brother?"

"Nothing to it. Just gossip, rumors."

"College? Other men? Women? Abortions? Bad debts? Something?" Liberty pleaded.

"Sorry, boss. There ain't nothing. She a perfect polygraph score. In fact, she is even more snow white than the public knows. There's no telling how many people she has helped here — all over the world, in fact — without anyone knowing. Sorry, boss. She's the real deal."

With a snarling look of sarcasm, Liberty said, "Great," as much to himself as to the phone.

Letting the robe fall off his body to the floor, he stretched out on the table, and bellowed "Hansel and Gretel! Get in here! Let's finish up."

Chapter 11

At the same time Liberty Fortune was being rubbed, buffed, and powdered by Hansel and Gretel, his brother had just past through Cincinnati and was heading northeast on I-71. He noted an exit for Xenia, a town just outside Dayton, and recalled that was where Phil Donahue began and perfected his audience participation format. *Quit while he was ahead. Wonder if he misses it?* Joey mused, as he pulled off the interstate to fill up with gas.

He hadn't noticed the man standing by the pump; he seemed to have just appeared. About six feet tall, slender, fair complexion, with a Marine's posture, he was nattily attired in an expensive looking grey glen plaid sport coat over a burgundy cashmere turtleneck sweater and charcoal slacks, with a crease that could cut glass.

"Can you believe these prices?" the man asked. "We'll probably miss four dollars a gallon some day."

Joey froze. The voice was unmistakable.

"Mind if I tag along with you?" the man said, sheepishly.

Joey was speechless as he cautiously turned toward Johnny Carson.

"Am...am I dead?" Joey asked.

Carson laughed and Joey noticed that his blue eyes twinkled when he laughed in person as they did on television.

"No, I am." He paused a few seconds then said, "But I've been asked to spend some time with you so you can decide if you want to be dead."

Joey replaced the pump, tore off his credit card receipt, and watched Johnny Carson get in the passenger seat of his Honda. Joey started the engine and looked at Carson. Suddenly they both broke up laughing. Carson was fastening his seat belt!

Joey headed his vehicle back onto the interstate. They drove on in silence for several moments. Then Carson looked over at Joey, and said, "Incidentally, I enjoyed your questions the other night. Good interview. Sorry I had cut out when the phone rang."

It took Joey several seconds to remember his dream of interviewing Johnny Carson, while he lay on his sofa two nights ago and the interruption when Rose called.

Joey asked, "You were there?"

"In your dream? Yes. I was there," Carson replied with his patented grin. Then he said, "Say, you wouldn't have a cigarette on you, would you? I left mine behind when I crossed over and, well…they don't allow them where I'm living now."

"No, I quit years ago. Sorry," Joey said.

"Don't be sorry," Carson said. "They took me out sooner than I wanted to go. I tried quitting dozens of times; never quite made it all the way. You know, it's funny. I always thought once you died, you're dead… you know, finished… out of here… 86 on the comic. To my surprise, that's not quite so. You actually do simply cross over."

"Where to?" Joey asked.

Carson thought for a moment then said, "To another place, another plane of existence. You know, I was always interested in studying the stars and the planets; spent a fortune on telescopes; stayed up all night just scanning the sky, looking, searching, for what I don't know, but it fascinated me."

Joey said, "Yes, I know that about you. So is the place you go to when you die one of the other planets?"

"I don't think so. No, it couldn't be because you continue to be a part of this one, except you're invisible, unless you are sent back on an assignment, like I've been. But even as a spirit, you continue to want the things you had — like cigarettes — and do the things you did. I mean you take across with you who you were in every way. Not like I thought, believe me! It's more like crossing the street to live in another neighborhood. If booze and broads were your habit when you were in the body, you'll be guzzling and chasing when you cross the street, so to speak. If you were a jerk here, you're a jerk there. I'm told that your personality and habits — that is, who you were — goes away after a while in the spirit world. But for those of us who are cosmic rookies, we're still pretty much who we were before we made the final exit."

Joey thought for a moment, then asked, "If I had a cigarette would you smoke it?"

Carson looked over, grinned, and said, "Great question! You are one terrific interviewer, my boy. But then, that's precisely the issue you're facing, right? And it's why I've been sent to you. You are great at what you do, can't do it anymore, don't know who you are without it, and never got to where you thought you deserved to get to, and you're not sure if life is worth living now."

"Yeah," Joey said, "And don't forget my wife's left me."

"My boy, I'm the world's greatest authority on that one." Carson waited for the laugh, which he got, then continued. "Seriously, your wife leaving you is a result of your professional woes. I mean, from my vantage point, it looks like you and Crystal would still be cooking if Joey were still working. Right? Or at least if Joey Robin had a better point of view about his life, during and after show time. "

"Yeah, I guess so," Joey admitted.

"Okay. Now, my time with you is limited. I've got to get back. Jack is…"

"Jack?" Joey asked, rolling his hand for Carson to explain.

"Oh, sorry," Carson said. "Benny. Jack Benny. He asked me to introduce him to a group of comics who came across bitter."

"Aren't they all?" Joey asked.

Carson nodded. "Yes, but some are worse than others. That's the group Jack works with. The ones who turned their humor into weapons near the end of their life. Jack is the best at that. Really gives of himself. I was never able to let it all out. Jack tells them what he thought, what he feared, his deepest self. Me? Can't bring myself to do it — not yet anyway. I'm still protecting the image. I fashioned the personality of the product known as Johnny Carson and kept the formula hidden from view. Subsequently, I lived my inner life as a loner and only gave Johnny Carson to the audience. Not good, I have since learned. Jack's been working with me"

"Were they all famous?" Joey asked.

"Some were; some never made it. Those are the worst cases. They not only have to contend with the comic's inherent bitterness gene, they have to deal with their personal angst as well."

Tell me about it, Joey thought.

"I am!" Carson said.

Joey laughed. "I keep forgetting. I've got a beam-me-down Carson sitting beside me."

"No. I'm really Karnack the Great!" Carson said. Instantaneously, he was draped in a long purple magicians robe, a turban on his head, and an envelope in his hand that he held to his forehead!

They both burst into laughter.

"You are the best," Joey said.

"Was," Carson replied.

Instantly, the Karnack costume disappeared and they drove on several more miles in silence. Eventually, Joey asked, "So tell me: Was it worth it— living behind that protective shield you put up— the loneliness, the failed marriages, the toll it took on you—was the prize worth the price, Johnny?"

Carson looked over at his driver, and said, in a serious tone, "When I was 'The Late Night King of Comedy', when I ruled the roost, when I walked out between the curtain and stood on my mark, performed the monologue — especially when it really cooked — nothing... I mean *nothing* else mattered. What ever I had to do to be in that magical place was worth every ounce of energy, personal sacrifice and, yes, loneliness. I simply basked in the light of being Johnny Carson."

"But you gave it up yourself," Joey said. "No one took it from you. You voluntarily retired, let it all go. That never made sense to me."

"That's because you never — and please don't be offended by this — but you never knew the pressure of fame. You craved fame. But you never got it, so you can't understand what it is like to have it."

Joey took a deep breath. He'd just been hit where it hurt the most. But he knew his passenger was right.

Instead of showing the pain, Joey let out a wild "HI YO!" like Ed McMahan used to do when Carson scored.

Carson laughed appreciatively. Then he said, "Look, I read the tea leaves. The business was changing. America's taste in entertainment and most everything else was sinking. I knew that soon, some young schmuck at NBC would ask me to do more filth, have more rock or rap or other tripe on the show. It was inevitable."

Joey butt in, "I know the drill."

"I know you know it, my boy. That's why I'm riding in this Honda Accord with you on some interstate highway heading who knows where? But let me finish this. I had two choices: One, I go with the flow, and the flow was flowing into the sewer. Or, two, I do a Marciano…"

"As in Rocky Marciano — the only heavyweight champion prize fighter to retire undefeated," Joey chimed in.

"Correct," Carson said. "So I chose to end it on my terms."

Carson sighed. He looked out the window for several moments. Clusters of road signs with restaurant and gas station names began to appear.

In a more solemn tone, Carson said, "There is another angle to the 'was it worth it' question you asked."

"Oh?" was all Joey said.

"Yes; 'Oh' is the right word. You see, when I crossed over, and the being of Light asked, 'What have you done with your life?' and I witnessed… no, more like *experienced* my life in review, I knew instinctively that what I did to be Johnny Carson had a down side that I never experienced when I was here. Most of what I saw in my life review were the opportunities I missed to do something worthwhile with my fame and my wealth, rather than using it to perpetuate the Johnny Carson image. It hurt so much to see what I could have done with the gifts I had been given but failed to do. I always thought I was the most important thing in my life. I learned I wasn't. I learned that fame is an illusion. Believe me. So now, I am an errand boy. I introduce Jack while he teaches, I get things, I fetch, I do what ever I can do at this rookie level, within the borders of what I know, to try to make up for my ego trip last time around. They give you a chance to make amends in spirit before you have to go back in costume for another show on earth. Does that make any sense?"

"I'm trying to understand. I really am. But you know I have always been suspect of this stuff."

"I know. I was, too. But recently you have had some things happen, which have been a bit bazaar. Am I right, my boy?"

Joey bellowed, "You are right, sir!" like McMahon did to Carson as Karnack the Great on the *Tonight Show*. They both laughed. But then Joey abruptly stopped laughing and widened his eyes, as if he had just realized something.

"Have you been e-mailing me?" Joey asked.

"Have I been e-mailing you?" Carson repeated.

"I asked you first," Joey deadpanned.

Carson broke up. He loved that old bit and was growing to appreciate Joey's timing, know-how, and showbiz savvy.

"I know you're being contacted," Carson said. "But it's not me." Then he paused, and said, "Wait, I do remember I was talking with Skitch…"

"Skitch Henderson, your band leader before Doc Severnson?" Joey asked.

"Right. Skitch and I were talking — he had passed over around the time I did — and someone came over and asked Skitch if a ukulele has four strings or five. Skitch kind of looked at the guy funny, like is this some kind of joke? And the guy said that they were working with some talk show host in Memphis and a uke' was part of the deal. I guess that must have been about you?"

"Was it ever!" Joey said almost under his breath.

"Well, anyway, I'd sure pay attention to what you're receiving. Like I said: I used to think I was the center of the Universe. Was I in for a shock! There's so much going on out there — stuff I'm just learning about."

Suddenly Carson seemed to become aware of something in the sky, or in the air, or in the Honda. "It's time," he said. "Carson the tour guide has almost completed his mission before he goes back to introduce Jack. I want you to take the next exit up ahead."

Joey's blinker light flashed to the right, as he steered his vehicle onto the exit ramp and stopped at the stop sign.

"Right or left?" he asked.

Carson looked at the restaurant signs. "Left. And just go a few yards… there… yes, there it is! Pull in there," Carson instructed.

The sign on top of the diner-looking building said 'Rita's Eatery'. Joey pulled alongside the other cars and trucks.

Carson looked at Joey with a smile of love and sadness, and said, "My job was to get you here. Several of the boys have come over for coffee. You'll be impressed. Crazy: I could never get a group together like that on the show. But now, under these circumstances, they are doing what they need to do for their own advancement. Maybe they will explain it better. Anyway, they'll be expecting you. Pay attention to them, my boy. You need them; and they need you."

He paused, and then said, "I wish I could ease your pain, my boy. Believe me, I understand. But my bosses make me promise not to give advice. They say I'm still learning the ropes. I used to buck the brass at the network, but I better not screw up here. So, I guess this is it. Goodbye, Joey. It was good being with you, doing old bits with you. It makes me remember how it was, how it felt." Carson sighed and shook his head.

"Okay," he said with resolve. "I gotta split. Just one more thing: Remember, my boy: Failure is as imaginary as fame.

Joey shut off the ignition.
Johnny Carson disappeared.

Chapter 12

Prior to leaving his office for the Waldorf to meet with Rose Barbelo, Liberty Fortune met with — and then later fired — Sam Saltsman (Fortune Holding's chief financial officer), ate lunch alone in his private dining room, approved the acquisition of an internet travel company, answered eighty-three e-mails, had twenty-nine phone conversations, approved an interactive video game concept for *Playing the Odds*, had his massage from Hansel and Gretel, received Mousy Powell's intel report on Rose Barbelo, spoke to his attorney regarding enforcing a provision in his pre-nuptial agreement with his latest wife, and chewed out the executive producer of *Playing the Odds* for the floor crew not laughing at his jokes during yesterday's tapings.

The Waldorf management provided accruements specific to the taste of each guest who occupied the space known as the 'Celebrity Suite'. Redecorating was done if the guest was of sufficient status to justify the time and effort. The expense, of course, was factored into the bill. Rose Barbelo's status justified a total make-over in accordance with her preferred ambiance.

Thus, the master bedroom was repainted an earthy mauve, while the two smaller bedrooms were done in lemon yellow and fuchsia. Each of the four bathrooms were papered in pink and scented with lavender. The kitchen was amply stocked with her favorite cereal, luncheon meats, cheeses, crackers and snacks for both she and Dharma, her grey and black Shih Tzu. Bottles of Rose's vodka of choice, Stolichnaya, plus other liquors and wines for her guests were stocked in the oak cabinet under the bar off to the side in the living room. The library, with its small but state of the art equipped office, was already done in dark oak and that suited Rose just fine. Each room of the large suite was brightened with a vase of fresh purple irises, her favorite flower.

Brenda Parker, Rose's executive assistant and close personal friend, was waiting for Liberty as he exited the private elevator leading to the Celebrity Suite. Brenda was a tall, shapely thirty-something with silky brown hair, dark expressive eyes and a warm but business-like smile. She accepted his extended hand and immediately felt uncomfortable with the way he held it.

"I'm Brenda, Ms. Barbelo's assistant," Brenda said more formally than usual. "Welcome to our home away from home, Mr. Fortune. Won't you come in? That chair by the fireplace is comfortable. Rose will be with you in a minute. Can I get you something to drink? Some wine perhaps? I've got it all here."

"You sure do, darlin'," Liberty said with a wink. Brenda's stomach turned.

He ambled over to the recommended, over-stuffed white easy chair by the fire and lowered himself in it. "Darlin', would you pour me a scotch and water — single malt if you have it — and just a couple of rocks?"

"No problem," Brenda said. She could feel Liberty's eyes on her as she moved toward the bar to fix his drink. When she brought it to him he took it from her by placing his left hand over hers while cupping his other hand around the glass. Looking up at her, he grinned slyly and winked. Now, her stomach knotted.

Brenda said a silent *thank you, God* when the slightly nasal, but still identifiable, voice of Rose Barbelo shouted with mock anger, "Liberty, you leave that girl alone!" as she approached Liberty laughing.

He looked around, stood up, smiled broadly, and hugged his host. Brenda looked at her boss, who rolled her eyes as they connected with her assistant's. Everyone in the business knew Liberty Fortune was a letch and he didn't let anyone in the room down. Brenda smiled, blew Rose a kiss, mouthed "good luck" and went into the library.

Rose gracefully eased away from Liberty, miming an instruction with her hand to re-seat himself then poured herself a cup of hot herbal tea from the sterling silver decanter resting on the coffee table, along with a plate of cookies. Rose sat down on the sofa across from Liberty's easy chair. Suddenly she was joined by Dharma, who snuggled up close to her mistress and was rewarded with a "Good, sweet princess" voiced in baby talk, followed by a Waldorf bakery oatmeal cookie.

Liberty watched it all with an insincere, pasted smile expressing a combination of *What am I doing here?* with *Who gives a six-dollar cookie to a dog!*

Quickly, he sized up the woman America loves seated across from him. Rose looked smaller than he remembered. Maybe it was the cold, but she looked somewhat worn down, weary perhaps. She wore silk, deep purple lounging pajamas, pink bunny ear slippers and just a touch of makeup.

He figured that here was a woman who did not feel the need to impress him. He felt oddly disarmed.

The modesty of Rose's appearance — a tactic she contrived in advance — offset her prideful guest and afforded her a degree of strategic leverage for the conversation to follow.

The 'Dharma' moment gave Rose a chance to get a sense of Liberty as well. He seemed larger than she remembered: black suit, red silk handkerchief, perfectly folded, crisp white shirt, red silk tie, black shiny shoes; nothing imaginative; nothing off-putting except his overpowering hauteur. His tan face showed her nothing about his soul. *This field's been plowed so often it's gone fallow*, she thought to herself.

Unobtrusively, she searched his eyes for a message, a feeling. They gave away nothing. Intentional or not, his was the quintessential poker face. She looked for any resemblance at all to his brother. She saw none. Rose smiled at the mere thought of Joey and missed him in her heart.

After Liberty asked some superficial questions about Dharma, her Waldorf accommodations, and Rose's head cold, which didn't seem so bad to Liberty that she couldn't have come to him, Rose inquired about *Playing the Odds*.

Liberty braced his back, broadened his smile, and proclaimed, "Fabulous!" followed by a recitation of the latest monthly, weekly, and over-night Neilson rating numbers, including those from various sections of the country, along with demographics, and trends.

"And your show, Rose? How're the numbers?" Liberty asked with feigned interest.

Rose responded, "We continue to be blessed beyond my dreams."

Then Rose eased her body to the edge of her sofa cushion and placed her teacup and saucer on the coffee table. Looking squarely at Liberty, she said in a quiet but firm tone, "I know your time to visit with me is limited so let me get to the point: How much will you take for your company?"

Chapter 13

Joey entered Rita's Eatery with a familiar sense of anticipation. It was the same sensation he felt every time he walked into a studio, moments before going on the air. How he loved that indescribable jolt of adrenalin, that exhilaration of focus, the feeling of control, of specialness. Was he experiencing this euphoric rush because he had just driven a hundred and fifty miles with Johnny Carson or because of what was awaiting him, he wondered?

Even his gait had a bit of a strut as he stepped inside, flashed a smile his face hadn't produced in months, and said to the lady sitting behind the hostess stand signing checks, "You've got to be Rita. Got room for one?"

The woman looked up and smiled. Joey thought she looked like Chris Farley doing a drag skit on *Saturday Night Live*. She was plump with several chins and cheeks splotched with red daubs of, what looked to be, clown rouge topped off with frizzled strawberry blond hair with a pink clamp on top. She was wearing a clean, crisp white uniform similar to the one Clara Ann wore.

"That would indeed be me, sweet thing. And I got room for one or one hundred. Sit where ever you like — counter, table, you name it."

Joey perused the room with an air of expectation. He spotted them right away.

"How about that large round table in the back?" he asked, his smile remaining unblemished.

Rita looked at him and frowned. "Sweet thing, that's an awful big table for just one cute man. And you don't want to take up so much room all by yourself in case Rita here gets a group coming in, now do you?"

"Actually, I am expecting several others, Rita. So, how about I just go back there and wait for them. Wouldn't mind some coffee while I'm waiting, however."

Rita beamed. "Sweet thing, with a smile like you've got, I think Rita would give you just about anything you asked for — except a free meal!" she exclaimed then howled an ear shattering high pitched laugh that made Joey wince.

Joey faked a responsive laugh and headed to the big round table at the back of the restaurant. Five men were sitting around it drinking coffee and engaging in a vigorously animated discussion. Joey's eyes widened with amazed disbelief, as if he had died and gone to talk show heaven. There at the big round table sat five of his heroes. One looked up and said, "And now, ladies and gentleman — and you too, Rita — is the star of our show. How about a big round of applause for Joey Robin!"

Joey took a seat beside the man who introduced him: Steve Allen, the originator and first host of the *Tonight Show*. Allen said, "Joey, welcome to our little get-together. I'm sure you know the others around the table. There's Dave Garroway over there. I'm sure you know that Dave was the first host of the *Today Show*. He set the tone for laid back naturalness in the early days of television." Garroway nodded. "And there's Morton Downey, Jr. whose provocative, hyper-style was the antithesis of Garroway's." Downey winked. " Speaking of provocative, you remember Joe Pyne?" Pyne's snarl did not change expression. "And the newest member of our cast, Mike Douglas, who sang as well as he hosted for what, over twenty-five years, Mike?" Douglas smiled broadly and saluted.

Just then, a waitress brought Joey some coffee. "You want to order something before your friends get here?" she asked, while licking some cake frosting off her finger. "You look awfully lonesome all by yourself at this big table."

Steve Allen said, "Hey Garroway. She's just your type. Want me to set you up?"

Everyone, including Joey, laughed. Garroway had been known for his intellectual, dry wit.

"Hey, mister," the waitress said. "That's pretty rude of you to laugh at me. I'm just trying to be friendly."

"I'm sorry, ma'am," Joey said. "I just thought of something funny when you came over. No offense. It's not about you. I didn't mean to offend you."

"Well, all right, then," the waitress said, lapping the last speck of chocolate off her finger. "I suppose I understand. Just let me know if you want something to eat. No offense taken." She turned and walked toward the kitchen.

All the boys at the table gave Joey a standing ovation and round of applause except Joe Pyne.

"Hey Pyne," Morton Downey, Jr. said, "What's with you? When are you going to lighten up? This isn't like it was before, you know. I mean, this is where we need to get over the stuff we brought with us. You crossed over in '70 and you're still a ticked off angry man. Joey here handled that terrific. Can't you show him a little appreciation? I mean, we're here to help the guy. Right?"

All the others mumbled "Amen", "Right-on", or other expressions of support.

Pyne shrugged his shoulders like a precocious adolescent. Suddenly, he stood up, poked his finger in Downey's chest, and hollered, "You got a lot of nerve barking at me like that, pal. After all, you stole my style; you ripped off my act! If it weren't for me you would have been nothing! Tell you what, Downey: Why don't you take your false teeth out, put them in backwards and bite yourself in the neck!" Pyne sat down and scoffed just as Downey swatted Pyne's finger away with his hand. The others shook their heads in disgust.

The false teeth line was typical Joe Pyne, one he had used dozens of times with callers to his shows that annoyed him. He was right, however. Joe Pyne invented the confrontational talk show host format in the '50's — at a time in America when civility and decorum were the milestones of broadcasting and an echo of society. He shocked the nation with his language, his behavior, and his downright audacity. Downey was a '90's Pyne—when broadcasting echoed a different, a more boorish generation.

Pyne had lost a leg in World War II and many people believed his bitterness and angst stemmed from that handicap. Pyne was killed in 1970.

"Come on, fellows," Steve Allen said. "That's no way to treat our guest. Sorry, Joey, every time Pyne joins us a fight nearly breaks out, just like his old show. The guy is a slow study." Pyne gave Allen an obscene gesture.

Joey said, "Hey, no problem. I'm just tickled to death… whoops, pardon me." The group howled in laughter. "I mean thrilled beyond words that you all would gather here for my sake."

From the front of the restaurant, Rita said, "Did you say something, sweet thing? I thought I heard you talking, or is Rita here losing what's left of her mind?"

"I was just thinking out loud, Rita," Joey said. "No problem. I'm fine."

"Okay dokie, sweet thing," Rita said, as she came around the front desk to greet a family of six people. She looked at Joey, sitting alone at the huge round table. "Are you sure you're friends will be coming, sweet thing? I could sure use that table."

"Won't be but a minute," Joey answered. "I'd appreciate if you gave me more time."

Rita gave Joey a thumbs-up sign and a wink and pushed two smaller tables together for the family.

"Joey," Dave Garroway said. "*Think* your words to us. Don't say them out loud. We'll pick them up. That's how it works here. One day it's how you'll be communicating, just like us. Think. We'll hear you."

"Took me a while to get on to it," Mike Douglas said in his casual, soft-spoken delivery, "Hey, you'll have a head start when it's your time!"

"Yeah," Joe Pyne butted in. "This way Rosy O'Donnell over there in the white uniform won't think you're a nut case."

"Now, let's get down to business," Steve Allen said. "I know you're wondering who called this meeting and why we're here."

Joey thought, *It had crossed my mind*.

"Terrific!" Allen exclaimed. "Did everyone get what Joey said… I mean, thought?"

"I did," Garroway said.

"So did I," said Douglas.

"He said he has to take a leak!" Pyne yelled.

The others ignored Pyne. Joey snorted a laugh.

Just then another group of customers entered Rita's Eatery. Rita looked over at Joey again. He looked at his watch and gave an 'I don't know what's keeping them' gesture with his hands. Rita's smile was a bit less obliging than before.

Allen said, "You're doing good, Joey. This won't take long. The gist of the story is this: When an individual loses their sense of purpose, loses their way, so to speak, a union of sympathetic guides, who are familiar with the individual's mission in the present lifetime, are assigned to help set the individual back on course. It happens more than you would expect. Disenchanted business people are ministered to by former business people; former athletes help athletes; former teachers help teachers; social workers help social workers; physicians help physicians; lawyers help… well, maybe not lawyers, but people from all positive and creative endeavors who get stuck in a spiritual rut are tended to by those who understand the elements, the nuances, the dynamics of the person's present task. Muses for the soul afflicted, I often say."

Joey thought, *You said people from positive and creative endeavors*.

"Yes. I'm glad you caught that," Garroway said. "No wonder you're a good interviewer. You listen. Yes. Positive and creative people are those ministered to. Forgive the ending preposition, please."

Pyne blew him a raspberry.

Garroway ignored him. "Anyone who causes harm, uses human pain for personal gain, who profits on human misery, who is in conflict with the natural order; those people are left to fend for themselves, no matter how much difficulty they are in."

A kind of hell on earth, Joey thought.

"Precisely," echoed Steve Allen.

Joey reflected for several moments. Then in his mind he asked, *Who's the assignment editor? Who says where you go and whom you go to?*

Joey noticed the fellows looking at each other. He got the feeling that they were communicating with each other but blocking it from him.

Finally, Morton Downey, Jr. said, "We think it's best we don't get into that now. Maybe another time. Certainly, when your time comes you'll find out. But for now, we'll take a pass on that one."

"But what we can tell you is that there *is* a system. It is far more intricate and yet far less complicated than I ever imagined," Douglas segued. "And it should come as no secret that it is all based on love; all held together by love. And the love that I'm talking about is incredibly awesome!"

A bus pulled up in front of Rita's and out poured about two dozen high school kids on a field trip. Nearly each one had some type of listening devise stuck in their ear. The rest were chattering into a cell phone. Two teachers, or counselors, walked behind them looking bleary eyed and stunned, as if they had just been released from a Turkish prison.

Rita came rolling back to the big round table. "Sweet thing," she said. "I'd love to let you camp here for the night if you liked, but Rita here needs the table for these folks. So would mind taking a seat at the counter or a small table over there? I know you understand. Anyway, I got a hunch your friends have stood you up. Will you help me out, sweet thing?"

"Ask for the picnic table outside," Steve Allen whispered.

"Sure, I understand, Rita. No problem. But could I take my coffee and sit at the picnic table outside on the grounds? I want to give it a while longer for them to get here. Is that okay?"

Rita blushed, smiled and seemed to form yet another chin.

"Sweet thing, you have won my heart. Out there is fine by me." She topped off Joey's cup with steaming fresh coffee.

Joe Pyne led the way, walking on two good legs — although he held onto a pair of crutches — followed by Dave Garroway, Steve Allen, Morton Downey, Jr., and Mike Douglas. Joey tagged behind and noticed that the pecking order was according to the length of time since each had died. When they reached the picnic table outside, they sat down according to the same order. Joey didn't know what to make of this.

"Courtesy." Garroway said calmly.

I'm sorry? Joey asked raising his eyebrows.

"You were wondering why we line up according to heavenly seniority, I guess you could say it's courtesy; respect — even if it is Joe Pyne at the head of the pecking order. He's been here the longest; he's had the most experience; the most lessons; the most time — so to speak — to adjust, learn, examine, and mature. We pay homage to experience and seniority here as it once was below.

Garroway then looked over at Pyne, and said, "Speaking of lessons, Joe, when are you going to nix the crutches? You know you don't need them anymore. Your body was made perfect the instant you crossed over. You don't need the crutches, you know that."

With a snarl, Pyne leered at Garroway, and fumed, "Pretty high-minded even for a snob like you, Garroway, a man who used to co-host his program with a monkey!"

Joey remembered that when Dave Garroway hosted the *Today Show,* he had a chimp he named J. Fred Muggs, who used to wonder around the studio. It was a great gimmick and played so well off Garroway's stoic personality.

Steve Allen rapped on the table with his fingers and said, "All right, boys. This meeting is back to order. We don't have all day, gentlemen." They all laughed. Even Joe Pyne broke a slight grin.

"Joey," Allen began. "We're here because we were told to come to you. I know it's your nature to want to know who sent us, who we work for. That curiosity is what made you good at what you did, but it is also the core of your problem. Get it? It's about *why* not how. This is about *you*, not about us."

Joey squirmed.

Morton Downey, Jr. smiled and said, "Believe me. We all understand. You are fascinated by this little show you're on outside Rita's Eatery; but you squirm when we tell you the show is about you."

"And therein lies your problem," said Garroway professorially.

Joey could not stop his mind from thinking about who he was sitting with, who was trying to help him. *I'm in the company of greatness*, he thought. *My heroes have come to rescue me. But from what? I don't get it!*

"From yourself, you idiot!" Pyne blurted out. "You became what you dreamed of becoming! Do you know what a gift that is?"

Everyone looked at Joe Pyne in disbelief.

Garroway's jaw dropped open.

Pyne didn't pay them any attention. He got in Joey's face and said, "Do you know how many people would sacrifice their grandmothers to have what you got? For nearly forty years you've done the work you dreamed of doing since you were a kid and you did it with skill and respect for the profession; you mentored a wonderful soul who is bringing light to this dark world of yours; and you followed your heart and married a woman who adores you and devoted her life to you. Do you have any idea how you have been blessed in this lifetime?"

Joey tried to avert Pyne's harangue by pulling back, but Pyne edged forward, his face inches from Joey's.

"And so the time comes when you had to give it up. It doesn't matter how it happened. It was time. What you need to know is that there are no accidents. The kid who fired you was doing the job he had been assigned to do. He was an instrument of the system. Just as you were, and are. Just as the five of us are right now."

Joey saw them nod in agreement out of the corner of his eye.

"We're all players in a huge philharmonic orchestra, pal. And lately, you've been hitting some sour notes. Instead of appreciation for the blessings of your lifetime, you have spent a lot of time ragging on the Universe for not making you a star, of defining yourself by your perceived failure rather than by your actual achievement! You've gotten everything you asked for, but you boil inside because it's not enough! And the worst part of it all is that, not only have you gotten what you asked for; you've gotten what you *yourself* planned! *You* wrote the symphony, pal!"

Pyne drew back a few inches. He allowed some space between himself and his subject. He hesitated several seconds, then in a voice with less vitriol, he said, "That is why your e-mailer is asking you if you want to die, Joseph. To reject the gifts of a life one designs, sends a cosmic message that one wishes to terminate that lifetime."

The group allowed Joey to process what he had just been told. They knew it was a lot for him to handle. Pyne had laid a heavy dose of metaphysical concepts on him.

Finally, Dave Garroway looked at Pyne and said, "Well done, Joe. You *have* been learning after all."

"Stuff it, four eyes," Pyne responded, reverting to his on-air persona. The others smiled.

Joey stood up and began pacing around the table. He rubbed his chin with his hand as he did when he was working through a problem. The others kept their seats.

The family of six came out of the restaurant, the father studying his receipt. The youngest child — a boy about six — pointed at Joey and hollered, "Momma, that man over there is crazy!"

The mother said, "Hush, Tony. Sal, stop looking at that piece of paper. I'll give you my share if you want." Keeping her eyes pealed on Joey, who kept circling the picnic table, deep in thought, with his hand still rubbing his chin, she ordered everybody to get in the car quickly. She didn't take her eyes off him until they pulled away from Rita's. Joey was oblivious to the whole incident.

After several rotations around the table, Joey mentally asked, *You said I designed my life. Do you mean like when I was a kid, hoping to become a talk show host? If that's what it's all about, why doesn't everyone get what they ask for?*

Steve Allen answered: "They do. Or, at least that's the way it's supposed to happen. But this goes beyond our childhood hopes and wishes, although quite often, as in your case, what you wished for as a child and what you planned prior to that were the same."

Joey looked puzzled.

"It works like this," Mike Douglas said, "and it blew my mind when I found out about it: In between lifetimes, in the world of spirit, we design our next life. The plan for our next lifetime is predicated on lessons we have yet to learn or didn't learn in previous lives."

"And here's the fascinating part," sequed Steve Allen, "We enter into agreements with other souls to play the needed role, just as we agree to play a needed role in *their* next lifetime. We literally cast the parts and create the circumstances — the triumphs as well as the tragedies — that we need to experience."

Pyne added, "The ultimate goal is perfection, pure enlightenment. The pathway to it are the lessons learned from multitudes of lifetimes."

Morton Downey, Jr. smiled warmly and said, "When I was where you are it all looked so chaotic and unfair. From here, it is so beautifully orderly and just."

Joey took several minutes to sort out what he had been told. Then he scanned the quintet of legends and transmitted. *Easy for you guys to say. All of you — Joe, Steve, Dave, Morton, Mike — all of you became famous. You got to the top. I mean, why not me? Why was I denied fame?*

The five looked at one another. Again, Joey had the feeling they were communicating among themselves and blocking him out. In a few minutes they all looked at Joe Pyne, as a committee looks at its chairman, to express the will of the group.

He said, "We could explain the deal about fame to you, but we feel it ought to come from someone else."

"Someone you know," Steve Allen said.

"After all," Garroway continued. "We're here to get you to consider your choices. That's all; to show you what you've been given, how you got it, and then for you to determine if you want to play out the string."

"Dave's right," Mike Douglas said, "After all, we're not angels."

You're not? Joey thought with surprise.

"No, we're guides. We're helpers," Garroway said. "Angels have always been spiritual beings. They operate at a higher level than us. We're a group of guys who did what you did and loved doing it. And when we crossed over, we were asked to help out our media brothers and sisters when they have a problem — especially when their lust for life is faltering — because we know the game."

"You need to go see your old friend Bernie," Morton Downey, Jr. said.

Bernie Frank? Joey thought with surprise. *You know I know him?*

Downey laughed. "We know a lot about you, Joey. A lot."

"You want to know on what basis fame is meted out?" Steve Allen asked. "We could tell you. It's not complicated. But we think if you heard it from someone you know, one of your peers, someone like yourself but someone who figured it out, it might have a greater impact. Coming from us, five guys who became stars, well, it might not go down as well."

"Go see Bernie Frank, Joey. I always liked him," Mike Douglas said.

"Anyway," Joe Pyne added. "The Florida sun will do you good. You look more dead than us!"

After a brief, silent interval, the five iconic broadcasters stood up and walked slowly to the edge of the lawn in the proper pecking order. As they approached the parking lot, Joe Pyne turned and gave a thumbs-up to Joey, still seated at the picnic bench. Joey smiled at him, and heard, "Thank you."

After they each dissolved into the air, Joey slowly stood up, and his foot kicked something lying on the ground. He looked down and saw a pair of crutches.

Chapter 14

Joey was uncertain what to do after that — push on further east, go back home, or head south to Florida where Bernie Frank was living these days. He glanced at his watch —3:56 PM. Joey time was always precise, to the second, an off-spin from his broadcasting life. Then he looked to the sky and scanned the varied white clouds as they slowly headed west. *At least they know where they're going... or do they?* Joey thought. *Maybe like me, they are simply drifting.*

The late autumn sun had lost some if its brilliance and an unseasonably chilly breeze wafted across his neck. *I hope Cris got home safely. I wonder what she's doing now. Maybe I ought to stay over. It's getting late. No use driving anywhere until morning. If I told her who I've been hanging out with today she'd have me committed.* The thought of how Crystal would react to hearing about his day made him laugh, followed instantly by a feeling of reminiscent love throughout his entire being.

After using the bathroom in Rita's Eatery — nearly empty now after the lunch bunch left and before the dinner customers arrived — Rita came out of the kitchen and said, "Your friends never showed, huh? Too bad. You sure looked lonesome out there at that big table all by yourself, sweet thing. I looked at you from time to time. Seemed to me you had a lot on your mind, like you were preoccupied with something. You ain't robbed a bank or nothing, have you, sweet thing?" Rita burst into that glass shattering, shrill laugh of hers. Joey winced again.

"No, I'm fine. No problems." Joey said, easing his way to the door.

Rita shook her head in disbelief. "Can't kid a kidder, sweet thing. I know better. You are a man in rebellion. I don't know exactly what you are rebelling against — a job, a wife, the law, maybe just yourself — but I know you are in rebellion. Something is eating at you, and it ain't Rita's food." Rita smiled. It was a wise knowing smile that caught Joey off-guard.

"No, ma'am. Everything is fine. Really. No problems," he said, almost like a student to a teacher who asked why his grades have suddenly fallen.

Rita shook her head back and forth and uttered "Uh uh," meaning I don't believe you. Then she firmly gripped Joey's arm and guided him to an empty booth and sat him down. Startled, he offered no resistance. Rita plopped down across from him and placed her chubby, pumice hands, with polish peeling off her nails, on top of Joey's. She closed her eyes and breathed deeply. After several seconds, she nodded, and her lips formed an expression of affirmation.

In a voice less shrill and more soothing, sort of like a nurse consoling a patient after the hurried doctor renders his diagnosis and abruptly leaves the examining room, Rita captured Joey's eyes with her own and spoke straight to them. "Sweet thing," she began, "Rita here was right. You *are* in rebellion. I knew it the minute you walked in that door." Then with a sly smile, she said, "Now don't get the big head. Rita here picks up a lot of stuff from folks… strangers, who just walk in her door. So you ain't special in that regard." Her smile dissolved and the reassuring expression returned. "But you *are* special in a way, sweet thing. You are special because you are the subject of a lot of attention these days. You do know what I mean, don't you, sweet thing?"

All Joey could do was nod and very softly say, "Yes."

With her hand still covering his, Rita said, "Good. Glad you were finally honest. Otherwise we'd all have more of a problem with you than we're already having. Of course you know what Rita here's talking about. No telling what experiences you've been having last few days."

Feeling a bit more comfortable and somewhat less astonished, Joey grinned on one side of his mouth and said "You wouldn't believe what's been happening."

"Oh yes I would," Rita responded with a tone of certainty. "Yes

I would. I'd believe it all."

For some reason Joey wanted to share what had been happening to him. He wanted to tell Rita about the e-mails, about encountering his wife with some guru at a place special to he and his wife, about the dark cloud coming toward his room, about the Arthur Godfrey set — uke'and all, about Johnny Carson riding with him, and about sitting with Dave Garroway, Steve Allen, Joe Pyne, Morton Downey, Jr. and Mike Douglas inside and outside her café. He felt a compulsion to tell this woman what had been going on the last few days, about who his brother is — *she'd flip like everyone else did if I told her Liberty Fortune, the host of Playing the Odds, the media and business mogul, was my brother* —and about Rose Barbelo — every man's sister and every woman's friend.

He was about to begin his story when Rita said, "I would believe it all, sweet thing, but I don't want to hear it. Some gifts are to be shared; others are to be stored away in secret. Keep what's been happening to you stored away in secret, sweet thing. They are precious gifts from God."

Joey's eyes moistened. Rita took one hand, keeping the other on top of his. Reaching in her apron pocket, she withdrew a tissue and gently dabbed the tear from his cheek.

"Now, Rita here's going to tell you some things before mom and pop and the kids start piling in here wanting their burgers and fries." Rita took her hand off of Joey's and slowly folded them in front of her with an air of authority. Joey nervously scraped at the skin around his nails, like he always did in stress except when he was on the air.

"Now, Rita here doesn't know you from Adam's cat," Rita said, evoking an involuntary tick in Joey's cheek, "but I do know this about you: You definitely *are* in rebellion. I don't know what, I don't need to know what, but you're at war, sweet thing. I suspect it is a war you began; one that you didn't have to fight. But you're in this war, and your life is in danger because of it. Now, I'm going to go out on a limb here and say…" she lowered her head so that her eyes could peer, laser-like, into his, "...that your friends actually did show up today and that you all had a nice meeting right back there," she said, pointing to the round table in the back of the room, where Joey had appeared to be sitting alone but was actually meeting with the fab five, "until I ran you out. And that you continued your party out there." She threw her head back toward the outside. "Now am I right, sweet thing, or has Rita here gone completely off her rocker?"

Without hesitation, Joey smiled and said, "Bingo!"

"Whew!" Rita exclaimed. "You win some and you lose some. This one I felt sure about." She clasped her hands on her ample bosom, took a deep breath, blew it out and said, "Thank you, God."

Joey said, "You wouldn't believe who they were." He still had a strong compulsion to tell this woman everything.

"Don't need to know, sweet thing. I told you: Hold your gifts from God close to your heart. They are yours, and precious. However, I do know that people you look up to, or people you trust are often sent when a person is in a crisis. Just the fact that they came to you confirms my feeling that you are in a war and your life is in danger. And that's why you are being visited. I bet there have been others, sweet thing."

Again Joey wanted to spill it all out, but he realized that Rita's statement was not a question, but her personal confirmation.

Rita looked up at the Pepsi Cola clock on the wall across from the counter. "Getting near time," she said. "But you need to know this: You've got friends at the top who are concerned about you. This war you are in — the one I call your rebellion — it's your choice whether you win or lose it. Your friends at the top know your story. They are trying to show you what your choices are; to teach you certain things about your life that you may have overlooked or help you remember things you might have forgotten. Sweet thing, my advice to you is to talk to them just as if they were right beside you... which they most likely are. Ask them to help you, to guide you, to show you the way. I bet you've never done that, have you?"

Joey shook his head and pursed his lips as if to say, *'fraid not*. He wanted to tell her about David Malak telling him how much help and protection is around him, but that would have brought up the whole Crystal thing and Rita was looking at the clock again.

"Then start doing it, sweet thing. From this moment on, you ask your friends at the top for advice and for direction and for all manner of what it is you need at the time. Trust me, sweet thing. All you need to do to get help is to ask."

Rita began the first of three efforts to slide out of the booth. Joey eased out and together they made their way to the door, just as a van pulled up with kids climbing out, whining that Rita's Eatery wasn't McDonalds.

"They're lucky just to be getting something to eat," Rita muttered under her breath.

Joey wanted to confirm and add to her observation — a talk show host's MO — but before he got a word out, Rita said, "Sweet thing, I suggest you stay the night. There's a Motel 6 right across the road and a Day's Inn just down the road, not far. It's getting late and you've had a busy day. And who knows what the night will bring?" she winked.

Then, looking across the road, she smiled and said, "See, they left the light on for you... just like they say on TV!" She let loose one of her shrill, ear drum splitting, howls, this time making Joey grimace and recoil.

Joey thought for a second, allowed for the acoustic vibration to subside, and then he said, "I believe I will. I'm getting a bit weary."

As the kids noisily piled through the door, brushing past Rita and Joey, she said, "Now don't forget what Rita here told you, sweet thing. Talk to your friends at the top. It's very important to you. Promise?"

"I'll do my best," Joey said.

Rita looked at him squarely, and said, "That's not a promise, sweet thing, but I guess it's the best I'll get."

Then she took a step back and looked at him. Joey felt the effect of the loving smile on her face throughout his body; it was a different look than he had seen from her throughout their encounter; like a balming of palliative calm. He felt loved.

Without hesitation, Rita put her huge arms around him and drew him to her in a bear hug of an embrace. The she turned on her heels and bellowed, "Welcome to Rita's, folks. Bet these hungry kids want some burgers and fries."

Joey chose the Day's Inn. His feeling of calm and love evaporated as he entered his room. Now he felt weary and forlorn. A rare headache developed inside both temples. And he was hungry. *Oh, but for a home cooked meal,* he thought. Then in a mental voice like a burlesque comic, he replied to himself, *Oh, but for a home!*

He placed his overnight bag on top of the nylon braided luggage stand, turned on several lights, and set the heater on medium.

To complete the lonely picture, Joey propped up several pillows on the bed, lay down, reached over to the side table and retrieved the bag containing his dinner — two Arby's roast beef sandwiches, curly fries and a medium Dr. Pepper. With a touch of sarcasm mixed with woe, he said to himself, "Just what the doctor ordered."

As he squeezed the horseradish sauce from the plastic tube onto the bun, his mind floated back to a roast beef of a different kind. Food often triggered Joey's memories of times gone by.

"Joey, stop picking at your food," he heard his mother say. "Do you know how much this brisket costs?"

He sees himself sheepishly look at his mother, then to his father, who gives him a soft *don't worry about it; let your mother be your mother* look with his eyes, then to Benny, who was shoveling in heaping forkfuls of his second portion of the brisket of beef, roast potatoes, and tzimas, preceded by the zesty hot chicken soup that comprised the traditional Sabbath meal at the home of Jacob and Rachel Rabinowitz.

Preparing the Sabbath meal was to Rachel Rabinowitz what

preparing to paint was to Picasso. It began with a discussion with the butcher regarding the size, weight, texture and — most of all — price of the brisket itself. Too thick and it would not cook sufficiently; too thin and it cooked up dry; trim too much fat and it loses its taste; don't trim enough fat and "I'm paying you for what I'll throw away!"

The potatoes were carefully peeled then sliced, just so, and placed artfully in the roasting pan around the brisket, like the moons of Jupiter, along with some onions to be roasted slowly together all day Friday.

Rachel's tzimas was her specialty. To the traditional mixture of carrots and raisins, Rachel added some walnuts, chopped scallions and "my own secret recipe of herbs and spices, you know, just like… what's his name? the chicken man; wears a white suit — he's a General or something."

At the beginning of the meal, Rachel would light the Sabbath candles and say the blessing. Jacob would say the Kiddush over the wine, and Rachel would hurry to the kitchen and bring out the steaming bowls of chicken soup. The challah, the Sabbath bread, was already in the center of the table waiting for Jacob to slice. After the soup, Rachel brought out the platter of brisket and friends, always with a pleasant smile on her face. This ritual reminded Joey of movies he'd seen about English kings. *All that was missing was Errol Flynn swinging across the room from the chandelier challenging Basil Rathbone to a sword fight,* he'd think.

The platter was passed around the table, followed by the tzimas bowl, then the challah and finally a small bowl containing white ground horseradish that would bring the uninitiated to their knees. Jacob seemed impervious to its lethal affect. Joey and Benny would hoot and howl after their first taste, followed by huge gulps of ice tea to put out the fire in their mouth.

After plates were brimming with food and the eating began, it was show time. Jacob, of course, hosted; conducting the conversation, usually about politics — national and local — and Rachel would add an occasional comment that Jacob would generally shrug off or totally ignore. It was his show. Benny would ravenously eat through it. Joey would watch and think of rejoinders to his father's commentary — sometimes, but not always, saying what he thought.

Often he would consider how one of his broadcast heroes would handle a certain topic his father raised. The seed of Joey Robin's love affair with the venue he spent a lifetime embracing was planted at his family's dinner table.

After he and Crystal were married, Rachel taught Crystal — who had previously thought a brisket was a line in an Ella Fitzgerald song that rhymed with basket — how to cook a brisket. "It's Joey's favorite," Rachel had told her, perhaps confusing Joey with Benny as parents often do as they age. The odd thing was that after Crystal began preparing brisket the Rachel Rabinowitz way, but with a touch or two of her own, it did indeed become his favorite meal. What he shunned as a boy he cherished as a man. And even though he and Crystal stopped celebrating the Sabbath after Michael died, a roast brisket became his meal of choice, his comfort food. Roast brisket and potatoes were his culinary symbols of home.

Sitting on his Day's Inn bed, he studied the remainder of his Arby's roast beef sandwich for a few seconds, shook his head, and set it aside.

Chapter 15

He fired up his laptop, logged on to AOL, and joined in the chanting of the "You've Got Mail" announcement.

By now, Joey assumed his mystery e-mailer had written one of the letters waiting to be opened. But, before he opened his mail, and without deliberation — in an act without reason — he Googled the name 'Rita'. After scrolling through Rita Hayworth, Rita Cosby, Rio Rita and assorted other variations on the word, he stopped at an entry that took his breath away:

In Hebrew lore, Rita is translated as Truth and Law and Order in the nature of things.

Watch for the signs, whispered in his mind.

He decided to check names of others he had encountered on his recent journey. He had never considered the meaning of the names of those in his orbit before. Now, he began to think differently. Still retaining a tinge of cynicism, his psyche was gradually tilting toward possibility.

For over forty years, he was married to a woman named Crystal, and he had never, ever considered her name as an indication of her place in his life. And yet, there she was; clear, sparkling, transparent, guileless, unique and solid. All these things his wife was… a gift from God that he had taken for granted for so long.

But it hadn't always been so. Through misty eyes, his mind played back to a time — an energetic, fresh and youthful time — when defying all the odds to win the heart of Crystal Faye Davis of Hendersonville, North Carolina was as compulsive a mission as becoming a media star.

Joey had been working at a small radio station in Ashville. Back when radio stations were locally owned, the owners expected their air personalities to promote their shows and the station by emceeing local events on the weekends. Most of the DJs liked emceeing the 'Miss This' or 'Miss That' pageants, or the high school proms, or sock hops, or what ever. The gigs provided an easy way to pick up a few extra bucks, and an even easier way to pick up girls.

To the maidens of Ashville, as well as to other young ladies in cities and towns all across America, local radio personalities — by way of some convoluted logic were looked upon as celebrities because they spun recordings of the stars. Most of the local jocks were in hock up to their elbows, but because their voice was on the radio, they were treated with honor, respect and gratuity by the local merchants, and by their sons and daughters with fanciful adoration.

Joey was not interested in the perks of local celebrity. He enjoyed the weekend work because — simply put — it was showbiz.

It was during one of these moonlighting weekends that Joey met Crystal. She was a sophomore at the University of North Carolina at Ashville, where her only grade above a D was in swimming. The rudiments of the undergraduate college student — lectures, homework, quizzes, and exams — thoroughly bored her.

In fact, her earliest memories were feelings of a child misplaced, like a wayward cosmic sojourner who has slipped out of orbit and become caught up in the energy of a noisy, chaotic self-serving planet. Recognizing and discerning truth from falsehood, real from phony, right from wrong, guile from honesty never failed her. It was her gift as well as her curse. Friends are hard to come by, and loneliness becomes one's companion when one is intolerant of anything short of honesty and truth.

Therefore, Crystal's failing grades were not an indication of her lack of intellect. Her acumen was instinctual and intuitive; a knowing from some inner light that radiated from within and emanated around her.

Joey was drawn to that light the instant he spotted Crystal. He had been hired to spin records at a UNCAA fraternity party at a private residence, one hot August evening, in the late '50's. The fall semester had just begun and the frat boys and their dates were behaving typically. The beer was being sloshed and guzzled, screaming girls were being pushed into the pool, while other couples disappeared into some private quarter, as Joey played Bobby Darin's, *Splish Splash*.

But one girl sat alone, and Joey could not take his eyes off of her. She wore a white, terry cloth, sleeveless top with matching shorts and was holding a glass of beer but not drinking it. Instead, she seemed to be staring off to somewhere beyond the din of the party.

When he was a kid, Joey's dream girl movie star was Virginia Mayo. There she was, he thought, sitting oblivious to the mayhem going on around her. Similar to the features of the Warner Brothers' dancer and actress, Crystal had lively green eyes, flowing blond hair, flawless smooth fair skin, and long shapely legs.

But Joey was drawn by more than just a childhood fantasy sitting gorgeously a few feet away from him. He didn't know what it was; the feeling was new to him. Nothing other than show business, broadcasting business, and building a career had ever interested him. He'd had a few dates along the way but nothing meaningful or memorable.

"Just a short break now to fuel up," Joey announced into the PA system to no one paying attention. "I'll be back in a flash with more hits on wax." He glanced over at the girl in the chair. He popped open a can of Ginger Ale and thought, *should I or shouldn't I?* Still pensive, there was a look of sadness on her face. Joey found the picture irresistible. He sidled over.

"Hi," he said.

Startled, as if slam-dunked back into the body after a near death experience, the girl turned her gaze away from whatever planet she was on, looked up at Joey, smiled and said, "Hi."

"I'm Joey Robin," he said. "I'm the guy playing the records over there." He pointed to his corner spot where his mike and turntables were.

She smiled, looked at him squarely — a look Joey would get to know for over forty years — and said, "I know who you are. I listen to your show at night."

"Thank you. I appreciate it, Miss…" He waited.

"Oh, I'm sorry. I'm Crystal. Crystal Davis."

Joey extended his hand. She accepted it. Her hand felt warm and soft in his. He didn't want to let it go.

"May I have it back, please?" she asked coyly. They both laughed.

"Of course, I'm sorry," he said, a bit embarrassed.

He grabbed a nearby chair and set it beside hers. A bold move, he knew, but it seemed the thing to do. And she didn't object or appear to mind.

"So," he said, after taking a swig of his Ginger Ale. "Do you live around here or go to UNCAA?"

She looked so lovely, and he was so mysteriously drawn to her that he felt off-center.

"We're from near here, Hendersonville, just outside Ashville. And yes, I go to the University. I'm a sophomore."

They talked a little about her difficulty with school, that she didn't know what she wanted to do with her life. She said she liked ballet but the University didn't have a dance major. "Anyway," she said. "My mom doesn't think much of dancing as a career." Her statement made her smile vanish. She looked away for a moment. But her smile returned as did her focus on Joey as she said, "It must be wonderful to have a goal, to know exactly what you want to do."

What is there about this girl?

"I'll admit it is wonderful to have a goal, as you say; to know exactly what you want to do. I've known all my life — as long as I can remember — what I wanted to do, wanted to become. The problem is getting there, you know, to the top."

Why am I telling her all this?

Crystal smiled a gentle warm smile. He melted. She said, "May I tell you something? I mean, I hope it doesn't hurt your feelings?

Joey's eyebrows lifted. "No," he said. "Go ahead."

"Well," she started, hesitating a few seconds, then she gave him that square in the eye look again, and said, "I told you I listen to your show, and... well... okay; I like what you have to say more than I like what you play. I mean, anyone can play those same records, but no one talks on the radio the way you do. That's just what I think. But I'm just a girl from Hendersonville who's flunking out of college. So don't pay me any attention." She looked to see if she had hurt his feelings. Then she looked away to the distance. Then she looked back at him quickly when she felt his hand on hers. Not only was this young woman in white shorts and top beautiful and warm, she had said exactly what Joey Robin had wanted someone to say since he took his first job in radio: Talk more. Crystal Davis was affirming what he believed about himself; that he was in league with his heroes. This validation did not come from an owner, a program director, or a station manager or from his peers. It was from this angel unaware from Hendersonville, North Carolina.

They stared in each other's eyes for a moment. Then, she said, "You're not hurt? I didn't hurt your feelings, did I?"

He smiled, leaned in, and gently kissed her on the cheek.

He said, "Hurt my feelings? All I can say about what you said is: from your mouth to God's ears."

"Good," she said softly. "I like that."

The feelings passing between them, as they gazed into one another's eyes, were suddenly broken by a gross, bellowing voice shouting, "Hey DJ. Where's the music?"

"Put some music on, platter man!" another yelled.

And then another, "Yeah, how about some Elvis?"

Joey got up from his chair. "Can I call you?"

"Yes," she said, smiling. It was the first time she seemed happy to him.

He took a pen from the pocket of his polo shirt and handed it to her. She wrote down her number on a napkin and handed it to him. He took it and squeezed her hand at the same time. They exchanged a second of eye contact, smiled, and he returned to his gig.

For the next six weeks Joey and Crystal saw each other as often as possible. Because his show was at night, most of their dates were late in the afternoon and early evening. Sometimes he'd pick a movie for them to see, followed by a bite to eat at a place that he selected, where he'd tell her the background of all the stars in the film, their real names, where they're from, who gave them their big break, even what they like it eat.

Crystal would listen attentively and forget most of it except when he talked about himself. He loved talking to her. She made him feel like he mattered, and that he would realize his dream.

They talked a lot in those early days. Joey introduced Crystal to Chinese food, and they'd eat from each other's plates and talk for hours on end. They would take long drives and talk. They would talk at Joey's small apartment and order pizza. They'd hold one another and talk. Generally the talk centered on Joey's career, his dream of stardom, of the big time. Sometimes they would talk about other things, but the conversation usually got back to "You know, honey, the way Cavett made it was to write jokes and bits for Carson. Maybe if I sent some of my stuff to...." and on and on.

After several months it was clear to both of them that they were deeply in love with one another and that there was no turning away from each other. But, there was a problem: Joseph Rabinowitz from Johnstown, Pennsylvania and Crystal Faye Davis of Hendersonville, North Carolina were from two different worlds. And back in the '50's, those worlds usually collided.

The vast distance between the two worlds became apparent when Joey asked if he could visit Crystal at her home.

"They don't know who you are," she said with a worried look in her eyes.

He raised his eyebrows for her to qualify the statement, an effective mannerism he used throughout his career when he wanted a guest to clarify the ambiguity of a statement made on his program.

"I mean," she qualified, "they know I'm seeing Joey Robin, the radio man." She made quotation marks with two fingers of both hands when she said 'radio man'. "But they do not know 'the radio man' is Jewish… and… a Yankee!"

Joey considered what she said for a moment without responding.

Crystal added, "And what about your folks, Joey? I mean, how are Jack and…"

"It's Jacob," Joey interrupted softly but firmly.

"Sorry," she said with a slight smile, which quickly vanished as she said, "Jacob and …" she held her hands out for him to fill in the blank.

"Rachel," he said, maintaining his soft yet firm tone.

"Sorry… again." She paused for a breath then said, "Jacob and Rachel Robin…o…wiz…"

"Rabinowitz."

"Right. What will those two think of their Joseph bringing home a… what did you tell me I was?"

Joey lightened up, and said, "A shikza. It means…"

"I know: a non-Jewish girl. In this case, a Southern Baptist non-Jewish girl. You think my side has problems with you? What about when your side gets a load of me!"

Joey's urge was to rush over to her and hold her tightly. She looked so adorable to him at that moment. He wanted to tell her how much he loved her, and that love will conquer all obstacles, that everything will work out all right.

Instinctively, however, he sensed that this discussion needed to be had for Crystal. She was the one most at risk, with far more to lose. The escapades of his brother had softened up his parents. The expectations of Jacob and Rachel Rabinowitz that their sons would retain the values of their parents vanished abruptly when Benny — shortly after taking the name Liberty Fortune — announced to the family that he had left Judaism and become a Catholic. "Brandy's wish," was his only explanation when his shocked father asked why. Brandy Sloan — formerly Evonalova Lutzkie — was Liberty's second wife and a former Miss Philly, an annual beauty contest sponsored by the Philadelphia Philly's pro baseball team. The marriage ended in two years when Liberty took up with the third runner up in the Miss Universe contest. So Jacob and Rachel Rabinowitz were primed and on alert for the emotional punishment only children can render to parents.

"My side will be okay, honey. They've already had their jolt. Tell you what: Just ask your folks if I can visit. Tell them who I am... not just the 'radio man', but a Jewish guy from the north who loves their youngest daughter. Will you just ask them if I can visit?"

Crystal said she would ask.

"Mom, Dad, I want to talk with you about Joey and I," she said tentatively a few days later after dinner.

"It's Joey and me," her mother corrected, after dabbing the corners of her mouth with a linen napkin. "The test is how you would begin a sentence. You would not say 'I want to talk with you about I and Joey' now would you, dear?"

Her mother had been an English teacher before marrying her father and devoting her time to having his children and maintaining a proper home for the plant manager of the Hendersonville, North Carolina branch of Dupont Chemicals.

Crystal looked at her father, a decent man, who rolled his eyes, giving Crystal some supportive comfort.

"You're right, Mom. I forgot. Joey and me. Can we talk?"

Her mother glanced at the clock on the mantel, and said, "All right, dear, but please say what ever it is swiftly. I have a D.A.R. meeting at the church in twenty-seven minutes, and I dare not be late. We have a speaker who has information about what might happen if that dreadful Kennedy fellow becomes our President."

Crystal cleared her throat and began by saying that she and Joey had been seeing a lot of each other and had fallen in love. While her father kept pursing his lips as if sucking on something sour, as he did whenever he sensed impending confrontation, his daughter, whom he adored, said, "…and he would like to meet with you both."

"I see no problem with that," her mother replied. "In fact, since you have been seeing each other frequently, it is only proper that we meet the young man. Is that all, dear? I really must be going."

"He's from up north and is Jewish!" Crystal blurted out.

The room turned deadly silent. Her mother's eyes widened with sheer terror, as her jaw dropped and remained open for several long moments. Her father's lip froze in mid purse, and his left upper cheek developed a tick, causing the eye above it to incessantly blink. Crystal started to cry. *I could not have done it worse*, she thought as a feeling of impending doom enveloped her entire being.

Her mother, naturally, was the first, and, as it turned out, only parent to speak. She took a deep breath, provoking a shiver throughout her upper body in an effort to regain composure and shake off the frightful experience she had just encountered from her daughter.

Using a firm, low-pitched tone of voice, selecting and enunciating each word as if conveying an order from on High, she said, "Crystal Faye Davis, you are not to see this person, talk to this person, or in any way communicate with this person ever again. Have I made myself absolutely clear?" Then, one more time louder, "Have I made myself absolutely clear?"

By now Crystal was sobbing uncontrollably. Her mother's edict felt as if molten lava had been poured over her soul. She did not acknowledge her mother's warning.

Her father attempted to reach out to his disconsolate daughter with his hand; but stopped short when he noticed the piercing eyes of his wife warning *don't you dare consol her*. He sat quietly, occasionally twitching.

Her mother added, "No doubt this Jew from up north is the reason for your failing grades at the University. I'm just thankful to

Jesus that we got this stopped before anything more serious happened. Now, I want you to go to your room and ask Jesus' forgiveness for what you have done, and for what you have thought of doing. Ask for his strength. And then, Crystal Faye, open your books and start studying. That is all of this we ever will hear about or discuss. This matter is concluded. I am already late for my meeting."

Crystal splashed some water on her face in the upstairs bathroom and went to her bedroom where she neither prayed to Jesus for forgiveness nor opened her schoolbooks. She carefully cracked open her bedroom door so she would hear the sound of the front door closing, and her mother leaving.

When she heard her mother drive away, she waited for the next sound she wanted to hear; that of her father going out the back door to his work shop in the garage. Instead, she detected the sound of footsteps coming up the stairs. She eased her bedroom door shut and lay down on her bed. Then there was a soft rapping on her bedroom door.

"Cris?" the voice said. "May I come in?"

She thought for a moment. There was no reason to deny the other man in her life that she loved a moment with her.

"Come in, Daddy."

He walked in as if on eggshells; as if his wife would burst in any moment and catch him being a loving father to his favorite daughter.

He sat down on the side of the bed. Did she see tears in his eyes? She had never seen tears in her father's eyes before. She felt so sad for him, for her. He leaned over and gave her a kiss on the forehead. Her eyes closed at the touch of his tenderness.

After several heaving sobs, she said, "He's a good man, Daddy. You would like him."

He smiled gently. "I'm sure I would, honey."

"All he wanted to do was come over, Daddy. He just wants to talk with you and

Mom. What's so bad about that?"

Her father sighed. "Honey, if it were left up to me, I'd say okay; bring him on over. But your mom… she… she has no place in her for anything that is out of the ordinary. Guess that's why she married me," he said with a sad laugh.

"You're not ordinary, Daddy. You're special. Just like Joey. Okay, he's from up North and he's Jewish. But you ought to talk to him, listen to him."

"I hear him on the radio, honey. He sounds like a fine person."

They both remained silent for several moments. Then Crystal asked, "Daddy, were you ever in love?"

He looked away to some place on the wall, smiled slightly, and said, "Yes, I was… once."

"With Mom?"

"Yes, with your mother."

She sat up and reached for the big teddy bear she slept with and nestled it with both arms against her chest.

"Are you still in love with Mom?"

Her father looked uncomfortable. She noticed a slight pursing of his lips, not as bad as during her mother's tirade, but he was definitely under pressure there.

"I… I still love your mother."

Crystal scooted closer to her father.

"Where did *in love* go?"

The question seemed to slightly jolt him. Then her dad's lips stopped pursing; he looked in control of himself; younger even. He found that spot on the wall with his eyes and seemed to be remembering something. Crystal thought he looked beautiful at that moment.

His eyes gazed down at his daughter. They were filled with love. Softly he said, "We let life make us forget how much we wanted each other."

Then he squeezed her hand, stood, and took a few steps toward the door. Stopping he said, "Don't ever allow life to get in the way of love, honey."

When she saw him walk slowly to his workshop, Crystal went downstairs and called Joey.

"How'd it go?" he asked.

"Awful," she said.

"Will they see me?"

"No."

"Are you sure? I'm a pretty persuasive…"

"No, Joey. And I was ordered never to talk to you or see you ever again."

"What?"

"It's an order, Joey. It's over. I can't go against my parent's wishes. I'm sorry." She started sobbing again.

"I'm not giving up on us, Cris. I love you. I always will. I'm not…"

"I love you, too, Joey. I always will. But this is… this is goodbye."

"Cris… don't do…"

"Goodbye, Joey."

Joey tried calling her back. She didn't answer. And for the first time in his life, Joey Robin broke down in a flood of tears. He wept until his sides hurt from crying. He'd try calling her throughout the day, but to no avail. He came by the university, but her mother had instructed the authorities that he was not allowed near her daughter. The officials told him if he came on the grounds again he'd be arrested. He wrote letters, but they were either returned undeliverable or not answered. He cried himself to sleep every night. Nothing in his life had ever mattered except being on the air. Now, nothing in his life mattered except being with the girl he loved.

Several months went by, with Crystal and Joey praying for a miracle — a miracle which would bring them together. Then the Universe interceded.

First, Joey was offered a job in Memphis, not as a DJ who talked a little and spun records, but as a full-fledged talk show host. Stations were just beginning to program the all-talk format and it was catching on. Joey's slot was the primo prestigious and lucrative morning drive time.

One of Joey's sponsors was the Teeter College of Performing Arts. On a whim, he mailed a brochure to Crystal in one of his daily unanswered or undeliverable letters to her. A week later, he was shocked to receive a letter postmarked Hendersonville, NC:

Dear Mr. Robin,

Over the course of the past months I have watched my daughter, who I love more than life itself, sink lower and lower in despair. Due to her emotional health, complicated by failing grades, she has withdrawn from the University of North Carolina at Ashville. She spends most of her time at home alone in her room. I am concerned for her state of well being, both emotionally and physically. Her mother has not allowed the letters you have been sending to reach her. However, Crystal is aware of your efforts to do so.

This week your letter containing the brochure from the Teeter College arrived while I was at home. Because Crystal has always expressed an interest in ballet, and I have been on the lookout for anything that may enliven her spirit, I took it upon myself to show her the brochure. Immediately she perked up. Her spirits soared even more when I made her the following proposal: that I would allow her to attend the Teeter College in Memphis under the provision that she neither sees you nor talks with you. She readily accepted my offer.

While her mother vehemently opposes this arrangement, I was able to convince her that this is in the best interest of, not only our daughter, but of our entire family, including her mother and me.

Therefore this is to inform you that our daughter will be arriving in Memphis in time for the start of the fall semester on Saturday, August 3rd at 9:30 AM on Trailways Bus. I am assuming and that you will honor the provisions of my agreement with Crystal, as she said she would honor it as well.

With my very best wishes for your continued success in all areas of your life, I am,

Sincerely yours,

Jonathan L. Davis.

Two months later, Joey and Crystal were married by a justice of the peace.

Chapter 16

Was it too late to reclaim this gift? Joey wondered with misty eyes, sitting in his Day's Inn motel room, feeling the stupor of squandered treasure.

Joey rewound the tapes in his mind of his encounter with David Malak; what he said, how he said it, how he seemed to virtually blend with and calm the energy in his space. For some reason, Joey could not stop his eyes from misting. It seemed as if the tears were coming from a deep well within him; a place untapped before this journey.

He thought of Rose. Spontaniously he googled 'Barbelo'. Instantly four pages of biography and other representations of the body of work of Rose Barbelo appeared on his computer screen.

Eventually there was this:

Barbelo is a female angel next to the Father of all.

He dabbed at his eyes with his handkerchief. *They're all around me*, he thought. *I never knew.* He considered Googling Michael, but quickly dismissed the thought. *Enough*, he said to himself.

Instead he clicked on his e-mail. He checked to see if Crystal had written. She had not. He deleted the one from AARP, a reminder from his dentist, a few from media sources that still had his name in their address book, plus four more Viagra-type ads.

And then he opened the one from howardcosell@badrug.com. The address spoofing the sports commentator, Howard Cosell, that Mohammed Ali used to kid about his toupee, brought a wide smile to Joey's face.

WOW! WHAT A DAY YOU'VE HAD! BUT IT AIN'T OVER YET. HOW ABOUT THAT RITA! SHE'S SOMETHING ELSE, ISN'T SHE? I JUST LOVE HER. AND CARSON RIDING ALONG WITH YOU? HOW SPECIAL WAS THAT! DO YOU

KNOW HOW HARD IT WAS GETTING HIM TO DO THAT? FOR A WHILE I THOUGHT IT WOULD HAVE TO BE ROBERT Q. LEWIS. REMEMBER HOW YOU LOVED WATCHING HIS AFTERNOON TV SHOW? BUT CARSON LOVED YOUR DREAM AND FINALLY SAID OKAY. IT WAS GOOD TO SEE YOU GUYS GETTING ALONG SO WELL. HE LIKED YOU, YOSELEY. YOU OUGHT TO BE PROUD. HE DOESN'T LIKE A LOT OF PEOPLE. HE SAID YOU HAD EVERYTHING IT TAKES TO MAKE IT BIG. BUT IT JUST WASN'T IN THE PLAN.

ANYWAY, GOOD JOB WITH THE GUYS AROUND THE TABLE. THEY ALL AGREED WITH CARSON... ABOUT YOUR ABILITY. EVEN JOE PYNE SAID SOMETHING LIKE 'HE'S OKAY.'

THE IMPORTANT THING IS THAT YOU ARE BEGINNING TO UNDERSTAND SOME OF WHAT IS SIGNIFICANT. I AM SO GLAD YOU LOOKED UP THE NAMES OF THOSE PEOPLE AROUND YOU. QUITE A CIRCLE OF PROTECTION AND LOVE, YOSELEY. YOU ARE VERY BLESSED.

BUT THERE IS STILL MORE FOR YOU TO LEARN. TIME IS RUNNING OUT. AND YOU STILL NEED TO ANSWER THE BIG QUESTION:

DO YOU WANT TO DIE?

BUT RIGHT NOW, AT THIS VERY MOMENT, YOU NEED TO DO SOMETHING. LOG OFF THE INTERNET AND TURN ON THE TV AND TUNE INTO LARRY KING. DO IT RIGHT NOW. BYE.

PS. YOU'RE NOT EATING RIGHT. AFTER THE KING SHOW, GO OVER TO RITA'S AND ORDER SOME VEGETABLES. DO I SOUND LIKE YOUR MOTHER, YOSELEY?

There's no way this could be my mother, Joey thought to himself. *She didn't even drive a car, let alone use a computer*!

Without any hesitation or obstinacy, Joey flipped on the TV and tuned it to CNN. The time was exactly 9pm. Without realizing it, for the first time ever, Joey leaned back to watch Larry King without wishing he were him.

"Tonight an exclusive interview with the woman who turned the media world on its heels today with the startling announcement that she is expanding her, already formidable, media empire, by acquiring Fortune Media. The woman some people call the most beloved woman in America, Rose Barbelo. Joining Rose Barbelo is the man who sold Fortune Media to her. As most of you know, he is not only the host of the longest running quiz show in America, *Playing the Odds*, but a business mogul whose vast holdings read like a Dow Jones directory — Liberty Fortune. Welcome both."

"Well I'll be damned!" Joey said out loud as he cranked up the volume on his set and moved to the edge of the bed.

"Rose, first you. Why did you buy Liberty's company?"

"Thank you for having us on, Larry. First, let me say, before my folks down in Memphis have apoplexy, I did not buy Liberty's investment companies, his real estate companies, his baseball team, his oil companies, his what-else-he-owns companies. Only God could afford that. I just bought his media company. That includes his cable television franchises, his radio stations, and his production company. And I am pleased to announce right here on your show that Liberty has agreed to stay on as host and executive producer of *Playing the Odds* for as long as he wants to. I hope he never leaves."

If there had been a studio audience, the applause sign would have flickered. No doubt the older demographic folks at home were cheering without prompting from a sign.

"Yes, but why? Why did you want it... his media company, that is?"

Way to go, Larry. Hang in till you get an answer, Joey said to himself.

Rose worked to look composed. Like most hosts, she asked questions better than she answered them. A frenzy of impulses synapsed across her mind. After all, this was a huge deal involving dozens of lawyers and accountants, a group of lenders and assorted other entities not to mention the personal high career stakes riding on what Rose had in mind.

"Well, without disclosing to the broadcasting industry and other media of my specific plans, let me just say, Larry, that I have some ideas that require ownership of outlets."

"Program ideas, I assume?" King asked.

"Yes, program ideas. I could either try to build — that is, try to start up a string of outlets one at a time, which would require a lot of time and energy — or I could just go to someone whose got stations and offer to buy them all. So I got in touch with Liberty; we talked; I offered; he agreed; and I bought." Rose punctuated the end of her comment with her most endearing smile. Hidden beneath the desk, her knees were shaking like a kettle before the steam blows out.

"Liberty, what made you want to sell your radio and television cable franchises?"

The close-up on his brother sent Joey's mind back to that day at Forbes Field, when they were both kids.

That's where I'm going to be, he remembered himself saying as he pointed to the radio broadcast booth.

That's where Benny's going to be, his younger brother had said pointing to the owners' box.

"You sure got there, brother," Joey whispered in the empty room. "You sure got there".

Liberty's face looked artificial to Joey, as if it were made from a mold rather than flesh and bone. Nothing in the face remained of Jacob and Rachel Rabinowitz. The white open collared shirt under a double-breasted navy blue blazer exposing a gold crucifix closed the case for Joey.

"Larry, have you ever heard that line from the movie, I think it was *Casablanca*, when Humphrey Bogart says 'I'll make him an offer he can't refuse?'" Liberty asked with the twinkle that made millions of women adore him.

"Benny, you shmuck!" Joey yelled. "It was Brando in *The Godfather*! There isn't a person on the planet who doesn't know that! How dumb can you be, Ben?"

Joey answered his own question in his head: *I'm calling you dumb and a shmuck, and I'm sitting here in the Days Inn with a cold Arby's and you just made mega millions to add to your mega millions.* For a second he considered what he had thought, then said out loud: "Millions, gazillions, you're still a dumb shmuck!"

"Yes, I've heard the expression." King said with a coy look and a wink at Rose, who let Liberty's faux pas pass.

Good for you, Larry. Joey thought. *Lovely nuance. You too, Rose.*

Within an hour, hundreds of thousands of viewers would e-mail Liberty correcting his mistake. Liberty's office would then add those names to millions of other names in a database. When the next Liberty Fortune book, CD, DVD or other product would go on the market, those millions of names would receive a 'personal' e-mail from him, inviting them to be the first to buy, at a special rate for Liberty Fortune Club Members. Making an on-air mistake was a devise to build a marketing base that he had used over and over through the years. Comics and critics, as well as his brother, called him simple-minded, a buffoon, a dumb shmuck. Liberty Fortune was as dumb as P.T Barnum.

"Well that's what happened. Rose came to see me and made me an offer. I liked the offer, and we made a deal." Liberty smiled broadly, exposing a mouth full of teeth as white as snow. Then he added, "I've been on your show many times before, Larry. And I've always told you the secret to success is not to fall in love with the merchandise. Rose wanted my stations more than I did and, well, she got them."

"And I paid dearly for the privilege," Rose interrupted, reaching out to put her hand on Liberty's arm as King did his laugh.

"Rose," King began. "Can you tell our audience and your millions of followers a little bit more of what you have in mind to put on your stations?"

Rose hesitated.

Careful Rose. Remember what I told you about revealing an idea before it's hatched. These are not kindred spirits, kid. Finesse, kid. Finesse, Joey thought, as if trying to send her a mental message.

"Of course we'll be making announcements down the road, Larry, about specific formats, personalities, and so forth. And I'm still somewhat in the clouds from working out this arrangement with Liberty, who — let me say — is every bit the warm human being to do business with, as the person millions enjoy every day on *Playing the Odds*.

Way to go, kid. That's my girl. Class. Now give King a bite but not the whole apple.

"I can tell you this, Larry: God has blessed my life and my work in so many ways. To work with Joey Robin for so many years and learn so much from him and to have his friendship and mentoring has been a God send."

Ironically, the camera did a cut-a-way shot of Liberty at that instant. His lips still maintained the pasted shape of a smile; but now there was a quiver at the corners.

"And then for *Pathways* to become the hit it has become is nothing short of miraculous. And so I am interested in creating more programming that serves human kind's search for meaning, like *Pathways* does. I have something more specific in mind, a special project — in fact, I have the whole package in mind — but I'll save that for another time. Maybe you'll have me back to talk about it."

Larry King was aware, as was the whole of the media community, that Liberty Fortune and Joey Robin were brothers. King and others in the business also knew that there was an unwritten rule, one that Liberty had dictated, that the relationship was never to be discussed. So pervasive throughout all of media was the influence, the tentacles, the control of Liberty that the edict had its own name: in the business it was known as 'The Rule of Fortune': If you wanted Liberty Fortune on your show, if you wanted the many commercial benefits Liberty Fortune's holdings could bestow on your network and it's board of directors, you never, ever mentioned or raised the issue of he and his brother.

Recently, Rose Barbelo tried to circumvent the rule. At the conclusion of their negotiations for the purchase of his media companies, she personally asked Liberty if, one time and one time only, he and Joey would appear on her show together to answer "whatever I might think of to ask."

"Rose," Liberty replied, with no resemblance to the charmer he was publicly. "If you want to kill our deal, bring the subject up again. If you want me to walk out now and tear up our letter of intent, bring the subject up again. In fact, I will have a stipulation inserted in our purchase agreement that there will not be any reference to my family, including my brother, in any formal or informal announcement of this transaction or else the deal is null and void. And I will expect you to abide by the terms of our agreement."

Rose's motive for wanting Liberty's media companies outweighed her disgust for what she considered his petty anger toward his brother — the man to whom she owed so much, and for whom she held such deep affection. Rose Barbelo, the interviewer, craved knowing what lay at the heart of their feud. However, Rose Barbelo, the businesswoman, had learned the art of choosing one's battles. Subsequently, her carefully worded reference to Joey Robin in her statement, without mentioning he was Liberty's brother, did not jeopardize nor violate their agreement.

"We'll play it your way," was all she said after Liberty coarsely reaffirmed his law.

He simply nodded once, as if to say, 'So there. Case closed.'

King said, "Rose, good luck with your new venture — whatever it is. I know all America is behind you."

"Thank you, Larry," Rose said graciously.

"And Liberty," Larry said. "Is there anything you'd like to add?"

"Tell him how much epoxy glue it takes to hold your face together, you phony!" Joey barked to the TV.

Stretching a broad smile, Liberty looked straight at the camera and talked for two minutes about what a great country America is. He never mentioned Rose.

"Thank you Rose Barbelo and Liberty Fortune," King said. "We'll be watching you both in the weeks ahead. We'll be right ba…"

Joey faded the sound, shook his head in disgust, and thought, *Benny you are not only a shmuck, you lack one ounce of good taste.* He sat on the edge of the bed for several moments holding the remote in his hand, unmindful of the image of Don Rickles sitting across from Larry King, who was breaking up laughing.

I wonder what she has in mind. he contemplated silently. He wanted to call Rose and tell her what a great job she did, but decided against it. *Maybe tomorrow, after the wind dies down*, he decided.

Joey felt unusually hungry. Remembering what the mysterious e-mailer advised, he combed his hair, and decided to walk across the road and have a bite at Rita's Eatery. *Maybe I will get some vegetables. Who knows? Maybe Rita has some more words of wisdom for me. She's some special lady.*

The café was mostly empty. Just a few tired-looking truckers eating steak and eggs while talking on their cell phones.

"Is Rita around?" Joey asked the skinny man with a toothpick in the corner of his mouth, adding up the day's receipts behind the counter.

The man looked up. He looked puzzled.

"Sorry," he said. "You asked for Rita?"

"Yes, I just thought she might still be here. I'd like to…"

"Fella," the man interrupted. "I guess you don't come around here much. I'm Rita's cousin, Josh. I own the place. Rita died about five years ago."

Chapter 17

"Hey, sweetie!" the familiar vivacious voice breezed through Joey's cell phone. He had been driving eastbound on I-70 for about three hours after a fitful night's sleep.

"Hi, kid. This is a nice surprise."

"Where are you?"

Rose knew Joey so well that she never wasted time questioning his behavior, peccadilloes, or reasoning. If what he needed was to take a drive, then what he needed was to drive without someone pressuring him to explain why he needed to take a drive because he wouldn't reveal his innermost raison d'être anyway.

"Just about to enter Pennsylvania," he replied.

"You're going to your home, right?" she asked.

"Going home is correct for two-hundred. Do you want to take the two-hundred or continue playing?"

She ignored the game, replying warmly, "Sweetie, I hope you find what you're looking for. I really do."

I wish I knew what I was looking for, he thought.

"I caught you on the King show last night. You were terrific."

"Oh, thank you, dear soul." And she meant it. Somehow a compliment or a good review from Joey still meant more to her than all the accolades she receives. Rose sought his approval of her performance as if she were still under his wing.

"Were you surprised?" she asked.

"Well, yes, to tell you the truth. I was, kid. And I must say; a bit intrigued. You want to tell me about it?"

"Oh yes. Very much. Because you are a… yes, I want to tell you all about it. Joey, I need to talk to you but not like this. First off, you know how you are driving and talking on the cell phone. You're libel to wind up in Canada. I've got an idea: Since you will be in Pennsylvania and I'm still here in New York, why don't we meet? I do need to talk to you about what I'm doing. How about I stop off in Johnstown on my way back to Memphis? Say... tomorrow night? We could have dinner and talk. I'm sure Johnstown is loaded with great places to eat." She waited for the laugh.

Joey gave the laugh she wanted, and said, "Won't that be too much trouble? I mean you..."

"Sweetie," Rose interrupted. "It's my plane. I tell it where I want to go. This'll be wonderful! Meet me at the Johnstown airport... they do have an airport, don't they?"

"With a runway, too," Joey deadpanned.

"Good. That'll make landing easier," she said, just like when they worked together. "Meet me at six at the airport. You can have the day there doing whatever it is you want to do. Oh, sweetie, I am so looking forward to this. It will be so good to see you and talk to you. So much to tell. So much to share. See you tomorrow. I love you. Bye."

"Goodbye, kid. Thanks. I'll be there waiting for you."

Joey felt a rush of energy. Just the anticipation of something other than the mundane his life had become filled him with an energy he had forgotten existed. It stayed with him until he approached the outskirts of Johnstown. Then nostalgia replaced the momentary high.

He navigated his way down the winding narrow roads leading to the valley where the city of his youth lay wasting — its pallor gray, its energy low — due to the closing of the steel mills that once gave it life.

Joey drove slowly past several significant places of his youth. The radio station where he used to hang out was gone. A tanning and tattoo parlor stood where his Uncle Morris's store used to be; his dad's store was now an adult bookshop. Five blocks away, on Iron Street, the site where the synagogue he grew up attending (where he had his bar mitzvah and used to sit and pray for a life in broadcasting and for stardom) was now a Goodwill Industries shop.

Joey headed for the road leading up to Southmont, the leafy

suburb where he grew up. Southmont was a 1950's TV sitcom, a time when Paw Cartwright, Ozzie Nelson and father knew best: all white, clean, safe and predictable. In fact, he once wrote a parody for his high school drama class called 'Leave It to Rabinowitz.'

It was just as he remembered it nearly fifty years after he left to follow his dream. The pall that cast its gloom and depression over Johnstown was instantly replaced by the idyllic ambiance of this small, middle class community, although now he spotted a few Neighborhood Watch signs denoting the changing times.

He drove down the elm tree lined, Luzerne Street and turned right past the fire hall and headed toward Grandview cemetery. There he parked in front of the Jewish section and easily located the gravesite of his parents with its two modest headstones. He began to recite the Kaddish but could not remember all the words, and so he simply stood there in silence. Off to his right and slightly behind, stood the solitary figures of a young man and older woman. Joey didn't see them.

Then he drove to the house at 722 Lakota Street where his body, mind and spirit were nourished and his later reality was fashioned. He parked his car across the street and stared at the house. *The remains of a day, just like me: out of style and in need of a face-lift*, he thought.

He got out of the car and slowly walked up the creaky wooden stairs leading to the porch where he used to sit in the warm evenings listening to his dad talk. He wished he had remembered the stories his father used to tell.

And then he saw him! A man, sitting on the old swing. The man didn't look up as Joey slowly reached the top step. *I ought to get out of here*, he thought. But something compelled him to stay.

"Hello," Joey said cautiously, more like a question.

The man didn't stir. Nothing. He just slowly swung back and forth, his head down, his chin resting on his chest.

Joey looked at him. He wore a double-breasted navy blue blazer with gold buttons over a white open collar polo shirt and a naval cap with some kind of gold embroidered insignia or emblem in front. His trousers were white linen with a razor sharp crease. His shoes were two tone black and white loafers. The entire outfit was the kind of get up yachtsmen used to wear, maybe some still do.

His one hand rested on top of the other in his lap. They were deeply tanned, as was the man's face. Joey took a seat on the rattan chair to the side of the swing. There were two chairs, each identical, each in the same state of disrepair as when Joey lived at this home, the same ones his dad and mom sat on each night, sometimes talking, often not, watching life go by, there on their beloved front porch. The chairs, like everything else on the porch seemed frozen in time, the time when Joey was the boy who dreamed of a life behind a microphone or in front of a TV camera.

Without a sound or movement of warning, without looking up, the man suddenly spoke. The voice sent a chill through Joey's body.

"Welcome home," the man said.

Joey leaned in and down so as to get a better look at the man whose voice he immediately recognized.

Joey said, "Jack? Jack Paar? Is it you?"

The man looked up and grinned a familiar, sheepish grin. His blue eyes smiled.

He replied, "I kid you not."

It was Paar's trademark expression. He'd use it after telling a story during his monologue. There was always some outrageous irony in the story — that's where he would implore "I kid you not" to the audience. Paar's stories in his monologue usually pertained to some experience, something outrageous, incredible, something that that had happened that week that could only happen to him. It was Paar one-on-one with the audience — personal, entertaining, endearing. A theatrical devise designed for the intimacy of TV. It took courage, talent, and wit to carry it off. Regis picked up the shtick many years later and still uses it today with much the same dynamic and sense of incredulity that Paar used when had the whole country saying "I kid you not." They still do.

Joey immediately understood the gist of the outfit Paar was wearing on the porch. Paar loved life on the water, and he could afford the expensive amenities that went with it. Often he would film his yachting excursions and show it on his program along with his witty voice-over narration.

"Should I ask what are you doing here?" Joey asked.

"You should if you are any kind of an interviewer," Paar shot back.

"Okay. What are you doing here?"

"I thought you'd never ask."

Joey laughed. Paar grinned.

Paar put his feet on the ground, stopping the motion of the swing.

"Mind if I sit next to you in your mom's chair?" Paar asked.

"You know it was..."

"Please," Paar disgustedly appealed, using the back of his hand to cast away some imaginary nuisance flying near him, which in this case was whatever Joey had started to say. "Can we skip the part where you are amazed with what I know about you and your life? Haven't sufficient surprises, seemingly weird paradoxes, and paranormal experiences happened to you in the past few days to convince you that you are the subject of significant interest to someone with sufficient clout, so as to bring the intercession of what amounts to the entire deceased membership of the Fryer's Club or the Broadcasting Hall of Fame appearing before you, as if you were a human vortex?"

Before Joey could answer, Paar added, "Can we move on from your shock and awe and let me do my thing and get out of here?"

No more than several seconds of reflection was all Joey needed to conclude that the past few days of his life were beyond reason.

With a slight smile, and a look in his eye of confirmation, Joey said, almost in a whisper, "Sure."

"Good," Paar said. "Tell you what: Instead of more sitting, let's go inside."

They moved slowly indoors. Everything looked just like it was when Joey was growing up there. The front foyer still needed more light because of Jacob Rabinowitz's warning that the chandelier uses too much electricity. The carpet was still frayed.

The living room was off the foyer to the right. Still adorned with the secondhand sofa, which Rachel covered with an off-white, chenille bedspread that was only removed "when company comes over." In front of the sofa sat a nondescript brown wooden coffee table with a glass top ornamented with a silver cigarette lighter, a large glass ash tray, and a bamboo coaster holder with cork coasters stacked inside.

Across from the coffee table was Jacob's easy chair and ottoman, covered with a green fabric; the arm rests nearly worn to the felt, and the spot where Jacob's head rested darkened from the Vitalis Jacob applied to his hair. Slightly behind Jacob's chair was Rachel's, with a rather new gray slipcover, decorated with men and women dressed to the nines, stepping out of horse drawn carriages.

At the front of the living room, boldly stood a Winter upright piano. A large clock with sloping wooden sides sat on one side of the top, and a brown wooden metronome rested on the other. A large photograph of Dinah Shore's sunshine smile beamed from the cover of a sheet of music titled *We'll Meet Again*. It was one of Rachel's favorite songs. Joey remembered his mother humming it as she prepared meals, did the laundry or tended to her sewing. "I heard this song the night you were born, Yoseley," his mother would often tell him. Hearing the song always filled Joey with a special warm feeling.

Just to the side of the piano was the focal point of the room: a television set. Before television, the sofa and chairs had been arranged for conversation. But when TV arrived, family conversation — as well as dining room mealtime — ceased to exist.

"I remember our first set… a Dumont," Joey said to Paar, as they stood in his old living room. "We were so excited just to sit and watch the test pattern," he laughed. Paar looked at him as if to say, *we all did that*. "Then Dad brought home an Admiral set after things got going with television. He watched wrestling matches from Chicago, and he had his favorite wrestlers. Let's see, there was Lou Thesz and Gorgeous George, somebody named Farmer something, I can't remember all of the others."

"Thank goodness," Paar deadpanned.

"After school, Mom and I would watch the *Robert Q. Lewis Show*. It was really one of the first TV talk shows I can remember, along with Peter Lind Hayes and Mary Healy. Funny how the format they laid down hasn't really changed. It's what you did back on the *Tonight Show,* right Jack?"

Paar put his hand to his chin and thought for a second. "Basically, yes. The genesis was really Godfrey on radio. He was the originator of the format. We all used it and adapted it to our style, maybe added a few wrinkles of our own. But even to this day, everybody's still doing Godfrey."

Paar escorted Joey from the living room back to the foyer where, off to the left, a stairway led to the second floor.

"I used to slide down this banister, much to Mom's chagrin," Joey said, as they made their way upstairs.

"How original," Paar responded. "Now if Mom had encouraged you to slide *up* the banister, that would be interesting." Joey laughed. Paar was doing Paar.

They looked in the first bedroom where Jacob used to sleep after he stopped sleeping with Rachel. Some detective magazines were stacked on the side table, along with a box of King Edward cigars on a shelf beneath.

Then they peeked into Rachel's bedroom, where blankets, quilts, and pillows were piled nearly up to the ceiling. Some bottles of Sea Breeze lotion, a jar of Noxzema, and a silver framed photograph of her sons smiling head to head, sitting on the living room sofa, was situated in the middle of Rachel's bureau. The photograph was inscribed, 'to the best Mom, from your boys. Love, Joseph and Benjamin.'

To the side, a smaller photo of a child, a young girl.

"Iris," Paar said, with a tone of reverence.

Joey raised his eyebrows and looked at him with amazement, but Paar held up one finger as if to say, *Remember what I told you… what you agreed to,* and Joey lowered his eyes, and softly said, "Iris."

Paar studied the photograph for several moments then delicately placed it back on the bureau top.

A tiny bathroom was off to one side of the upstairs. Joey glanced in and saw the familiar jar of Barbarsol shaving cream alongside a Gillette double edge razor on the side of the sink. On the other side, a bottle of Vitalis hair grooming lotion. They headed for the smaller bedroom at one end of the hall.

Across from the bed, almost touching it, stood an old brown wooden table used for a desk with a metal corkscrew lamp and a small photograph inside a gold frame.

Beside the bed, on an old wooden table, was Joey's northern star — a Crosley radio.

"I'd lie on this bed and listen and dream and wish and pray," Joey told Paar, who just stood by the door observing Joey remembering. "In fact, Jack. I listened to you the first night you filled in for Jack Benny. When they introduced you, everybody said, 'Jack who?'"

"Wow! What a memory!" Paar said. "I had just gotten out of the Navy. Filling in for Benny was my big break."

Joey shook his head disconsolately and started to say something but Paar jumped in. "I know, I know. You never had a big break. You believe you deserved a big break, but it never came. Why others and not you? You've been putting up with that vexation for a long time, haven't you, kid?"

Joey snorted a laugh sound, but didn't reply. Suddenly his familiar woeful thoughts were diverted. He thought he noticed someone — no, several some ones — in the doorway beside Paar. One was looking over Paar's shoulder, another peeking around Paar's side, and still another peering in over the crouching one. It looked like a poster for a Marx Brothers movie or the Beatles' *Sgt. Pepper Lonely Hearts Band*. Joey craned his neck for a better look. But whatever or whomever it was he thought he saw disappeared, or, he concluded, wasn't there in the first place. Paar just stood there with the quizzical expression of a magician reacting to the puzzlement of an audience.

"Listen to me, kid," Paar said. "The first thing you've got to do is for you to remember how much you wanted to be what you became. It all began in this room, with that radio, writing letters to stations at that desk. Now take a deep breath. I want you to remember how much you wanted the life you were given. Like the song says, try to remember."

Similar to the experience recalling how much he wanted a lifetime with Crystal, Joey felt himself lying in bed, listening to Jack Benny, Fred Allen, Red Skelton, Amos & Andy, and other comics. He saw himself pressing his ear against the receiver late at night, as he fished on the dial for WMCA in New York and Barry Gray, who practically invented the art of celebrity interviewing, and WOR and Long John Nebel, the first broadcaster to talk seriously about UFOs, and then listening to sports, not for the event, but for the way Bill Stern, Mel Allen, Red Barbour, and, of course, Rosy Rosewell and others, brought the games to life with their talent for pacing, shading, nuance, drama, and tension; all delivered through the unique and stylistic quality of merely their voice.

And he'd listen to musical variety shows staring Eddie Cantor, Buddy Clark, Al Jolson, Bing Crosby, even the *Grand 'Ol Opry* and *Sunday Down South* from Nashville, featuring a young singer named Dinah Shore.

And the dramatic shows, *The Lux Radio Theater*, which dramatized hit films, and *The Big Story*, depicting how various journalists investigated and reported a major news story, and *Inner Sanctum*, which scared millions of listeners with the adroit appeal to the theater of the mind, and on Saturday mornings, *Gunsmoke*, a western for adults, which dramatized the old west as vividly without pictures as its latter television adaptation did with costumes and scenery.

How he craved being a part of that world! How his soul longed for that Universe of broadcasting! How fast he wanted time to fly so he could fly to that planet where his heroes lived! He could feel his childhood yearning inside himself, permeating throughout his essence, as he sat on the side of his childhood bed all these years later. His seventy year old body and mind resonated to the instant regression of his spirit to a time when he hungered for the life he eventually attained.

After several moments of time travel, Paar broke the silence. "Let's go back downstairs, kid," he said, with a twinkle in his eye.

Joey slowly rose from his childhood bed. Suddenly, his jaw dropped. The photograph, the one in the gold frame on the table desk, he didn't pay any attention to it earlier, but now it stunned him like a taser to the belly. He reached for the frame.

"Jack," he said to his guide without looking at him, with a voice filled with awe. "This is no Woolworth frame. This frame's *pure gold!*"

Then he brought the photograph closer to his face. "Oh my God!" he cried out.

It was a photograph of Joey, as his present day self, sitting at an outdoor picnic table in front of a restaurant, obviously engaged in an animated conversation. But no one else is seated at the table.

Staggered, Joey carefully returned the photograph to the table. Paar came over and offered his arm, which Joey took hold of.

"There's more," Paar said. "Can you make it?"

Joey took a deep breath and hesitated. Then he said, "Make it I can do. Take it? I'm not so sure." Paar grinned.

They made their way back down the narrow staircase.

"Please don't slide," Paar said, with his giddy tone of feigned agitation, the devise with which he'd jibe Charlie Weaver or Hermione Gingold or other regular characters so effectively on his *Tonight Show.*

To the rear of the small foyer was the dining room separated from the foyer by only a cheap, blue, linen curtain, hanging from a rod his father had put up. Behind the dining room was the tiny kitchen. From the foyer, Joey thought he heard someone in the kitchen but shrugged off the thought just as he did upstairs, when he thought he saw people peeking around the doorway.

Still a tad unsteady from his bedroom regression experience, Joey approached the dining room with Paar behind him, "I'll show you where I used to pretend to be Arthur Godfrey."

Paar said, "Kid, you better sit down for this."

Chapter 18

Paar slid open the curtain and held out his hand as if to say 'behold'.

Sitting in the chair young Joey used to sit in, pretending to be Arthur Godfrey, was the old redhead himself! With a beaming smile on a face full of freckles, wearing a loud Hawaiian shirt, and holding a ukulele, Joey's avatar said, "How warr ya, how warr ya," in that unmistakable, nasal baritone Radio Guide listeners fifteen times voted the most recognizable voice in America.

"You can forget our agreement on this one," Paar said with a chuckle. "Just please don't faint. I refuse to do mouth to mouth on any man."

Joey blinked several times. Yes, it was real. There at the table where he conjured himself as Arthur Godfrey sat the man he conjured. The man from whom all talk show hosts came.

"Sit down, Joey," Godfrey said, pointing to one of the chairs at the dining room table. "Be my guest... literally!" he chuckled. So did Paar, who sat down in another seat at the table.

Godfrey strummed a few chords on the uke', and then said, "Let's see now. We've got three seats occupied and one available." Raising his voice a tone, he chanted to the direction of the kitchen, "We need another guest at the table."

Seeing Godfrey and Paar turn toward the open doorway to the tiny kitchen, Joey turned his head toward it as well. In an instant, a radiant, smiling figure, holding a silver tray of what looked like sugar cookies entered singing "We'll meet again, da-da dee, da-da dum... I just love that song, don't ya'all?" asked Dinah Shore, in her lilting southern accent, as she placed the silver cookie tray in the center of the table.

"And no one sings it like you, Dinah," Paar said, as he stood for his Hollywood hug and air-kiss on the cheek, as if she were guesting on his show.

Godfrey slowly rose to his feet as well and got his instant hug and faux kiss from Dinah. He sat down gingerly, twisting his bottom against the seat, and said, "I keep forgetting I'm not crippled anymore. I still repeat the habits of when I could hardly walk even though now, I'm as spry as a wiper-snapper."

Godfrey, an avid pilot, had miraculously survived an airplane crash in his younger days, leaving his body literally broken. Through the years, his body repaired itself to the extent where he could walk — he even danced on his television show — but with considerable effort and constant chronic pain.

Dinah moved toward Joey, who stood up to do the hug-kiss bit, but instead, Dinah faced him and said, "Now listen here, you old stick-in-the-mud, we've got to get you straightened out before it's too late, ya hear?"

It was a tone of gentle reprimand that only southern women carried off effectively. The recipient didn't miss the point, but wasn't offended either. Crystal used to call it the 'honey and mustard' treatment.

Joey wondered why she didn't want to touch him. *Come to think of it, neither did the boys at the picnic bench outside Rita's Eatery, and Carson never shook hands before he disappeared,* he thought to himself.

"Now sit down and let's get started, boys. I've got an *American Idol* loser that wants to kill herself to get to before the day is over.

Joey looked at Dinah Shore admiringly as they both sat down at the table. Her daytime television talk show was the epitome of class. She interviewed as she performed — with taste, perfect timing, and sensitivity. Dinah could get more out of a guest with her affable gentle approach than all the others who prosecuted, harangued and interrupted the answer. To Dinah, doing an interview was like finessing the lyric of a beautiful ballad.

Godfrey began. "My boy, you are confronting one of the worst offenses in the Universe. Your life was blessed and protected from the moment you were born — even before, I have come to learn." He waited for Paar and Dinah to finish nodding confirmation before continuing. "But instead of gratitude, instead of appreci-ation, instead of looking ahead, you look back in anger and resentment at your life. What you are doing, my boy, is cursing your blessings. And that is a Universal offense. That is why you are being asked if you want to die."

Godfrey made his points in that distinctive delivery that moved millions to buy products he touted or support causes he championed: sincerity with a pinch of puckish wit, a slow cadence, enunciating each word as if they were from Mt. Sinai.

Joey felt a serge of confidence, of the need to defend himself, to explain himself, to plead his case, to justify his despair. He leaned forward, put his elbows on the table, raised his hands, moving them slightly as a preacher behind a pulpit gestures for emphasis and attention, and said, "Easy for you to say Mr. Godfrey, and for you Jack, and you, too, Dinah. Easy for Carson to get on my case and for Steve Allen and Garroway, and Downey, and Douglas and Pyne. They all — you all — were stars! You made it, for crying out loud!" Appearing bereft, tears began to form in Joey's eyes. "Even my dense brother, who has as much affection for his cattle as he has for this business, even *he* became famous. Me?" he sniffed, and dabbed at his nose, "I'm a failure; a has-been who never was. A poor schnook who loved broadcasting with his heart and soul; gave it everything he had; and winds up unemployed, unemployable, and unknown."

Joey looked at the faces of his audience. He saw empathy.

"Sounds like time for a commercial," Dinah said, getting a laugh from the fellows. "Anybody want some sweet tea?" Dinah asked. "I can make some in a jiff."

"I'll bet you can," said Paar with a laugh.

"I'll pass," Godfrey said. "Although I made a fortune for the Lipton folks."

"And they treated you kindly, I recall," Dinah said, with another dose of honey and mustard.

"I guess I'll pass, too," Paar said, enjoying the repartee.

Dinah said, "Okay. Then let's go on."

Joey said, "See what I mean? You all decide who's having tea. Why? Because the rich and famous call the shots. You're so used to living your privileged lives you forget the ones like me who wait to see what the ones like you decide to do."

There was a few seconds of silence.

Paar spoke. "Arthur, the boy here really has a problem. I don't know if we can… I mean, maybe this was not such a good idea."

"The tea bit was a throw-a-way line, honey. Didn't mean any harm. Really," Dinah said, reaching for his arm, then, as if remembering something, pulled it away.

Godfrey ran his hand down the back of his red hair but the cowlick that was part of his personal logo persisted in sticking out. Taking a deep breath and slowing blowing it out, he said to Paar, "No Jack. We promised we'd do this. We're staying with it."

He turned to Joey, who wore an expression of vulnerability, and said, "My boy, I'm here to tell you that none of the people who have been sent to you received their bliss from fame. Their bliss was garnered from using their gifts. Bliss is comprised of all good and fame is not one of its components. Fame, unlike bliss, is situational." Dinah and Paar nodded affirmatively.

Godfrey continued, "Carson was as happy when he was doing magic tricks as he was on the *Tonight Show*. Steve Allen was as happy when he was writing songs or books as he was hosting the *Tonight Show*. And Jack…" he looked over at Paar. "Well, were you *ever* happy, Jack?" Godfrey asked with a clever laugh. Paar had a reputation for being a malcontent, a worrier, a performer filled with disenchantment about most all of life.

Paar smiled and said, "I was happiest with my family. Show business gave me a way for me to give them more. I enjoyed communicating. Talking to an audience about what I saw, what I thought… that was fun, most times. Talking to smart people, people of accomplishment, or people who had an outlook different from the norm… that was fun, most times. But the whole star thing is the reason I gave it up, quit, retired."

He paused, reflected a moment then said, "Someone once said, 'be careful of what you pretend to be because eventually you may become it.' I built the Jack Paar monster, it made money for a lot of people, but it constantly needed feeding. Eventually, when the demands of what I liked to do required those things that stardom demanded, well, to paraphrase Howard Beale, I got sick and tired and couldn't take it anymore. I tried to be a star, but I found being me and being a star were incompatible. Now I am correcting the fraudulence by trying to get folks like you back on the right path before it's too late."

Dinah chimed in. "Honey, I *wanted* to be a star. I admit it. I dreamed of stardom back in Winchester, Tennessee when I was a little girl. I wished for stardom when I sang on WSM in Nashville. And I plotted my stardom trail when I got to New York. And do you know what stardom got me? Fame? Yes. Fortune? Pretty much. But the thing it got me the most was loneliness. Honey, when I think back on the joy I felt when I was simply the girl singer in front of some orchestra, singing her little heart out and the emptiness a life of stardom brought me, I could… well, it's why I'm doing the work I'm doing today. Doing what you love is the blessing, honey. Becoming famous at it is a bonus at best — or it can be a miserable curse."

Joey's thoughts went to Rose. *I never heard Rose talk about becoming a star*, he thought. *She would talk about the effect a good program had on people, or how excited she was that her idea about a show about spirituality was catching on and the good it was doing. But she never spoke of her fame. It is as if it never was part of her agenda. Interesting*, he mused.

"And so, my boy," Godfrey said. "It seems your misery is caused by misplaced values. You have confused craft with celebrity, a gift with fame, skill with stardom."

Godfrey paused to let Joey process what he just absorbed. At precisely the right instant, Godfrey said, "Let me ask you something, my boy. I want you to tell me something. Go back to when you were the little boy in this house. What were you feeling sitting here at this table pretending to be me? What was your primary feeling? Think back now, here you are, being me. What are you feeling?"

Joey closed his eyes. Instantly he was a young boy sitting at the table with the fruit bowl, the salt and pepper shakers and the candle sticks as the set of the show. And he was pretending to be Arthur Godfrey. It felt so good. He felt so happy. *To be able to talk on the radio would be so wonderful. Oh, how much I want to do that in my life*, he was thinking. It was a feeling of blissful euphoria that he had forgotten since later on emotions of fear and resentment replaced the feeling of that childhood fantasy.

His eyes were still closed. Then he heard the familiar voice. "What were you feeling? Godfrey asked. Paar and Dinah waited.

"Joy," Joey said in almost a whisper. "I felt pure joy."

"Did you want to be famous?"

Joey sighed. "No, I wanted to do what you did. Being famous wasn't part of it."

Paar spoke. "I'll say it again. Be careful what you pretend to be because eventually you may become it. You pretended to be the man himself here…" Paar paused and waited for Godfrey to react. In a second he did, and with a belly laugh. "The man himself" was the phrase with which Godfrey's announcer, Tony Marvin, used to introduce Godfrey to the radio audience. 'Now here's the man himself' was to Godfrey what 'Hereeee's Johnny' was to Carson.

Paar continued his thought, obviously pleased with his perfor-mance. "Eventually you morphed Godfrey — as just about every other talk show host has — into your own style. Joseph Rabinowitz — the boy with the dream — got lost. You became Joey Robin — talented but frustrated. And when Joey Robin could be Joey Robin no more, well… here we are, are we not?"

Then, in a voice more gentle than Joey had ever heard Godfrey use, he said, "You see, my boy, to know what you want to do in a lifetime is a blessing far more profound and much deeper than is generally acknowledged. To find your métier is a remembering of one's agreement with the Universe before we return for another lifetime. The millions of poor souls who do not know what to do with their lives have simply forgotten — or have chosen to forget — the promise made before their return."

Godfrey paused, cocked his head and raised his eyes somewhere upward and slightly squinted, as if listening for what he wanted to say next. Then he leveled his head and slightly smiled, as if saying 'I've got it'.

"We have learned," he said, opening his arms, so as to include Paar and Dinah. "As you will one day learn, that it is no accident you wanted to become a broadcaster. It is the fulfillment of your soul's desire for expression."

He leaned in and held up his index finger. *What I'm about to say is vital*, his body language transmitted.

"Whatever level of fame you achieved during this lifetime is irrelevant. Fame is like all the awards given out — the Oscars, Emmys, Grammy's and so forth — they are awarded on a human scale of achievement, based on an arbitrary and fluctuating set of circumstances, values and — let's face it — manipulation. Remember, my boy: fame — unlike bliss — is situational.

With a slower cadence and more deliberate enunciation, Godfrey said, "Self expression performed purely for its own sake is a Universal precept. It is a prime component of bliss because the expression is devoid of motive. To bring forth one's self expression is to be in harmony with the Universe. It is the way to life. To deny one's self expression in one's lifetime is to smother one's spirit. It is the way to death."

Do you want to die? echoed through Joey.

"Nicely said, Arthur," Dinah said in her sweet southern drawl. Paar nodded with a thumbs-up. Godfrey held up his hands in a stop the applause motion. Taking a deep breath and slowly releasing the air, he moved his body back in a more relaxed, less intense position in the chair.

He grinned a warm, empathetic grin at Joey, and said, "Between each lifetime, when we reside in the spirit realm, we are informed by higher beings what we will need to learn in our next lifetime on earth. To enable us to learn those lessons, to have the experiences we require, we write the story of our next life." Godfrey paused a beat to allow Joey to absorb what he had just been told. Then, he added, "And we make agreements with other souls—our supporting players—about the role they will perform in our next incarnation, and the role we will perform in theirs. You get it, my boy? *We* are the authors of our destiny! God produced an awesome system, Joey—absolutely fair and perfectly reciprocal. To manifest what we need to learn, correct, or experience, we write the story of our next lifetime during our life between lives in the spirit world!"

Paar broke in, the sudden interruption startling Godfrey. Paar said, "The Hindus have a name for that plane of spirit existence. They call it the bardo — the plane of existence, where souls reside between lives. In the bardo, we are all Trafalmadorians. In Kurt Vonnegut's *Slaughterhouse 5* they saw past, present and future all at once, like a landscape, each moment ever-present."

Godfrey laughed. "Jack loves this stuff — he eats it up since he came across."

"He was ready for it, Arthur," Dinah said. "That's what made his show a hit: Jack's natural curiosity, his willingness to expand his intellect. Not like us song and dance folks," she said, with a bright, toothy grin. "If it didn't have a verse, sixteen bars, a bridge, and a final eight bars, it was way beyond us."

Godfrey laughed and nodded his head, adding, "Yep, plus, in my case, if it wasn't something I could sell on the air within a thirty second live pitch, it didn't interest me."

"And then you crossed over," Paar said with a slight tone of satisfaction.

"And then we crossed over," Godfrey and Dinah said almost in unison, like the voices from the amen corner of a rural church.

"And what we found," Dinah said, "was that we either stuck to our pre-written script during our lifetime, by honoring the agreements we made with other souls and other souls honoring agreements they made with us, as joyful or painful as the role we agreed to play was, or we ad-libbed."

"Ad-libbed?" Joey asked, his mind working hard to process all he was being told by some of the masters of his Universe.

"Showbiz for free will," Paar responded. "One can make all kinds of agreements in the bardo. But once you re-enter a body and mature, you can stick to them, stick to some of them, or, as Miss Dinah said, ad-lib... make it up as you go along... use your free will."

"It's quite a beautiful system" Godfrey said. Like Einstein said so wisely, 'God does not play dice with the Universe'."

Paar jumped in. "If He does, the dice are loaded!"

"Good one, Jack!" Dinah said.

Paar grinned in that pose so familiar to his television audiences that conveyed *I just can't help myself from being so witty and clever.*

Joey said, "I never understood what Einstein meant."

Paar said, "He meant there are no accidents — unless, of course, someone ad-libs and pulls one out of the hat, so to speak, without prior agreement. But in the main, you meet who you are supposed to meet; you do what you are supposed to do; you are who you agreed to become. It appears chaotic; but each human being is playing a role his or her soul previously agreed to play. We are all interconnected, Joey. It's all one big theater in the round."

"Think of it," Dinah said, her clear blue eyes shining, "How else can the law of reciprocity, or karma, operate other than through experience? How can experience manifest other than through opportunity? How is opportunity provided and by whom? It seems to me that we, being authors of our life, answer the questions."

Joey scratched his head, and said, "So you are saying we are the authors of the script of our life; that what happens or does not happen was blueprinted by us before we were born."

"Again," Paar added.

"So an infant that dies of SIDS, a person dying with AIDS, a starving child in Africa wrote and got others to collaborate in their misery?"

After a momentary hush, Godfrey looked at the others, returned his eyes to Joey and sadly said, "Yes."

With eyes expressing incredulity, Joey shook his head in disbelief as he picked away at the skin around his thumbnail. The others remained silent and calm.

He pondered for a moment then asked, "So what about the law of attraction? I remember my interviews with Earl Nightingale and others who claimed that we become what we think about. They said the secret to getting what you want is to focus on it, concentrate on it, and you will attract it to you. Is that all bogus or what?"

Paar smiled his wry smile and replied, "We do attract what we think about. The law of attraction is authentic. 'As a man thinketh in his heart' is valid as well. But the deeper question is: *Why* do we think about what we think about? What prompts us to think about what we want? Why? Because the soul remembers what the mind forgot."

Joey mulled over what he had been told for a few moments. Then he said, "Just one more question: How do you pry the secret from your soul? How do you remember what you wrote?"

"By watching the signs, darlin'," Dinah replied. "Most of us go about our lives as if in a daze, unaware of the symbols in our present moment that our angels, helpers and guides are constantly providing for us... sort of like flash cards to trigger our memory of what we promised."

Sweeping his eyes across the three, Joey asked, "Who sent you?"

They looked at each other as if asking *What shall we tell him?*

Then Godfrey replied, in a soft, sincere voice, "Someone who loves you."

He paused. "And Joey," Godfrey added. "You are not your

shattered dreams; you are the dream."

The room turned silent, taking on the aura of a hallowed place. Godfrey, Paar and Dinah folded their hands against their breasts, closed their eyes and bowed their heads. Joey looked at each one of them. He replayed and tried to process their message. *Did Dinah agree to have her heart broken by Burt? Did Godfrey agree to be anti-Semitic? Did Jack Paar agree to quit at the top? Is it possible that my life has been the terms of an agreement I drafted? Did I agree to be the child of Jacob and Rachel Rabinowitz, to marry Cris, mentor Rose, be Benny's brother and, oh my God, Michael's father? Is that how it works? Are we the authors of the scripts of our lives and hire the supporting players and agree to a supporting role for ourselves in their lives? Who's directing all this madness? Wait, don't tell me. I think I know.*

At that moment Joey became aware of the room gradually becoming brighter and brighter. The light was unlike any he had ever seen before. As it grew in incandescence, the light began to gradually blot out his three companions. They seemed to become one with the light, as if disintegrating into it. Joey sensed their presence was still in the room, but they were somehow melded in the light. Soon it became impossible for Joey to look at the light because of its intensity and an overwhelming feeling that compelled him to look away, to not look into the light.

Closing his eyes he heard sounds, harmonious sounds emanating from the light. Keeping his eyes closed, he laid his head back, his face facing upward. The music from the light anointed him with a feeling of love, such as he had never felt before. It penetrated his entire body, filling him with a happiness: a bliss: a euphoria he had only heard about from the accounts of mystics and others he wrote off as nut-cases.

Suddenly, amid the effect of the awesome light and tranquil harmony, he was in a different room. No, he was not *in* the room; he was somehow looking at the room, a sterile room reeking of the odor of bodily waste, a room that emitted anguish. A woman —

old, emaciated, alone — is lying in her nursing home bed. On a table beside her bed is a radio. She's listening to a program; her eyes are closed. Then, something she hears brings a slight smile to her thin, dry lips. Joey can hear it, too. He remembers that show because after it one of his bosses asked him if he couldn't try to be more up to date and "less yesterday" with his material. On that show he described how his mother used to try to trick him into eating eggs by mixing them in his chocolate milk. "But she couldn't fool me," he had said on the Joey Robin Show that day, "those yellow speckles floating on top of the glass gave her away every time!" Watching that feeble woman lying in her bleak depressing nursing home room, Joey could feel — virtually experience — that brief moment of joy he had brought to her fragile life. *The only thing I felt after that show was that that young jerk wouldn't talk to me like that if I was a star. The effect of the program or the story on anyone — least of all a decrepit old woman in a nursing home — never crossed my mind.*

With his head remaining tilted back, his eyes closed, and the room — still bathed in a brilliant, incandescent light — emanating sounds of loving harmony, Joey suddenly felt a swoosh sound, and he was instantly sitting beside a man driving his Buick faster than the speed limit on the interstate highway. He's in his mid-fifties, overweight, with not much hair left on the top of his head. Even though he has the air conditioning running full blast, he's sweating as if he were in a sauna. He's got the radio set on *The Joey Robin Show.* As he blows by trucks and other vehicles, he talks to himself.

"Listen to that guy, will ya? There he sits in some plush studio somewhere, must have gorgeous dames running all over the place, raking in, what? a hundred Gs a year? At least. Not to mention all the... what do you call those bribes those guys get? Payola? I bet he hasn't bought a car in his life! What does he know about a real job? About people who have to really work for a living out there, hustling every minute of the day. Man, he's got it made. Sitting there talking for a living! Can you imagine a job where all you do is sit down and talk about whatever is on your mind? And get paid for it to boot! I've got two hours to get to Clarksville, close the sale or I'm toast. This is my life. This is the hand I've been dealt. I surely didn't ask for this life. No sir. Not this life. Two kids in college, a wife who believes if she misses one week at the beauty parlor she's sinned against the Almighty, and a job I hate. Him? Sitting there talking into a microphone for a living? I sure hope the man knows how lucky he is. If he doesn't, he's a fool."

For what seemed like hours — even though only several moments elapsed since the light appeared — Joey was shown four-dimensional scenes of the impact his life as a broadcaster has had on others. With a sense of sacred urgency and spiritual obligation, he deeply reflected on what he saw and on what he felt.

After sufficient time allowed in that ethereal zone, an inner-prompt beckoned him to open his eyes and level his head. The light was gone. So, too, was the sound of harmony. And so were Arthur Godfrey, Jack Paar, and Dinah Shore.

Joey sat alone at the dining room table. He glanced at his watch. It was time to go meet Rose.

Chapter 19

Frank LaCosta gripped the phone in his hand in front of his face as if he were about to crush the larynx of an assailant, and barked into the receiver, "Look, this is the third time you called. Three strikes and you're out, pal! I got enough problems without you wasting my time with your shenanigans. Now don't call again. Understand? I got a friend of mine with the phone company and…"

"Mr. LaCosta," the voice of a woman on the other end of the line interrupted his tirade. "This is Rose Barbelo. I'm sorry for the problem."

Frank LaCosta recognized the voice immediately. "Oh, sweet Jesus! It is you! I just thought…"

"I know. I certainly understand how you thought someone was pulling a trick on you, Mr. LaCosta. I should have placed the call myself to begin with. I apologize for any inconvenience. Hope your blood pressure is back down," she said with a laugh.

LaCosta fumbled for the bottle of aspirin buried somewhere in the heap of trash on his desk and flipped the top off with his thumb, spraying aspirin tablets in all directions.

"No problem, Ms. Barbelo," he said, downing several aspirin with a swig of cold coffee left over from the morning. "So what the guy… the gentleman who called said was right? You need a limo?"

"Yes, sir. We'll be touching down in about an hour. If you could meet us then and be available for the evening I'd be very grateful."

"No problem, mam. I will be there and will personally be at your service."

"Wonderful," Rose said. "See you soon. Bye"

Frank LaCosta collapsed in his wooden desk chair, his face sopping with perspiration. The owner and proprietor of The Johnstown Limousine and Taxi Service, which consisted of one limo and two taxicabs, had not had a customer for its limo since the prom season five months earlier. Most of his income was derived from his car wash and detail business.

He hurriedly scampered to the shop area and began polishing the exterior and vacuuming the interior of the 1999 stretch Lincoln Continental. A quick visit to the bathroom, where he mopped his face with a grimy towel, splashed Old Spice lotion all over himself, and changed into a pair of black slacks, black shoes, white shirt, and black necktie and topped it with a black blazer. Then off he drove to the Greater Johnstown Airport to await the arrival of Rose Barbelo — the person of whom he will forever refer to as "she's a very close friend of mine."

After she spoke with LaCosta, Rose phoned Joey and told him that she had hired a limo, and that it would be easier for all if they just met somewhere for dinner so he wouldn't have to make the trip to and from the airport, which sat at the top of a steep and winding hill. "Just find us a place where we can talk," Rose had said.

Joey chose a restaurant located at the crest of the 'World's Steepest Incline Plane' overlooking the city of Johnstown. It had opened after he left town, but he had heard the place was quiet and the food was better than average.

Joey's nostalgia gene was on overdrive. By nature a backward thinker, revisiting places he had been at other times in his life often gripped him emotionally. Over the years Crystal would grit her teeth and roll her eyes every time Joey showed her places he used to live, eat, work, walk — whatever. When she'd kid him about his infatuation with places and events in the past — especially since her favorite moment was the present — he used to say, "I'm not living in the past; but the past is living in me."

Supported by two heavy steel cables — which passengers always feared would snap — the Johnstown Incline Plane lifted people and vehicles up to Westmont and Southmont — the suburbs above the city where the middle and upper class lived — and back down again to the city where they worked.

As he drove up to the Incline Restaurant, his mind streamed video of his childhood. The most vivid was the one where he would wait with his sled on snowy Thanksgivings for his father to disembark the cable car. Jacob Rabinowitz would try to squeeze one more needed dollar into the family coffers by opening his store on holiday mornings "just in case someone needs a tie or a shirt at the last minute." By noon he'd give up, close up and walk to the incline plane where he would be hoisted up the mountain where little Joseph and his sled would be waiting. Jacob would plant a smile on his face — even as a young boy Joseph could detect the worry behind it — and pull his son, who was stretched out on his sled, the half-mile to their home for the holiday.

Being Thursday, there were not many people dining out in Johnstown. In small towns going out to eat was for weekends. Joey wondered if Rose's people had made a reservation. They had — under his name.

A stocky man in his fifties — with tired eyes and a dark complexion, wearing a maroon J.C. Penny blazer over a wrinkled white shirt, open at the color — forced a friendly greeting, as Joey entered the restaurant. It looked better than he imagined it would. The tables were covered with maroon tablecloths and neatly set with maroon napkins displayed from inexpensive goblets. Photographs of historic Johnstown — the floods of 1889 and 1936, the iron mills and steel mills, a once bustling Main Street, the downtown park with men in straw hats reading newspapers on benches, the VFW, people waiting in line to see *Gone With the Wind* at the Rialto Theater, among others — hung on the walls throughout the dining room. Elevator music played in the background. *My kind of stuff*, Joey thought. He loved elevator music.

The man showed Joey to his window side table with a view of Johnstown below. Before he sat, Joey looked around the restaurant, a habit he had acquired since the start of his days as a public personality. A sponsor, potential sponsor, or fan should never come away from dinner without a smile and a wave or a tableside visit from Joey Robin. Rather than a public relations effort, Joey's conviviality was a manifestation of the fear he lived with all his life. Not getting fired was a dominating force in Joey's psyche.

At a small table near the back of the room, he noticed a young man having dinner with an older woman. Something about them felt oddly familiar, but both their faces were shaded from the light so that Joey could not identify either of them, nor did he particularly want to. *Probably old high school chums*, he figured. *Hope they don't recognize me. What are you doing these days is not a question I want to be asked from folks who knew me when... It's tough enough to come up with an answer to the question back home in Memphis.* He looked away and let the curiosity pass.

Not far from Joey's table, a middle age couple was finishing their desert and coffee. He noticed the couple never spoke to one another; it was as if they were alone together. Joey had an impulse to approach their table and say to the man 'Why aren't you talking with her, laughing with her, enjoying her? Don't you remember how much you wanted to be together years ago? Why did you let life make you forget?' He decided it wouldn't be a good idea. *Why ruin their night out*? he smiled to himself.

Typically, Rose was late, once again a loser in her constant and frantic competition with the clock to allow just one more task before an appointment.

Fourteen minutes later, Rose entered, moving at her usual brisk pace while talking into her cell phone. She wore tastefully-fitted, black designer jeans, black boots, and a bulky, black cashmere turtleneck sweater. A crucifix designed in gold filigree hung from her neck on a gold chain. She looked as good as her net worth. Her eyes lit up when she saw Joey. After a few more words into the phone, she stuffed it into her large black leather tote bag with her initials embroidered in gold on the side.

The tired maître d', obviously not knowing who she was, escorted Rose to Joey's table. They embraced and kissed one another on the cheek. As the man turned to leave, Rose said, "Sir, there is a man — a Mr. LaCosta — outside in a limousine. Would you mind asking him to come and have dinner? You might seat him over there," she said pointing to a table near the entrance to the lounge, "so he can see the TV in the bar. Tell him to have whatever he wants to eat and put it on our tab. I'd appreciate it."

The man nodded and did as he was told. *The nobility are different,* Joey noted. *The very air around them seems to await instructions as to the direction to blow. But this was not a manner Rose had acquired since becoming rich and famous. No, she had always had an air of authority, of bidding, even when she had none. Is it an absence of fear?* he wondered. *An unquestioned expectation of results that make the nobility different?*

Joey ordered drinks — she a Stoli martini, straight up, with olives — "but if you don't have Stoli, Smirnoff will do." Which it did; and he a George Dickle on the rocks — "but if you don't have Dickle, Jack Daniels will do." Which it did.

After the drinks arrived and they exchanged some trivial chit-chat, Rose looked at her martini glass as she casually stirred it a few times, then looked at Joey, and said, "You look tired, sweetie. More than tired, you look drained. Is anything more wrong than I know about? Is it Crystal? You miss her something awful, don't you? Is there a chance…?"

Joey cut her off, "I do miss her something awful, as you say, kid. Is there a chance we could get back together?" He paused and dropped his eyes. "I don't know. The problem is that I don't think Cris understands what happens to a man whose dreams are dashed."

Rose shook her head as if she understood, but in her mind she thought, *And I don't think you understand how unpleasant it is to a woman to live with a man who constantly broods.* Always cautious about treading in waters close to Joey's personal life, especially his family life, she kept her thought to herself.

Instead, she said, "Other than that, you feeling okay? Your health, I mean. You really look beat, sweetie. All systems working?"

Joey hesitated. *How do I tell her what's been happening to me? Or, should I tell her?*

He decided to say, "I haven't slept a lot," and see where it would lead.

Rose lowered her head a bit and peered at her friend. "Because…." She was leading him as an interviewer leads a reluctant guest. Joey knew the drill and was willing to play. He needed to play. And Rose was the perfect playmate for this game.

"Because I have been having some… experiences."

"Experiences…?" she left the word hanging, using her head and shoulders to coax the answer from him.

Joey took a sip of his drink. *Should I go for it? Should I just spill it out? Someone needs to know, and Rose is the precise person who would understand; who wouldn't get scared or say I'm crazy. This is the stuff that made her famous, for crying out loud! It's what she knows, what she does.* His thought direction suddenly swerved. *But then I can't just say, yeah, Rose, Johnny Carson rode with me through Ohio, and then he left and I stopped at a joint to eat and Dave Garroway and Steve Allen, Joe Pyne, Morton Downey, Jr. and Mike Douglas sat around a picnic table with me and shot the breeze. And oh, yes, Arthur Godfrey, Jack Paar and Dinah Shore met me at my home and we talked. Oh, one more thing: I'm getting e-mails from someone who knows all about me, someone who has sent me on this wild journey! He keeps asking me if I want to die. Something about a promise I haven't kept. I can't just figure…* A man standing at the side of their table interrupted his thoughts.

"The special tonight is roast pork loin, your choice of potato, coleslaw or green salad for fifteen ninety-five. Soup is navy bean with pork only two ninety-five extra. Care for some bread?"

Rose looked at Joey and simultaneously they burst out laughing. The man in the maroon jacket looked too tired to care. He was obviously the owner, maître d', cook, waiter and bouncer, if they needed one.

"Sweetie, my time here is short. I need to be back in New York by midnight. How about we just share some appetizers? Unless you're starved for some of that pork?" They both laughed again, although Joey thought the bit was precariously close to losing its nuance.

"No… that'll be fine, kid. But we will take the bread… and another round of drinks," Joey said to the man.

After they ordered appetizers, Rose looked up at the man and said, "Oh, and what about Mr. LaCosta? Has he been taken care of?"

The man rolled his eyes, and said, "Yes, mam. He is now on his second porterhouse. He asked me to ask you if it is alright if he had a beer."

Without hesitation, Rose said decisively, "Tell him I would prefer that he not have any alcohol while he is driving. Thank you."

Joey noticed how Rose's "thank you" dismissed the man.

The nobility are different.

Rose waited until the food arrived and consumed before she began to adroitly navigate the conversation back to where it was before the man appeared. She did not want the focus of their dialogue interrupted again. *You've learned well, kid*, he thought to himself. He harked back to times when she had changed the subject too quickly during an interview. "Never leave a topic before it is fully explored and probed. Wring it out before you hang it up," he would tutor.

When the man came to bus the dishes, Rose informed him she wanted the bill for both she and her friend and Mr. LaCosta. She also informed him that she and her friend would be occupying the table for an hour or so and they would prefer to not be disturbed.

The waiter presented Rose with the tab. Joey made an effort to reach for his wallet, but Rose waved him off saying, "It's on your brother!" She hesitated a split second, then said, laughing, "Just kidding." Joey could have done without the joke.

Rose paid with an American Express credit card and gave the man a gratuity of a crisp one hundred dollar bill. He looked at it, cleared his throat, thanked her, and walked away staying out of sight as she had requested.

The nobility are different, Joey thought again.

With the table cleared, except for their drinks, and the dining room empty, except for the couple in the corner finishing their dinner, Rose reached for Joey's hand. She held it for several moments. Finally, she said, "Joey, something has happened to you. Something very important. Something that has permeated your very soul. I'd like you to tell me about it. I think you *need* to tell me about it. In fact, I think you are *supposed* to tell me about it."

And so he did. He told her everything. He left nothing out. Her reaction was what he had hoped for. She was not blown away nor was she shocked. She listened fully, totally and intently. It felt good to tell her. It felt right.

"So there you have it. That's what's been happening," he said finally.

Rose sat silently for several moments playing with the tooth picked olive in her martini glass. Joey waited. He wanted her to fully process what she had learned.

And then she spoke. "Before I tell you what I think, I want to tell you how privileged I am to be the one you told, and how blessed I am to be here when you needed to tell. Whatever it is that has been special between us since I walked into your world, and you gave me a life, has never been more special than it is at this moment. And I hope you'll understand when I tell you that I love you, Joey. We are exactly where we are supposed to be at exactly this moment in time. I had to fly my jet to get here, and you needed to drive your car to get here, but we came just as we were supposed to come. Perhaps this is why we met in the first place. Maybe this is what all the shows, all the ups and downs were about. And I have a strong hunch that it is what my good fortune is all about as well."

Joey breathed a laugh. "That seems to be the message of the week," he said.

Rose repositioned her body. From leaning in slouched and touching Joey's hand, she now rested against the back of her chair; and with her elbows on the armrests, she placed the tips of her fingers together forming a pyramid.

In a soothing, comforting tone of voice, she said, "What you have shared with me is not foreign to me, Joey. It is what I do professionally; and it's how I live personally. So while I am invigorated that entities from the spirit world have visited the best friend I have in this world, the events you shared are not weird or crazy to me. On the contrary, I consult and am in touch with my angels, helpers and guides constantly. I don't make a move without sounding them out, asking their advice, and seeking their protection. They are my constant companions; my board of directors."

"I didn't know that," Joey said quietly.

"Would you have hired me if you knew?"

"Probably not."

Rose chucked.

Staying on point, Joey locked his eyes on to hers and said, "Rose, I feel like I've been denied something... a prize that I've been promised or — this sounds nuts — something I've agreed to accept! My visitors told me being a star doesn't matter. It's doing your thing that counts; that in the Universal scoreboard, bringing forth your ability rings the bell, not whether you win some award on earth. They said fame is a human value not a cosmic value. Intuitively, kid, I know they are right. Heck, I even witnessed the effect my work has had on people I never met. And yet, there is this unsettling feeling inside me that I've either been promised or agreed to attain something great. Does that make any sense?"

"We'll get to that part in a moment," Rose answered. "But first, I think you have confused success with fame. Your spirit visitors may have seen them as one in the same as well. You *know* you are successful. You succeeded at what you set out to do, and you are one of the best at it. You know that. So did your visitors.

No, Joey, it is not *success* you feel you've been denied. No, it's deeper than that. Much deeper. It is *relevance*. Relevance! You want to be consequential; you want respect; you want to matter. Reminds me of the line from... oh, what was that Robert Redford movie about the baseball player?"

"*The Natural*," Joey said.

"Right. Remember when the ball player... what was his name?"

"Roy Hobbs," Joey said softly with certainty.

"He's asked what he wants out of being a ball player, and he says, 'When I walk down the street, people will look at me and say, 'There goes Roy Hobbs — the best there ever was!' That's you, sweetie. That's what you really want."

Joey placed his right hand to his chin and rubbed it.

"Now, I agree," Rose went on, "the only way to get respect — to matter, to achieve relevance in this materialistic world — is to become famous; a star. If you are not a star in whatever profession you are in, you are not relevant; you are inconsequential. You are, as you would say, a schlemiel."

"A schlemiel?"

"And that is what is eating at you, dear soul. You *are* successful. But you are not famous, not a star. And fame to you is being relevant, of being looked upon as the best that ever was — or at least *among* the best that ever was."

Joey thought a moment, and then said, "It seems to me, kid, that you are using the word *relevance* for the word *ego*. Am I right?"

"In your case? Forgive me, sweetie. Yes. With you it's been about ego. Your desire for respect, to be important, to matter, to be relevant, has been driven by ego."

"Like Roy Hobbs?" he asked.

"Like Roy Hobbs," she replied.

"But I've done the best I could, Rose." he said pleading with his eyes. "You know that. You've seen it up close. I have done the best I could."

Rose's eyes softened, her lips formed a tender smile as she said, "Yes, I know you have. But, sweetie, the conscious intention of your entire body of work has been the glorification of Joey Robin."

Startled, Joey's body jerked, his eyes widened, as Rose bored in.

"Yes, others — like the old women you experienced seeing in the nursing home, who was listening to your show — have derived benefits from your talent, but to you, it was about your self veneration." She paused to allow him to consider what she was saying. She noticed a slight affirming nod of his head.

"Now here is where we get to all that has been happening to you, sweetie, as well as to that nagging feeling you told me about a few minutes ago, about sensing some agreement or promise you made. Ready?"

"Go for it," he said. "By the way, do you pay your guests?" he asked, trying to lighten up the moment.

Without hesitation, Rose replied, "Sweetie, you have no idea what this is worth to you!"

He returned her smile, and waited for Rose to continue.

"Instinctively — somewhere deep inside you — you knew you had agreed to be more than the praise-seeking performer you were. You sensed you had agreed to do something with your talent that gave your life meaning. That's what *I* mean by relevance, Joey: Not importance — Meaning!" Rose shifted positions in her chair and took a quick glance at her watch. "The reason you are being ministered by your heroes in spirit is because of an unfulfilled agreement; something you agreed to do that you have not yet done; most likely with your talent. And I feel like I'm here to help you fulfill your promise, dear soul. You *do* deserve relevance, Joey Robin, not based on past performance but on future returns."

"What future, Rose?" he blurted louder than he intended. "I've got no future!"

Rose smiled knowingly, and said, "You think all your work is behind you, but it is not." Joey looked at her with a smirk as if to convey *easy for you to say.*

"Joey, most people are suffering from a kind of amnesia… trying to remember who they *really* are, what they are *really* supposed to do with our lives. Many people die before they complete their story, either due to the temptation of ego or getting side-tracked. Except for a few Masters along the way who remembered their mission and fulfilled it, most of us wonder through this life in a fog. We mindlessly miss the signs along the way that are provided for us by our angels, helpers and guides.

"You are not alone, sweetie," she went on. "Many people who feel they have not been given what they deserve in life are really intuiting an unfulfilled agreement they made in the bardo."

Joey leaned forward, and eagerly said, "You know about the bardo?"

Rose smiled and said softly, "Sweetie, where do you think we met?"

Joey replied, "I thought it was in a studio."

As if on cue, Frank LaCosta approached their table. "Miss Barbelo, you wanted to be back at the airport at nine."

"Right. Thanks. Another few minutes, Mr. LaCosta, and I'll be ready to go," Rose said. "By the way, did you enjoy your meal?"

LaCosta nodded and said, "Yes, ma'am. Steak's a little over-cooked, but I managed to get it down. Excuse me. I'll go warm up the car."

"Good," Rose said, and returned her gaze at Joey while returning to a more formal, business-like, sitting position; her hands folded, resting on the table, her back squarely against the seat of her chair.

"Now. Enough about you; a little about me. Okay?" Rose asked.

Joey laughed. "Deal," he said.

"Everybody wants to know why I bought your brother's media companies and what I'm going to do with them."

"Right."

"*Pathways*, as you know, Joey, is more than my television show. It has become a brand, an imprint in millions of people's minds. Well, I am going to create the Pathway's Cable Network. It will feature programming focused on body, mind, and spirit."

"Great idea, Rose. And I think you were smart to buy an existing cable network rather than start one up."

Slowing her cadence, she said, "One of the first projects of PCN will be a weekly program about creative people. People, who by virtue of the quality of their work, deserved to become famous, but who, for one reason or another, never achieved fame. I'm calling it, *Artists Without Honor.* And Joey, I want *you* to be the host. Remember when I called you the other morning at your apartment and told you I had an idea? Well, this is it! I just had to go out and buy me a cable network to make it happen!" She smiled a light-up-the-room smile, the one she had for times when she got something big accomplished that she said she would do against all odds.

Joey's mind raced. *Is she doing this to pay me back for what I've done for her? Does she feel sorry for me so she went out and bought a cable television network?*

"Now before you say it, let me deny it," she said. "This is not payback or sympathy. It is good, sound, professional judgment. No one understands or empathizes with the fame denied issue like you do. Takes one to know one applies here."

Joey thought a moment, and then said, "Rose, this whole world is about success these days. That's all anyone gets excited about: winners, not losers. The Universe belongs to the Liberty Fortunes. Who's going to watch a show about people who never made it? You want to be the anti-Trump?"

"Let me worry about who's going to watch it," she said. "The intent is sound, the concept is novel." She paused then added in a coy manner, "Sweetie, I came all the way to you tonight to ask you to do this show. Now, you know you already accepted the job."

Joey looked at her quizzically. "I have?"

Rose smiled. "Didn't you tell me you've had a gut feeling that you either promised or agreed to attain something great?"

Rose lifted her shoulders with the palms of her hands upward, raised her eyebrows and cocked her head as if to ask, "So what else is new?"

"Okay, I'll do it. Got any idea for guests?"

Rose reached down for her tote and scratched around it until she found her cell phone.

"I know who I want the first one to be," she said as she stood.

"Do I interview myself?" Joey asked

"Almost," Rose replied with a smile. "I want you to interview, Bernie Frank."

Chapter 20

While Joey Robin and Rose Barbelo were sitting at their window table at the Incline Restaurant, high above the featureless vista of downtown Johnstown, Pennsylvania, Joey's wife, Crystal, and her friend, David Malak, were sitting under the stadium lights at the AutoZone Park in downtown Memphis, Tennessee.

AutoZone Park is home to the Memphis Redbirds, the city's Triple-A minor league baseball team. When David called Crystal after appearing again on *Pathways with Rose Barbelo* that day, he said, "How 'bout we do something fun?"

Rose didn't hesitate a second. Fun was what she was seeking these days, what she had lacked with Joey the past nine months.

"Would you take me to the baseball game?" she asked, childlike.

"Cool! I'll pick you up at six." he instantly replied. She liked that. No deliberation, no hesitation. Decisiveness. She liked that a lot.

"And buy me a hot dog?" she added.

Malak laughed. "Darlin', you can have a hot dog, pizza, nachos, what ever your lovely heart desires."

"Just a hot dog will do fine, David. I'll be ready at six. See ya."

Funny, she thought when she hung up the phone, *he says let's do something fun and the first thing that pops into my head is the place where Joey used to take me when he wanted to unwind and relax.*

She smiled, thinking of she and Joey walking into the stadium, sometimes with his arm around her, some times they'd hold hands. How he loved when folks recognized him. He'd beam like a new moon each time someone would come up and say they liked his show or asked for his autograph or just stared at him.

"Hey, Joey," one guy once yelled as they took their usual seat in the grandstand on the first base side. "You go robbing the cradle again?" Joey would give a thumbs-up and a big smile when some fan made a joking remark. They were usually good-natured jibes.

This was Memphis, the south. Not the Bronx.

During those times there with her husband, he was comfortable, confident, self-assured, and seemed happy. But was he? She thought he was happy when they would go to the ballpark; but she was never completely certain. Was he acting or being? She never really knew. There was always that vague inkling of charade about him that she felt even at AutoZone Park.

Sometimes he would look up to the press box with a far away look in his eye. And during the game, when a player would hit a home run or strike out, he'd mutter the expressions Rosy Rosewell used, the ones he heard on the radio when he was a kid, a kid with a dream of a life imagined.

Crystal wasn't going to tell David why she impulsively selected AutoZone Park when he said 'let's do something fun'. *Let's see how intuitive he really is*, she said to herself with a smile as she showered.

Three hours later, after watching three scoreless innings of the Redbirds playing the Louisville Bats, with Rocky the Rockin' Redbird zipping around on an ATV in between each inning, and eating half of a Redbird dog — that *didn't taste as good as they used to* — Crystal put her hand on David's arm, and said very softly in his ear, "David, can we go somewhere else?"

"Sure," he said, turning his head to look into her eyes. He gave her a knowing smile, and then they gathered their belongings and made their way to the exit.

As they walked up the aisle, they turned at the unique sound of the crack of the bat followed by the roar of the crowd mixed with cheers and applause.

Crystal said to herself, *Open the door, Aunt Minnie, she's comin' home*! and her eyes grew misty.

In the car, David asked, "are you cool with Chez Philippe?"

"Perfect." She waited a few seconds, and then said, "David, I'm sorry. The first place I thought about when you said lets have fun was the ballpark. It just wasn't... I don't know... I hope I didn't make you..."

Malak turned his head toward Crystal so she could see the expression of understanding in his eyes. Then quickly he returned his focus on the road.

Using the tone of voice he used when speaking with a caller when he was a guest on a talk show, or to a member of a TV audience, he said, "People often try to recreate special moments they experienced with someone else, Crystal. Seldom, if ever, is it the same. Obviously the ballpark was a special place for you and Joey. But that was a time for the two of you. As you meet new people — that is, if you choose to have other relationships — you must not try to fit what you had with Joey into your new situation. The new situation needs to create its own special moments."

"You're right, David. I know you're right."

She had also wished that he hadn't talked to her as if she were a caller or an audience member. She didn't like the feeling of being one of David's clients. *Maybe he's been doing this so long it's just natural for him to switch into his psychotherapist mode*, she thought. One trait among many that she appreciated about Joey was that when he was with her he wasn't 'Hi, this is Joey Robin, what's your question'. Sometimes he spoke so softly to her she could hardly hear him. She liked that. He was *her* Joey then.

Leaving some seconds of silence for his words to sink in, he said, "Something I once heard someone say seems to fit what we're talking about. The man said, 'Love is like a cigar: When the flame goes out you can light it again; but it never tastes the same."

"That man was very insightful. Who said it?" she asked.

"Richard Nixon," Malak replied. "Is that not awesome? Nixon!"

"I wonder where he stole it," Crystal quipped.

They shared the laugh and drove on to the restaurant.

The Chez Philippe is one of Memphis' most elegant restaurants. Located in the Peabody Hotel — where the ducks parade through the lobby at appointed times of the day and night — the bistro is run by its animated master chef Jose' Gutierrez. The cuisine is French; the prices are upscale; the clientele consists mainly of old

Memphis money and their offspring, the nuevo-rich, along with out of town business people with broad expense accounts.

David Malak had called ahead and, being the middle of the week, was able to secure a reservation. As they made their way to their table behind Ramon', the maître d', Crystal was fascinated that so many people strained their neck to gawk at David. Even though he was not widely popular or recognizable outside the New Age community and Rose's audience, Malak had that special air about him — a magnetic attitude of self assurance mixed with a vibrant physical bearing — that made strangers think he *was* somebody. *The deep tan in October didn't hurt either*, Crystal thought. David just looked, dressed and evoked a sense of the extraordinary.

A sudden impulse drew Crystal's attention to a man in his early forties having dinner with a woman who appeared to be somewhat older in the back of the room. Something about him felt oddly familiar; but his face was shaded from the light and she could not make him out. So she let the whim pass.

"Please tell me you and Joey did not like to eat here," Malak said laughing, as the maître d' unfurled a crisp white linen napkin and placed one on each of their laps.

Crystal fully laughed. She looked and felt more relaxed now.

"He hated it. 'Too many sauces,' he would say," She paused, then added, "I really think it was the prices." She laughed again.

Actually it was because he didn't feel special there — unlike the ballpark, where he felt like a celeb — the Chez Philippe corroborated Joey's conviction about his inadequacy.

They ordered wine and the server brought a basket of warm bread. Crystal ordered an appetizer of oysters Rockefeller for her entrée. David selected trout almandine. Their conversation was mostly about his work and Crystal listened intently. At first she was impressed with his report of how well his latest book was selling; how may people showed up at his latest signing; who had called him about hosting his own network show.

But as Malak prattled on, her adoration wavered, eventually

being replaced by feelings of disappointment. While her patronizing smile and slowly bobbing head gave outward appearance of accolade, they disguised her inner thoughts: *What is it about me that draws men who want to praise themselves? Joey, at least, I can understand. He's a ham. But my New Age teacher? The man who tells audiences and readers to rid themselves of ego?... that going beyond self is the key to enlightenment? I wonder who is more authentic: my maharishi or my husband?*

When Malak concluded his first person narrative of accomplishments, he extended his hand across the table and placed it on Crystal's.

"But enough about me," he said, "let's talk about the love of my life."

I think we just did, Crystal thought. Instead of saying what she thought, she smiled condescendingly.

Malak looked straight to her eyes, squinting somewhat with that total focus gaze he used when counseling one-on-one. "That's not a 'love of my life' smile," he said. "That's a southern lady smile for 'aren't you sweet but that's all you are'."

The waiter removed their dishes and poured what was left of the wine bottle in their glasses. Malak waved off the desert menu after consulting Crystal with his eyes. When the waiter asked about coffee or an aperitif, Crystal asked for a cappuccino and Malak ordered a double espresso.

"Crystal," Malak began, with a manner that made Crystal dread what was coming. "Have I ever talked with you about soul mates? I know you've heard the expression — these days it's become a rather casual term — but there is a specific metaphysical definition for soul mates. Essentially, a soul mate is a soul with whom one has shared many, many lifetimes. Not all have been good experiences. In fact, some lifetimes together have been quite terrible. But throughout the eons, the two souls have been together... sometimes as lovers, sometimes as parents to one another, sometimes as enemies. The point is that they have shared every lifetime in some form of a relationship."

Crystal finished the last drop of her wine, looked at Malak, and asked, "And your point is?" almost scared to hear his answer.

Malak slightly squeezed her hand and said, "You and I — we — are soul mates."

"David," she said, wishing he'd let her hand go but not wanting to pull it away for fear of offending him, "you and I — *we* — hardly know one another."

"On this level, yes, I agree with you. But on the cosmic level, the level beyond this one, we know each other very well. These are things I know, Crystal."

He removed his hand to give her time to process what he has just said. She relished getting her hand back. For a moment they silently sipped their coffee.

Oddly, she wished Joey were there to say something funny, make a comment, or to ask one of his questions to alter the circumstances. *He was so good at handling thorny situations*, she thought. *I feel like a hostage here.* She played back the time an evangelical Christian cornered them at a ball game one night and angrily warned him that he's going to be left behind when the world ends and not go to heaven unless he becomes a Christian. Without hesitation, Joey replied, "Too bad. And all this time I believed Jesus made it in!"

The man thought for a second and then walked away in disgust.

For the next ten minutes or so, Malak professed his love for Crystal, telling her how he adored her, needed her, that "we need to travel the path in this lifetime that we traveled before, only this time as lovers," nearly pleading for her to acquiesce. He used his entire arsenal of charm. But none of it took root.

When he was finished — at least for the opening round — Crystal downed her cappuccino, while mentally begging for the right way to respond, a way that neither encouraged nor offended him. *Joey! Somebody! Help!*

Suddenly, the man dining with the older woman, the one

Crystal thought she recognized but could not make out, got up and approached their table. Crystal craned her neck to get a look at him but the reflection of the lights from the chandeliers and other sources created a translucent effect making recognition impossible. He paused behind Crystal's chair. She felt a strange sense of peace come over her. She looked at Malak, who was staring up at the man as if transfixed. Then the man quickly walked away.

"Crystal," Malak asked, in voice of one just released from hypnosis. "What is a shalom chalet?"

The question took Crystal by surprise. "Shalom chalet? Oh, dear Lord. Why did... where did you come up with that?"

He said, "Just tell me. What is it?"

Crystal shook her head bewilderedly, took a deep breath, and said, "Years ago — well, really up until the time he lost his show — Joey and I used to dream of buying a cabin in the woods, a home away from the city, a get-a-way where he could read his books and relax and I could, you know, do gardening, put out bird houses, just kick back. We used to drive out on weekends looking for the perfect place. I said that if we ever found the place we both liked and we bought it, I'd name it Shalom Chalet. Joey always liked the name."

She paused and searched Malak's face. There was something different about it... less intense, more serene. She asked, "Now tell me the truth, David. Where in the world did you come up with that name, Shalom Chalet? I don't think anyone except Joey and me ever used it or talked about it."

Malak looked deeply into Crystal's eyes, the fingers of his hands forming a pyrimid, as he contemplated what he would say next.

"Crystal, you remember what I was saying about soul mates a moment ago, just before something broke my train of thought?"

Oh, no. Here we go again, she thought. *Joey! Help!*

Without waiting for her response, he said, "Well, I think I may have had *it*... or had *us* wrong."

Crystal's eyes widened a bit.

"Remember I said soul mates have different roles in different lifetimes?"

She nodded.

"That they can be friends, relatives, lovers, enemies, partners, whatever, but they have a role in each lifetime of the other?"

She nodded again, her eyes even wider now.

"Well, I failed to add that a person has more than one soul mate in each lifetime. For example, a person's business partner may be one of his soul mates, while his wife may be another. And there are others in the small circle of souls that transmigrate together lifetime after lifetime, exchanging roles, gender, race and all other permutations; each one doing a dance in the other's life that was pre-designated, pre-agreed, and pre-planned by each member."

"Crystal, I think... no make that I feel, that we *are* soul mates, that we *have* played roles in each other's lifetimes throughout the ages. But in *this* lifetime, in the *present*, we are to be friends — good, trusting, solid friends. Not lovers."

Crystal sighed. Her eyes moistened and her lips formed an approving smile.

"In this lifetime," Malak continued. "You know — we both know — who the person you love with all your heart and soul is, don't we?"

Crystal reached across the table with both her arms. He took her hands in both of his and squeezed them gently, then released them.

Malak leaned back and took a deep breath, and slowly let the air out. Crystal remained beaming across from him. For a second she closed her eyes and said a silent *Thank you*.

The waiter caught Malak's eye and he ordered a brandy for himself and a Frangelica for her. And for the next ninety minutes, they talked. Actually, she talked. Crystal told her friend things she had never told anyone before. She talked about her life before Joey and with Joey. She shared her feelings, her emotions, and her thoughts. And it felt so good to release, to evacuate, to vent what had been pent up for so long. Finally, after years of emotional isolation, Crystal had found her Rose.

And Malak listened with every fiber of his being. And because he listened so intently, she trusted him completely, just as his audiences trusted him. Trust, he had learned, was a product of listening rather than talking.

"And tell me about Michael," Malak said, in a soft tone of compassion.

Crystal hesitated, then closed her eyes and shook her head.

Almost in a whisper, Malak said, "Try."

Crystal bit her lip and nervously twisted her wedding ring as she contemplated her response. Her eyes seemed to change color with her emotions. Now they were a watery blue.

"Okay," she sighed.

For the next five minutes or so, Crystal told Malak about her son as a baby, as a child, as a young boy, how he looked, what he thought, how he acted both physically and emotionally. She pointed out Michael's sensitivity, and described Joey's seeming lack of appreciation or perception of his son's special nature and how they both missed his silent cry for help. She told Malak about the events after his death, and explained how it affected her and Joey. Without holding back, Crystal allowed and conveyed her deepest and most guarded emotions and feelings about her son's life and death, including the part she and Joey played in each.

"Did you and Joey consider having another child?" he asked at one point.

"Odd that you ask," she said. "Yes, after a year or so, I brought the subject up. I remember saying to Joey that the death of his little sister — Iris...? Yes, her name was Iris — when she was only five didn't stop his parents from having more children." She paused. "But, he brushed the subject aside. 'Out of the question,' he said. That's when I learned of his hasty vasectomy."

Leading her, Malak said, "And then, after many years, Joey lost his job."

"Yes," Crystal said, as if repeating a sad mantra, "Joey lost his job."

She started to describe the woeful mood Joey cast over their lives when suddenly, from out of the blue, Crystal's attention was distracted by a dish a lady at a nearby table was being served.

"Excuse me," she said to the waiter. "What was that you just served that lady?"

The waiter replied that it was grits pudding with peaches and honey.

Malak asked if she wanted some. Crystal thought for a second and asked if he would share it with her. Malak nodded affirmatively. When the waiter disappeared, she asked Malak what she had been saying. He reminded her that she was expressing how much of a turn-off it is for a woman to live with a man who is constantly sulking and feeling sorry for himself.

"The worst part of it is," she said, "that Joey thinks I don't understand what happens to a man when his dreams go up in smoke. He's wrong. I *do* understand. But there is nothing I can do. He's the one who has to fix it. What he doesn't understand is how his despair affects us… me… the woman he says he loves."

The grits pudding arrived, which the waiter put between them with two spoons, like two kids in the fifties at the malt shop after school. However, this malt cost twenty-one dollars.

Malak had a couple of spoonfuls and said he had enough. Crystal ate the rest; emitting erotic sounds of pleasure with her eyes closed after each spoonful entered her mouth. And then, like a starved POW who has finally been given some food, she took a crust of bread from the basket and sopped up the remaining mixture from the bowl. Malak watched her voyeuristically without saying a word, vicariously enjoying her moment of absolute joy.

After the waiter removed the bowl and the spoons and replenished Malak's double espresso and Crystal's cappuccino, Malak looked at Crystal, and she returned his gaze. Their platonic understanding felt right to her. As opposed to whatever it was she felt he threatened within her earlier, their relationship now seemed natural, cozy. She liked her friend.

They smiled endearingly at one another. Then, Malak said, "So, friend, what is it: Guilt? Remorse? Longing? Missing?"

Without taking her eyes from his, she said, "You ought to know; you're the psychic."

"All right," he said. "Then let me try to read it." Casting his eyes to someplace upward and to the side, he then returned them to connect with hers, and, as if deciphering a code, said, "It seems to me that you are feeling a mixture of emotions."

And while Malak performed his reading of Crystal, she thought, *He knows some; but how could he know all? How could he know that after forty-some years of marriage to Joey Robin, I have so much of him a part of me, absorbed in me and my thoughts, in my very essence? Across this table sits the most charming and charismatic man I have ever known. He enlivens me. He enlivens everyone around him. What a contrast to what Joey has become. But yet, there is something... something that almost seems meant to be or intended or something I can't quite figure out about Joey and me. It is as if there is a bond between us that was made somewhere in a time or place that I can't even recall; and meeting him that evening at college was a... what was the title of that show Rose did with Deepak a week ago about things preordained? Oh yes, I remember: Rendezvous with Destiny. That's what meeting Joey felt like: a rendezvous with destiny. So strange. So strange.*

She allowed the volume on her thoughts to lower, while permitting Malak's voice to enter the vacuum.

"...and so, my dear friend, I feel you and Joey are about to enter a new phase of your relationship; one different from the way it has been for so many years; but one rich and fulfilling to you both. Before I go on, tell me, Crystal, I know things began to go bad for you two when Joey stopped working. But surely it wasn't that abrupt; there's must have been signs."

Crystal picked up the small spoon resting in the saucer of her espresso cup and nervously used it like a talisman as she reflected on Malak's question.

Then, with a far a way look in her eyes, she said, "It started way before Joey lost his job, David. It began with the death of Michael. Michael's passing changed everything — not with a shout, but with a whisper. It was gradual. Very, very gradual. Eventually we let life make us forget how much we wanted each other. We forgot our story. Losing his job and becoming so depressed was simply the tipping point."

Malak took a moment to process the information, and then asked, "Crystal, did anyone ever explain to you what happens when a young person takes their own life?"

Crystal shook her head and said, "No," then off-handedly added, "After all, David, people don't usually come up to me and offer to tell me such things," and immediately regretted saying it. A slight pause. "Sorry," she said, childlike.

Malak seemed to ignore her flare-up. His mind was focused on the subject at hand.

"Metaphysically one of two things occur following a suicide: One, after crossing over the soul of the person is informed that they made a horrific decision, and they immediately reincarnate without the normal time off in the spirit world. It's a quick round trip, so to speak. Do you follow me so far?"

Crystal nodded that she was with him.

"Good. Now, with other young people who take their own life, the suicide act is actually a part of the agreement the soul made in the spirit realm—or 'bardo', as Eastern mystics call it. See? The person was actually keeping faith with the plan or the promise it made prior to re-entry into another earthly lifetime. Are you with me, Crystal?"

Again, she nodded. He definitely had her full attention.

"Now why would a soul bond itself to an agreement that it would end its own life at a young age? Remember, we're talking about young people suicide here. With older folks, it's a different story."

"I understand," she said.

"Okay. So why would a soul agree or promise — and keep in

mind the agreement was made with the compliance of the soul's mates and circle of brother and sister souls with which it would be associated during the next lifetime — to take its own human life at a young age? Here are the choices: One motive is that the soul needs to return to the spirit world in order to fulfill or carry out some mission that it cannot perform in the body." Malak paused. "Another motive is that those in the soul's circle — soul mates, family, friends and so forth — need to learn a lesson through the suicide of that person. Or…"

"Both," Crystal broke in exuberantly.

"Bingo! You've got it. The soul might need to perform some duty in the spirit world, *and* it needs to provide a lesson through its suicide to those he or she leaves behind." He paused to let the message sink in then added, "Now here's the tricky part: We're not just talking suicide as the method of a young soul intentionally leaving the earthly world. Many infants, young children, teenagers — acting on a prior agreement made in the bardo — sacrifice themselves through accident, illness, whatever, for the purpose of returning to the spirit world to perform some task, and to teach those left behind in it's circle a needed lesson."

Crystal's eyes welled with tears. She dabbed at them with her napkin, staining it with lines of dark mascara.

"What good did Michael's death do for anyone?" she sobbed. "Or, for that matter, Joey's sister? I mean, it leaves a bad wound, David. A wound whose pain you could not possible imagine. And you see what it did to us, to Joey and me. Michael, our beautiful son had so much to give. It doesn't make sense, David. I'm sure in your world the suicide of a bright young boy or the death of a lovely young child is grist for your mill to write books about or go on shows and talk about; but to those of us affected by those deaths, I ask you, David: What possible good does the death of a child do for anyone?"

Just then the lights in the room suddenly dimmed.

"Oh my God!" Crystal blurted out wide-eyed. "Did I say

something wrong?"

"No," Malak replied calmly. "They just want to close the restaurant."

They both broke up laughing.

"We'd better go," Crystal said.

Malak said, "I agree. You've had a lot of information dumped on you. Your head must be swimming. I can only try to imagine how you must feel. Just think about what I said, and let's see how things pan out. And remember if you want to talk at any time day or night, as Carly Simon says, 'You've Got a Friend.'"

"And I can't begin to tell you how much that friendship... this friendship means to me, David," she said, putting her hand on his. "Sorry if I went off the deep end or offended you. It's just that..."

Just then the waiter brought the bill. As Malak was signing the credit card receipt, Crystal casually said, "Oh David. That man, the one who was eating with the older woman and came by our table and stood behind me, did you know him?"

Malak looked up, cocked his head, and looked at Crystal with a puzzled expression.

"What man?" he asked.

The phone was ringing when Crystal entered her apartment. She ran to pick it up.

"Cris?" the anxious voice said.

"Joey?"

"You've been on my mind all evening. Are you all right?"

Crystal remembered calling out to him when she thought David was coming on to her.

"Yes, I'm fine." She thought of saying she missed him, but didn't. Instead she said, "Where are you?"

"I'm in a motel room in Johnstown."

"Johnstown?" she asked. "Pennsylvania?"

"It ain't Wyoming," he responded in that familiar Joey Robin way.

"Listen, Cris. Can we talk? I've got a lot of things to tell you."

Tears came to Crystal's eyes.

"And I you," she said.

She kicked off her shoes and with the phone crooked between her shoulder and her ear, got out of her clothes, slipped on a terry cloth robe, flung herself on the bed, and talked to her husband all night long.

Chapter 21

Joey got less than three hours sleep in his knotty pine-paneled room at the Southmont Inn, but he woke up feeling better than he had felt in months. He and Crystal had talked until five in the morning. They had covered it all — what had been happening to him, and what had been happening to her.

Before the last 'I love you' of many was said, they agreed to meet at the AutoZone Park in five days, after his interview with Bernie Frank was in the can.

Prior to checking out, Joey fired up his computer to check for mail. There were two from Rose — one wishing him good luck and another asking him if he wouldn't prefer to fly to the shoot on the company jet with the crew rather than drive by himself.

Joey wrote her back thanking her for the offer and then added: ANYWAY, KID, HEAVEN KNOWS WHO MIGHT BE RIDING WITH ME!

And he was serious; Joey had become totally open to the possibility of unexpected visitations, twists of logic, and meaningful signs along his pathway.

This was followed by another e-mail from one of her staff with directions to Bernie Frank's home in Florida. And then there was an instant message from donmcneil@breakfastclub.com.

Whoever is writing me knows their broadcasting history, he thought. Don McNeil's Breakfast Club from Chicago was a staple of morning radio listeners throughout the '40's and '50's. With a format similar to Godfrey — band, singers, foils, studio audience — McNeil, unlike Godfrey, never indulged in serious matters, always keeping the banter light and frivolous, carefully avoiding controversy. Also, unlike Godfrey, Don McNeil, although he tried, couldn't make the transition to television. But in the glory days of 'live' radio, Don McNeil was huge.

Joey clicked on the e-mail and read:

YOU DID GOOD.

Joey wrote back:

THANKS. IT'S BEEN QUITE A TRIP!

I KNOW. THERE IS JUST ONE MORE LESSON. ONE MORE THING FOR YOU TO DO AND THEN IT WILL ALL MAKE SENSE.

THE BERNIE FRANK INTERVIEW?

YES... MOSTLY.

MOSTLY? WHAT'S WITH MOSTLY?

SOON YOU'LL KNOW.

I STILL NEED TO KNOW HOW IT WORKS... THE FAME GAME. I UNDERSTAND A LOT MORE THAN I DID, BUT I STILL DON'T UNDERSTAND HOW THE AWARD SYSTEM WORKS. FOR EXAMPLE, WHY MY BROTHER AND NOT ME?

SOON YOU'LL KNOW.

OKAY. THEN LET ME ASK YOU THIS: ARE YOU THE ONE WHO SENT THE OTHERS?

SOON YOU'LL KNOW?

ONE MORE: WHO ARE YOU?

SOON YOU'LL KNOW.

HMMM. HOW'S THE WEATHER WHERE YOU ARE? DON'T ANSWER. SOON I'LL KNOW!

FUNNY! ENJOY YOUR TIME WITH BERNIE. IT'S A TWO-FER. YOU ALWAYS WANTED TO HOST A NATIONAL SHOW. SO ROSE MAKES IT HAPPEN. AND WHO'S THE FIRST GUEST? THE PERSON THE BOYS ADVISED YOU GO TALK TO BECAUSE HE HAS SOMETHING YOU NEED TO KNOW! TALK ABOUT A SYSTEM! DRIVE SAFELY. AND ENJOY THE TRIP. ALWAYS WATCH FOR THE SIGNS. I'LL BE SEEING YOU.

Joey's mind lingered on the e-mailer's last line. *I'll be seeing you. Does it mean he'll be watching me? Or was it just a way to sign off? Or will I be meeting him? Hold on! How do I know he's a him?*

Joey's drive south was uneventful. No iconic talk show hosts sat beside him in the passenger seat, no legendary broadcasters sat around the tables of the places where he stopped to eat, and the waiting staff at each place appeared to be certifiably alive in the present moment.

But now he was keenly aware of what he saw, how he felt, to instinct, to head-voices. The experiences he recently encountered had attuned his body, mind and spirit to a sharpening of his senses. He felt fully and unambiguously alive; and he relished the feeling.

He spent some of the time in the car listening to the radio — Rush, O'Reilly, Hannety — all the ones he couldn't stand before his recent experiences. No longer did they make him angry; no longer did he resent their fame with bitter bile, or wallow in woe with toxic misery over the lack of his own. No more *why them and not me when I'm so crafty and they're so crude?* While hoping he would find the answer to the riddle of the seeming inequity between celebrity and obscurity, the vexation had ceased to metastasis in his spirit. Now they made him laugh! He listened to Rush, O'Reilly and

Hannety and others and he laughed... out loud...! while cruising south on I-65 toward the gulf coast of Florida.

When he wasn't listening to the radio, he was envisioning the up-coming interview with Bernie Frank. This was a Joey Robin technique. Whenever he had an important program coming up, he would spend time alone visualizing how it would feel — feeling it was critical to the process — what he would say if they said this; or they answered that; what he would wear; how he would make a planned remark seem off the cuff or ad-libbed? Like a finely tuned athlete imagines the game he wants to play while sitting alone in the locker room, or the artist imagines the performance they will give sitting quietly alone in the dressing room, Joey Robin always visualized his act prior the program.

And where did Joey learn this art of visualization? From the man he was going to interview.

Bernie Frank was Joey Robin's coeval, his contemporary. Both emerged from similar families and culture. And both performed in a similar manner, with veneration for the institution of broadcasting and assuming themselves part of its legacy. In many ways Joey would be interviewing himself, as Rose had suggested.

Beyond that, Bernie Frank was the only living interviewer Joey Robin considered superior to himself. "Bernie Frank is the best there is," Joey would reply when asked who his favorite interviewers are." The immediate response would invariably be, "Who's Bernie Frank?"

"Bernie knows all the tricks," Joey said to Rose many times over the years. "All the subtle touches and gradations that set the artist apart from the mere professional. For example, watch how he does that inexplicable thing with his eyes that the camera catches — like Tom Snyder did so effectively — that connects the host to the individual viewer. *Nuance*, kid; artistry's secret ingredient."

Through the years, they would occasionally call each other and mainly talk shop; exchange interviewing tactics and techniques; share observations about craft; trade tips and tidbits about mutual guests — 'you might want to ask her this, or ask him that.'

Their conversations were never personal; never 'how's the wife, how're the kids?' That's why Joey was not surprised that Bernie had not called to tell him he got fired in Nashville. After all, Joey had not called Bernie to tell him he got fired in Memphis. *They* were never what they talked about. It was all shoptalk with these two.

It was during one of those conversations that Bernie revealed to Joey his visualization exercise in preparation for an important show. Joey used it ever since.

In visualizing the set up of the show with Bernie, Joey had decided to use the story of his father and his Uncle Morris. What better way to introduce a show called *Artists Without Honor*, about gifted people who never made the big time, than to set the scene with two older men arguing in the living room of a home about whether success is about luck or ability? Joey liked the feel of the picture of his introduction that he saw in his mind. The way the picture *felt* was the key to the process.

The format Rose and her executive producer had formulated for each thirty minute *Artists Without Honor* program would be the same each episode. With twenty-two minutes of actual program — after breaks for commercials — there would be a set-up shot on location with Joey hosting; a post production background segment of the artist and the artist's work, including comments from various people who have known or worked with the artist; a one-on-one interview segment with the artist on location; and a wrap up.

Rose had instructed the director to "Let Joey be Joey. Don't write for him; don't direct him. Just follow him and listen to him. We can edit in or edit out later. Just let him roll." And so, Joey Robin drove the final miles of a trip to do a job his student Rose Barbelo had hired him to do; and, unknown to his employer, to learn a lesson he was advised he needed to learn from the boys at Rita's Eatery and the mysterious e-mailer.

The site of the shoot was a house Bernie Frank and his wife Peg —
who was away for a few days visiting with their daughter in
Tallahassee — had been renting on St. George Island since his
show had been cancelled. Just off the gulf coast of Florida, St.
George's six pristine miles is one of those rare stretches of beach-
front property that have been thus far sparred the blight of devel-
opers and franchised food places.

Bernie was watching the news on TV while the crew were
lighting the area around two chairs facing each other on the deck,
where the interview would take place. He wore a T- shirt with
Nashville YMCA etched across the front, grey gym shorts, and a
pair of old canvas, once-white deck shoes. His legs were scrawny
and pale. He got up slowly — his eyes remaining focused on the TV,
extended his hand for Joey's, gestured to the TV with his head, and
said, "Do you think she regrets her decision?"

Joey glanced at the screen and saw Katie Couric anchoring the
news.

"I tried anchoring once," Bernie continued. "Hated it! Takes a
completely different skill set. I couldn't wait to get back to interviewing."

Then he turned to Joey, smiled warmly and said, "Welcome"
followed by a genuine embrace.

In spite of their many telephone conversations throughout the
years, they had met only once — at a state broadcasters' association
convention in Nashville, where they only had a chance to exchange
a few words, nothing consequential. Neither had wanted to be
there; neither were convention types.

The director told Joey the sun setting over the horizon would
provide a perfect backdrop, and fuse its light just right with the
artificial lighting they had set up, if they could get started within
thirty minutes.

Before she had left for Tallahassee, Peg had prepared a bountiful
platter of fresh shrimp and coleslaw and pitchers of ice tea for
everyone and left a note for Bernie to take it out of the fridge before

they got down to business. Joey and Bernie — alumnae of the school of don't eat before a performance — passed on the food, while the crew, like the gulls, ate their weight.

While the crew gorged, Bernie and Joey schmoozed in a corner of the main room.

"You know," Bernie began. "When they do an autopsy on us some day and test our DNA, they're going to find the gene that holds the secret to good interviewers."

Joey looked at him with a wry smile as if to say go on.

"That's right," Bernie said. "It's called the Talmudic gene. The Talmudic gene is the one that believes that there is validity to all points of view; but that there is only one point of view acceptable to the Universe. The good interviewer, possessed with the Talmudic gene, probes to find that Universally accepted point of view."

Joey nodded in appreciation, but then added, "Bernie, I'm surprised at you. You have violated the talk show host's creed: Never say your good stuff till you're on the air."

Bernie threw up his hands. "Three months off and rust is forming on me already," he said with a grin.

The director told Joey it was time for him to tape his intro-duction. Positioned symbolically against the deck railing, with gray sudsy waves ebbing and flowing against the sandy shore, and a glorious bronze setting sun in the distance, Joey set up the show. He told the story of the Sunday afternoon debates between his father and his uncle and concluded by asking, "So, what manner of justice sprinkles fame and fortune on the sinner as well as the saint without remorse, guilt or reluctance? About the only redemptive conclusion one can draw is that the server of celebrity does not discriminate. After this brief time out, you'll meet the subject of our first in our series of *Artists Without Honor.*

After three seconds of silence, the director said, "Keeper."

Bernie said, "One take! I'm impressed."

Then the director seated Bernie in one chair, positioned at a forty-five degree angle against the setting sun, and sat Joey in another chair at the same angle, facing his guest.

"It's not going to be as easy answering as asking," Joey said, as a production assistant attached tiny microphones to their shirts and handed him an IFB to insert in his ear so he could hear the director's instructions during the taping.

"You trying to make me nervous?" Bernie asked with a grin.

He had changed into a casual blue denim shirt with the sleeves rolled up twice; and Joey wore a white long sleeve linen sport shirt.

"I don't think anything could make you nervous, my friend. You are the quintessential Mr. Cool."

"I used to smoke them," Bernie said.

Old codger jokes like that is why we were both fired, Joey thought, but didn't say.

Just seconds away from the countdown, Joey noticed a young man and an older woman strolling on the water's edge of the beach. The man looked toward the lighted deck, held up his arm and gave a thumbs-up sign. The woman swiftly put her arm on the man's hand and pulled it down. A feeling of odd familiarity swept across Joey as he looked at the couple in the distance; their faces obscured by the rays of the setting sun.

The odd feeling vanished when he heard the director's voice through his IFB, counting "ten, nine, eight, seven..." and Joey asked his first question. Everyone around understood what was riding on this first show in the series, of the need to do a quality show, a Rose Barbelo-type quality show.

But no one knew how vital this encounter was to Joey Robin except Joey Robin. Could the answer to his lifelong frustration with the system of justice in his profession be only a few answers away? What he could elicit from Bernie was as important to him as it was to the success of the show. So much was riding on the next twelve minutes.

Without any preamble, Joey fired away. "Bernie, what does it feel like to go through a life watching those less gifted achieve fame and fortune and be denied it yourself?"

Bernie turned his head toward the ocean, then cast his eyes downward, then to the ice in his ice tea glass, shook his head, looked back at Joey, smiled slightly, and said, "Not good."

Joey leaned forward to the edge of his chair, and with his flailing arms assisting his wide-eyed disbelief, shouted, "Not good? That's all you have to say, 'Not good'? Here I drive five-hundred fa-kuckta miles through every town in the Confederacy to see you and ask a question that has confounded me all my life, and I finally get to seek the answer from the person who personifies the issue, the premier guest on the premier show, personally chosen by Rose Barbelo herself, and he says, 'Not good?'" Joey slumped back in his chair, feigning exasperation.

Playing Joey like a Stradivarius, Bernie said, calmly, "So what's the question again?"

That's Bernie Frank at his best: Using shtick as personal camouflage.

But Joey was no Russert come lately. He knew when to play, and he knew when to work. He'd give Bernie his Bernie Frank moment. After that, it was time to get answers — for the show and for him. It was time — as the saying goes in Tennessee — to belly-up to the buzz saw. Playtime was over.

Leaning in, he said intently, "Bernie, let's get real. Have you ever considered that your career rewards have not matched your ability?"

Bernie waited then said, "Alright. Relax. I'll answer your question." He took a sip of tea, crossed his legs and folded his hands and brought them to his chest. "Of course I've thought about it," he said. "I've thought about it a lot. Who wouldn't? Haven't you?"

Long ago Joey learned to ignore attempts of guests to make him an ally or accomplice during an interview. In fact, it was one of the subjects he and Bernie had discussed during one of their shoptalk phone conversations. The focus must always remain fixed on the guest, never on the host. Nowadays, the formula is reversed, to their vexation.

Bernie paused and smiled at Joey with his eyes — a subtle acknowledgement of Joey's adroitness. Then he got back on track and said "But you know what? I've figured it out; I've discovered the answer; or at least one that satisfies me to the extent that I don't fret about it anymore."

Bernie paused for Joey to ask what the 'it' was that he discovered; but just as he sensed Joey was about to ask he resumed his response.

"But yes, frankly, I have had my struggles with the tenth commandment. I've coveted, I've envied, I've moaned, I've spent a lot of nights cursing God for what I felt He denied me. For a while, I reconciled my lot — or lack thereof — with the fact that I never lucked up on a manager, a person to guide and move my career. I never had anyone like that. I never had a Leo."

He waited.

"A Leo?" Joey asked, on cue.

"Yeah, a Leo. You know, like on *The West Wing*, the television series. The character named Leo McGarry who recognized the talent and potential of a Governor and guided his career all the way to the White House. There was a love, a respect and appreciation between those two: one the mover; the other the shaker. To make it in this business, everyone needs a Leo. I never had one. I looked, but never found the right person, or was never found by the right person. Did I look hard enough? I don't know," he said, shaking his head.

Inwardly assessing his own lack of a Leo throughout his career, Joey thought, *I was usually the one mentoring — like with Rose — rather than the one being mentored.*

"Quite honestly", Bernie continued, as if he hadn't taken a break, "in recent years I have come to terms with the 'why not me' question, and have stopped beating my breast over what didn't happen in my career; what I should have become and what I didn't, and all that. In fact, I have not only accepted my lot, I have come to believe I'm the one who caste it. And with that belief, I am at peace with me."

For an instant, Joey thought he saw Godfrey, Dinah and Paar and a few of the others leaning on the railing of the deck applauding. Inexplicably, Joey smiled in their direction, as Bernie took another sip of tea, and went on talking.

"Now, before I share my discovery with you, we've got to define success as we are dealing with it here. What you and I are really discussing is fame, stardom — which may or may not be an element of success. For example, most all of us would agree that a woman or man who has raised good children is successful. The cleric who attends to the sick and the downtrodden is, on the Mother Theresa scale, a huge success. I readily acknowledge that those who follow the prophet Micah's admonition to do justice, love mercy, and walk humbly with thy God are unequivocally successful in the world devoid of time and space. Their reward awaits them. I truly believe that," Bernie said.

Now we're getting there, Joey thought. *He's getting on a roll.*

Then Bernie raised his index finger for emphasis, and said, "But our world is *not* devoid of space and time, Joey. In our world, time is sold by the second, and space is sold by bandwidth. And in our world, *this world*," he enunciated, opening his arms inclusively, "one is measured not by beneficence, mercy or righteousness. A local show means you have a job; a national show means you're a success. To be known as excellent at what one does, or the merit of what one does, is not necessarily related to being famous for what one does. In our world, popularity has far greater value than craft. In our world success is measured by size — your ratings, your house, your car, your paycheck. In our world, size matters!"

Bernie paused to silently stare out at the ocean and to allow what had been said up to that point to process, as the lights of the shrimp boats on the distant horizon glistened like stars resting on the water.

Joey did not try to fill the dead air. He welcomed its theatrical value. He looked over at Bernie as a first violinist in a symphony orchestra looks at the conductor awaiting the motion of his baton. He was aware that postproduction editing would dramatize the moment.

With perfect timing, Bernie resumed his discourse. "But understanding and acknowledging the terms under which we operate down here don't solve the puzzle. If the system is corrupted down here, we must look elsewhere."

Joey raised his eyebrows and pointed a finger toward the sky as if asking, 'Up there?'

Bernie nodded half-smiling. He said, "It seems to me that in order to solve this mystery we have to reconcile both systems: that of the world in which we operate, and the Universal system… up there." he pointed, mimicking Joey's gesture. "Let me put it this way — it's the best way I can think of to illustrate my point… my discovery: I use a Mac. Most of my friends use a PC. PCs and Macs use different operating systems. Until recently a Mac program couldn't be run on a PC, even though the data on the disc was identical. Why? Because PCs couldn't read and translate the Mac operating system. Follow me so far?"

Joey nodded thinking *Not only me, my friend, but some of our heroes are lapping this up as well.*

Bernie continued. "Recently a software program came on the market that can read and translate PC data to Mac and Mac data to PC, making the systems interchangeable. Both operating systems — both worlds — can now read one another. Voila!" he said, with his bottom lip turned down, his eyebrows lifted, and his hands vertical as if asking 'So what's the question?'

He held the pose long enough for his camera to catch it and for Joey to react.

Resetting himself, Bernie said, in a slightly slower cadence and with a tone of assurance, "I am convinced that the bestowing of success *is* perfectly fair, and in accordance with the Universal system by which it is operating. Any perceived inequity depends on which operating system we are using to translate the data. What we deem here on earth as unfair seems perfectly fair to the Universe in the long run, in the karmic run. The Universe deems success as one bringing forth one's talents, gifts, and abilities. That's it! Period! The Universe agrees with Nike: 'Just do it!' Planet Earth, on the other hand, deems success as becoming *famous* for bringing forth one's talents, gifts, and abilities. Earth disagrees with Nike. 'Just do it' isn't enough. One needs to become famous and rich from doing it or else you're... well, you're Bernie Frank and Joey Robin."

Joey gave his camera his best humble cut-away smile and waited for Bernie to continue.

"You see? The Universe and planet Earth use different operating systems. I am hopeful that we are heading for a time when the operating system of the Universe will be interchangeable with the operating system of Earth, like the Mac and the PC have become. We will then be able to penetrate the veil separating above and below, so that the seemingly unjust world we have been born into this time around will make sense because the operating system of the Universe will be translated for us. All the apparent inequities of life on earth would appear to us in a new logic, manifesting the ancient wisdom, 'As above, so below'."

Joey asked, "So on what basis, on what criteria, is fame and fortune, stardom and all that goes with it meted out and awarded?"

Contemplating for a moment, Bernie said, "Remember a moment ago I answered your question about whether I angst over my lack of celebrity by saying I have not only accepted my lot, I'm the one who caste it?"

"Yes," Joey replied.

"What I was implying was that I believe that we are the authors of our own life story. Who gets to be famous and who does not? If, when in the spirit world, the soul becomes aware that it needs to experience fame in its next life, then stardom is included in the script... not as a reward but for an experience, a lesson." Bernie paused and leaned toward Joey. Using an assertive tone of voice, he said "But remember; the Universe places absolutely no value on stardom or any of its perks. Only performance matters. If fame is included in the package of success, its purpose is solely experiential, simply for a lesson needing to be learned for the advancement of the soul and the soul's mates."

Joey felt a tingling sensation throughout his body. It was as if he had breathed in light. He looked over toward the railing where he thought he had spotted some of his visitors. They were still there; several were giving each other a high five.

Joey asked, "Have you figured out the basis on which the two systems operate — the one used by the Universe and the one we use?"

Bernie smiled in appreciation for the question. "Yes I have. The operating system of the Universe is based on love — unconditional, without terms, without expectation, non-judgmental pure and absolute love."

"And ours?"

"Ours is based on fear. Fear is at the root of ego, anger, all petty self-centeredness and aggrandizement."

Joey added the closer: "The question then becomes, when we learn to read the operating system of the Universe, will we change ours? Will fame be regarded here with the same irrelevance it is regarded by the Universe?"

The next morning Joey came in the living room to say goodbye after spending the night in the guest room. Bernie was watching the TV wearing the same YMCA T-shirt and grey shorts he wore the day before. His scrawny legs were just as pale.

He got up slowly; his eyes remained focused on the TV. Extending his hand for Joey's, he gestured to the screen with his head and said, "Part of Regis' brilliance is using female co-hosts. Kathy Lee and Kelly make Regis' star shine brighter."

Prior to last night's conversation with his colleague, Joey would have reacted internally thinking, *Why couldn't it have been 'Live with Joey and Rose'*? Today, he simply nodded in agreement.

Bernie turned his attention to Joey. He smiled warmly and the two men genuinely embraced.

"I hope I gave you what you wanted last night," Bernie said, as Joey reached for his overnight bag and briefcase.

"My dear friend, you gave me more than you will ever know," Joey replied.

The blue sky was decorated with patchy cotton clouds as he drove across the St. George causeway toward the mainland. The gulls swooped down and waved goodbye then banked to the left and flew across the road to greet new arrivals in their baggage-stuffed SUVs.

As Joey approached the mainland, he thought of his quest and the answer he was given by his alter ego. Silently he said *thank you*.

Casting his eyes upward he spotted a vaguely familiar cloud figure. With a loving heart, he acknowledged the contented face of his father.

Chapter 22

The morning began as most mornings began at Shalom Chalet. Crystal and Joey slept until about eight, and while Crystal performed her morning ablutions, Joey lingered in bed recollecting each moment of each of the thirteen episodes of *Artists Without Honor*, which he completed filming three months earlier. A feeling of harmony and serenity permeated his mind, body and spirit.

Downstairs, Crystal pushed the button on the coffee maker. Joey would be downstairs before four cups dripped into the glass canister. He'd stand beside the kitchen counter waiting for the dripping to end, like a homeless person at a soup kitchen, holding his favorite cup — a thick-handled, heavy off-white porcelain mug, the old in-artful kind that road-side cafes such as Rita's Eatery and Clara Ann's Country Cooking set in front of its patrons.

He'd pour a cup for himself and one for Crystal. It was spring so they could stroll out on to the newly-built deck high above acres of tall oak, maple, sycamore and elm trees plus a variety of saplings eager to attain the brawn of their elders.

Seated in twin Adirondack deck chairs they would watch the black-capped chickadees, red-breasted nuthatches, mountain bluebirds, warblers, Baltimore oriels, cardinals and wrens feed from the myriad of bird houses Crystal had hung from the eve of the house they had grown to cherish.

Finding Shalom Chalet was proof of Joey's newly acquired ethereal sensitivity, and it was love at first sight. The day after their reconciliation at AutoZone Park, he and Crystal took a long drive. After several hours, Joey pulled over to the side of the road and asked Crystal to get behind the wheel.

"Joey, are you alright? I mean, we're okay now; you don't have to push it. I know you always like to do the driving. I'm fine. Really," she said, her bewildered eyes searching his for an explanation.

Joey laughed and casually opened the driver's side door. Bending over slightly, he beckoned toward the driver's seat with an elegant rotation of his hand miming the supplication of the driver of a horse drawn carriage to his passenger.

They rode and talked some distance further when Joey abruptly interrupted what Crystal was saying.

"Turn right here!" he said firmly, but without a tone of urgency.

Crystal looked over at him and then did what he commanded. The road was narrow but paved. They traveled three or four pastoral miles. Cows grazed off in the distance. Barbed wire was strung seemingly forever. Crystal wanted to observe the rustic scenery, but the frequent blind curves demanded her focus remain riveted on the road. Joey sat alert but seemingly calm, a slight hint of a smile at the corner of his lips.

"Hang a left at the broken fence post," he said, now in an airplane pilot's pacifying tone.

"What broken fence post?"

"The one we'll be coming to in just a few feet."

Five seconds passed.

"There," he said, pointing. "That's it."

She turned left onto a road the width of one vehicle, with weeds growing between the middle of two dirt and rock ruts. A few feet up ahead on the right, a wooden sign with PRIVATE ROAD carved into it was nailed to a fence post. Just a few feet beyond that sign, on the other side of the road, a plank of wood warning KEEP OUT was nailed to a tree. One could not help but notice and give pause to the three bullet holes clean through it.

Crystal stopped and looked at her husband over the top of her sunglasses as if to ask, *Are you sure we should go on?*

Without saying a word, Joey raised his index finger and summarily pointed it forward like a cavalry officer in a Western film, hollering 'Yo-oh' to a platoon of soldiers.

Crystal shrugged, put the SUV in four-wheel drive and slowly eased along the twists and turns of a road, obviously, less traveled. They drove by a culvert containing an assortment of abandoned appliances and auto parts; passed the charred remnants of a stone fireplace and chimney marking where a small cabin used to be; and what looked to be several undecipherable grave stones — some turned over — smothered with undergrowth. Then the road elevated for about thirty-feet and leveled off.

Just a few yards ahead stood a barn in good repair. Beyond it were at least fifteen acres of recently mowed, thick, green grass over mostly flat land that occasionally undulated, giving it a lovely pastoral postcard look.

Crystal sighed, "Joey."

"It's there, just ahead," he said, pointing forward, a gentle smile on his lips. He closed his eyes, and said silently, *Thank you.*

Thirty or so yards past the barn, the road led to a cattle fence. It was open and they drove slowly along a shaded promenade lined on both sides by twenty-six huge straight and true loblolly pine trees. A well-maintained dirt driveway led to a cedar shake, two stories home, nestled on a point high above a ravine, overlooking a lake below. A sign stuck in the ground said, 'For Sale by Owner' and listed a telephone number.

"How did you know?" she asked, as they walked around the property, 'ooing' and 'awing' at every magical discovery.

But before he replied, she said, "Wait. I know: Eddie Albert from *Green Acres* was riding in the back seat! I just didn't see him. Right?"

Joey smiled, comforted by the manner with which Crystal had processed all that he had told her about his visitors. Until her quip, he wasn't quite sure how it had all gone down with her. Typically, his moment of comfort was replaced by a feeling of regret over the many years he wasted by not sharing his total life with her.

"Right," Joey said, adding, "and Eva sat beside him."

Without bargaining, Joey and Crystal accepted the price the owner — a physician from the Germantown section of Memphis — was asking and Crystal immediately set about renovating it while

Joey was off filming *Artists Without Honors*. When he was finished, the home was completed, and they moved into their haven — Shalom Chalet.

But there was no time for bird watching this morning. This morning was a special morning. Joey was thinking what lay ahead as he routinely brushed his teeth. The coffee was perking and Crystal had gone outside on the deck to fill the feeders with plenty of food to last while they were gone.

Three hours later Crystal and Joey arrived at the private airplane terminal adjacent to Memphis International Airport. Rose welcomed them on board her jet with hugs and kisses. She introduced them to several Barbelo Production executives, then pointed down the aisle toward a couple sipping soft drinks, and, with a gleeful smile, Rose said, "I think you know those folks."

"Peg! What a nice surprise," Crystal said, leaning over to hug the wife of her husband's professional twin.

Bernie raised his hand to Joey's, looked up at him and said, "She picked us up in Nashville. So far, not even pretzels!"

They landed at Los Angeles International airport four hours later and poured into a stretch limo waiting on the tarmac that whisked them to their hotel to freshen up. At five o'clock they arrived at the Beverly Hilton Hotel, the sight of this year's Emmy Awards.

As he entered the gigantic dining room, Joey felt as if he were walking on air. He paused to look around the room and breathe in the atmosphere of a literal star-studded Universe — a Universe to which he had aspired for so long and now to which he belonged.

"Honey," he said to Crystal as they took their seat at their table, near the front of the room. "If this isn't heaven, I don't know what is."

Dressed in a beaded blue violet gown with sweeping over-skirt, she looked enraptured. She softly kissed his cheek and the scent of her Shalimar fragrance added to his euphoria.

Rose had been busy working the crowd, elegantly attired in a black off-the-shoulder tulle Valentino gown with black and silver sequins. When she worked her way to the Barbelo Productions table, she took her seat on the other side of Joey, the one assigned to her by the assistant director of the Emmy Television production staff, whose responsibility it was to line up cut-away shots of the audience reaction to the various awards. Crystal reached across Joey and squeezed Rose's hand. Rose looked at Crystal and silently formed the words, "I love you." Crystal touched her heart with her hand and mimed sending her love in return. Their eyes exchanged a moment of coded feelings, emotions and thoughts that only these two women would understand on this special night.

To break the love fest, Rose said, "They've assigned me this seat for the last couple of years to catch my reaction when Oprah wins our category."

"Not this year, Rose," Crystal said. "Tonight's your night."

"No," Rose said. "Tonight's *our* night. It's not the Best Daytime Talk Show award I care about: Best Original New Series. That's the baby my heart is riding on."

While Joey scanned the room, marveling in his mind at the miracle of his being there, he looked over at Bernie Frank, who he thought would also be enthralled with where he was. But Bernie, to Joey's amazement, was reading the menu to Peg, who had forgotten to bring her glasses. Crystal scratched around inside her purse — which contained gear akin to that of a survival kit no matter where she was — found a spare pair and handed them to Peg.

And then it was showtime! Joey's heart jumped when the music came up and the announcer read the voice-over to the pre-produced video open to the telecast of this year's Emmy Awards Show.

When the Best Daytime Quiz Show category was announced, Joey searched the room and finally spotted the table where his brother was seated next to a buxom woman who Joey thought could not be more than eighteen years old.

"And the winner of the Emmy is... who else? Liberty Fortune!"

As the camera caught cut-away shots of Pat Sajak and Bob Barker applauding and forcing smiles, Liberty strode up to the podium, smiled broadly, thanked nobody except the fans of *Playing the Odds* and concluded by saying, "this being my seventh Emmy, I might have to buy a small country so I can house them all." The audience loved it and carried him off stage on the wave of their applause, as the program cut to a commercial break.

Then Joey did a remarkable thing that drew the attention of this media-savvy congregation who knew and obeyed 'The Rule of Fortune'. He stood and hastily made his way over to his brother's table as Liberty made his way to it from the stage—hand clasping, back patting and high-fiving along the way. They both arrived there at the same time. For a moment the two Rabinowitz boys just stood and looked at one another. Joey's eyes and lips conveyed a warm tender smile. Liberty seemed unsure what to make of the moment, or of Joey's smile.

Joey spoke: "I'm proud of you, brother." He paused. "I'm really proud of you."

Liberty seemed nonplused. "Joey?" he said. "Have you been..."

"Drinking?" Joey laughed. "No, Liberty, I'm as clear-headed as one of your champion contestants. And my pride in you is as honest and sincere as it is newly acquired."

"Oh yeah?" was all Liberty could muster.

"I know that after all that we've been through, since we've grown up, what I just said seems odd, maybe even suspicious. You've always been the suspicious kind. That's probably why you've done so well in business. But what I learned recently is that you have been true to yourself in your life. You made your plan a long time ago, and you stuck with it. I judged you on how I thought you ought to live; on *my* set of values; *my* criteria. What I didn't realize, until recently, was that my resentment of you and your success was simply a toxic spill of my own reflection. I was not the *me* I wanted to be, Liberty, and instead of simply enjoying who I was, I resented you for being you."

Suddenly, Liberty came forward and threw his body around Joey in an enveloping bear hug. The people in the vicinity of Liberty's table stared, nonplussed at what they were witnessing.

"We're two branches out of the same tree, brother," Joey said. "And we each sought the sun the best we could."

If Joey could have seen Liberty's reaction — which he could not because the men were still body-locked in a head-to-head embrace — he would have seen Liberty's brow furl as if trying to figure out what Joey had just said.

Releasing one another, Joey brushed the wrinkles of his tux jacket with his hand, and said, "See how it works? I just learned the system. It's credible! If you had not acquired all the wealth that you acquired — the wealth and fame that I resented for so many years — you would not have had a company that Rose would buy, so that I could have this moment! You get it? It's so fantastic, Liberty! *You* are partly responsible for *my* being nominated for an *Emmy*! Imagine! You! My little brother, Benny, shared in the plan that got me here tonight! And you know what? It was all blueprinted somewhere in time. I know that doesn't make sense to you, brother, but I'd stake my life on it!"

Obviously, Liberty's level of metaphysical tolerance had been exceeded. Making a grandiose gesture of swiping his hand across his forehead, he said, "Whew! That's strong medicine, brother."

At that point the music welled for the next segment of the Emmy ceremony. The public address announcer asked the audience to quickly return to their seats. "We'll be live in five, four, three…"

Joey leaned in to his brother, and said, "I love you, Benny," and he rushed back to his table as the countdown finished and the show was back on. To his surprise, Bernie was gone. David Malak was now sitting next to Peg.

"Where's Bernie?" Joey whispered to Crystal.

She glanced at Malak and put her hand on Joey's and patted it. "He had to leave," was all she said.

Joey looked across at Peg who was being consoled by Malak.

He felt bewildered, light headed. He wanted to know what happened to his kindred spirit. But aside from Peggy's silent sobs, no one else seemed concerned.

He started to say something to Crystal, but she gently put her finger on his lips and whispered, "Don't worry, honey, he'll be back."

Then she motioned for him to look up to the stage, and said, "Look, it's Sara Jessica Parker. Oh, if I could only be that thin."

The *Sex and the City* star began reading the nominees for Best Daytime Talk Show. "And the winner is… *The View!* —ABC Television, Barbara Walters, executive producer."

As tuxedo-clad, hand-held camera operators kneeled to get close up shots of Oprah Winfrey, Rose Barbelo, Montel Williams, and Ellen DeGeneres smiling and applauding, and Barbara Walters and the rest of *The View* cast took their place behind the podium to accept the kudos of the audience and the Emmy statue from Sara Jessica Parker, Rose leaned across to Joey while continuing to smile and clap, and said between her teeth, "Like I said, sweetie, this is not the one I care about; not the one my heart is riding on. That one is coming up next."

"And now, to present the nominees in the category of Best New Original Series, here is the executive producer of *60 Minutes*, Mr. Don Hewitt."

Rose reached over and grasped Joey's hand and Crystal took hold of his other hand as the distinguished television journalist read a brief description of the category and then listed the five nominees.

Joey looked over at Peg, whose tears were amazingly replaced by a smile of contentment. The chair beside her was empty. Malak was gone. At some point in time, with all the focus on the festivities on stage, he had left the table.

As Joey looked past the empty chair out into the room, he thought he saw Johnny Carson, plus all the other legends of broadcasting that had visited with him along his journey, gathering at a table off in the distance. His eyes widened as he watched the group welcome two other gentlemen with hugs and handshakes. Joey starred in disbelief. The two newcomers appeared to be disoriented. They were smiling but they kept looking around as if to try to get their bearings. Arthur Godfrey pulled up two chairs and motioned for Merv Griffin and Tom Snyder to sit down and join the others.

Impossible! Joey said to himself. He blinked. They were still there, out there in the dark, with all the other stars.

And then he returned his focus to the stage as he heard Don Hewitt say, "And the Emmy for the Best New Original Series for this year goes to... *Artists Without Honor!* —Pathways Cable Television, Barbelo Productions, Rose Barbelo, Producer, Joey Robin, host.

His first and instant reaction was utter detachment of body and mind, as if cocooned in a pocket of space devoid of sound and emotion. He had just observed the awarding of an honor to a show called *Artists Without Honor* hosted by someone named Joey Robin. It seemed meaningless.

In seconds, however, the infusion of applause from standing attendees pierced his insolated bubble, and he felt slam-dunked into the reality of his experience. Joey turned to his wife and kissed her fully on the lips.

"I love you," she said, "forever."

"Forever," he said.

Seemingly floating on air, like having his soul dancing around his body, he emitted the charismatic vibes of the *joie de vivre* now infused in his being once fraught with joylessness. Joey navigated his way between the round dinning tables toward the stage in a caravan of Barbelo people, headed by their ebullient leader while acknowledging the winks, blown kisses, fist taps and assorted shouted kudos of the applauding stars and the moons in their orbit, looking up at their newly discovered planet.

After recognizing the work and contribution of the individuals behind the scene of *Artists Without Honor*, Rose paused a moment and looked downward, away from the camera, as if to assemble the pieces of thoughts she wanted to express next — a tactic picked up from Joey years ago.

Holding the Emmy statue in her arms, as if cuddling an infant, Rose spoke:

"Many years ago, a local radio and television personality took an untrained girl and gave her the confidence, the opportunity and the encouragement of ten thousand angels. Amazing what happens when given the permission to try. And because of his belief in me, later on I was able to provide an opportunity for him. And thanks to you, tonight, an artist without honor is receiving that which he has so long deserved."

Rose turned to Joey and handed him the Emmy, and said, "Joey, dear soul, this completes the promise."

As the applause erupted and echoed throughout the room, Joey took the Emmy from Rose and paused to face her and look deeply in her eyes. "I know," she whispered. Then, with the stature firmly held in one hand, he leaned in and tenderly kissed her on the middle of her forehead. Rose's eyes remained closed for several seconds after he backed away. Then he stepped forward towards the podium.

Knowing the high that a cocktail of anticipation mixed with a jigger of silence can induce, Joey allowed the accolade of the audience to fade and then to settle. He waited another minute before he spoke.

Gazing out into a vast roomful of stars shining their light on him, he said, "Thank you, Rose. Had I known all this would happen I would have gotten fired years ago!" The room erupted with a tsunami of laughs, cheers, and then applause.

"And thank you, ladies and gentlemen, for bestowing this honor to this artist. But while my gratitude to Rose and to you all fills this room, my heart is with those of you out there watching this program on television; those of you who feel you deserve to be in this room tonight; those of you who believe life has not given you the award you feel you earned or deserve. I know you. I know your aching heart; the bitterness and resentment; the hollow bored in the gut by unrequited dreams.

"But what I also know — what I have recently learned — is that as unjust as the system of fame and reward appears to us, there is another level of justice, a system that makes perfect sense and is profoundly fair. On that level, only bringing forth that which is within you to the best of your ability matters; only doing the work counts. Reward is measured only on the basis of doing the work. In that system awards and fame are unfamiliar, unheard of, and unknown elements... like an undefined word in an unknown foreign language. Fame, on that level, is not only without value, it is without meaning.

Beyond that — and this one's hard to accept — I must tell you that you are exactly in the place you are supposed to be because... because you wrote the script."

Joey paused a few seconds to allow the thought to process, then he added, "There's an old saying that if you want to make God laugh, tell Him your plans — meaning, of course, that our lives are out of our hands, out of our control, that plans are futile in the eyes of God.

"Well, what I have learned recently is that if you want to *please* God, *remember your plan. And work your plan.* Because you wrote it. At a place somewhere in time and space, you planed the course of your life — of all your lives. The poet was right when he wrote, 'I am the master of my fate, the captain of my soul.' So, where ever you are now is where you need to be, where you are supposed to be. And the work you love doing is the work you should do."

Joey paused, looked down at Crystal dabbing her eyes with a tissue as she mouthed *I love you,* and over at Rose standing beside him, her watery eyes harboring a myriad of emotions.

"As for me, I must have written this lovely ending. From the deepest place in my heart and soul, I thank you for appearing in the story of my life."

The orchestra struck up the theme to *Artists Without Honors*, and Joey and Rose strode off the stage hand in hand. Turning his head for one more look at the glittering audience, he thought he saw the table with Carson and the others jumping up and down, pumping their fists, giving the thumbs-up and victory sign. All except Joe Pyne: he was making an obscene gesture. Joey shook his head in amusement.

Backstage, with Rose, he asked, "Do you think they got it?

"You said it, sweetie; that's all that matters."

"You know," he said, wiping his brow with his handkerchief. "It all seems so unreal. I mean, you, me, Cris, other things that happened. I wish Bernie had stuck around to see all this."

With a warm smile, Rose said, "I'm sure he watched somewhere."

"I hope so," he said.

Rose took a deep breath, let it out and with a look of knowing said, "What matters is that we played by the rules, and we got a chance to learn why we were in each other's lives."

While they were talking, two more awards were given out, and the evening came to a close.

Joey kissed Rose on the cheek, and she kissed him back. "Now," she said with a tone of valor. "You'd better get back to Cris. I need to go deal with the press."

Crystal was talking to the waiter, who quickly dispersed when Joey returned to the table. They embraced and kissed and said "I love you" to each other a dozen times.

Then they sat down facing one another knee to knee at the, now abandoned, table, his hands enveloped in hers and resting on her lap, silently gazing deeply into each other's eyes.

A few moments later, Joey said, softly, "I don't want to leave here."

She said, "I know. It's been such a special point in time for you, for us. I'll never forget it. I'll always remember."

He cocked his head, and said, "Promise?"

"Promise," she whispered. Pausing a second, she added, with mock confidence. "Anyway, I'll be right behind you."

Looking over her shoulder for an instant, he returned his focus to Crystal and said, "Come with me."

Joey had spotted him from the stage while he was making his remarks. That's why he said what he said during his acceptance speech. He wanted him to know that he got it.

Taking Crystal's hand, he led her to a table on the far side of the room. Sitting there was a man in his early forties outfitted in the latest style of formal wear. Seated with him was an older woman wearing a white off the shoulder gown, radiating a beatific beauty. On her head, over her smooth silver hair, a tiara of glittering diamonds added even more radiance to her warm, inviting translucent blue eyes.

"Hi folks. Have a seat," the man said in a resonant, welcoming tone of voice.

Joey and Crystal sat down at the couple's table.

Crystal's eyes filled with tears, and she was barely able to get the word out of her mouth. "Michael?"

"Hello, mom," he said tenderly. She reached out to place her hand on her son's face but something held her back. She just stared at him in marvel, mixed with disbelief.

"Hello, Micah," Joey said.

"Hi, Dad," Michael said. "Congratulations. You did well tonight." Michael paused, grinned and said, "I especially enjoyed your remarks." He followed it with a sly wink.

Joey chuckled and said, "I thought you would. Anyway, you have no idea how much your mother and I appreciate you and your friend taking the effort to come here tonight. I don't know how you did it — heck, I don't know how anything that's happened to me happened this past year — but it means so much to us that you came here."

Michael cocked his head and said, "Dad, I don't think you understand. *We* didn't go anywhere."

Joey looked at Crystal quizzically. She smiled back at him warmly. He was about to say something when Michael threw up his hands as if to ask forgiveness. "Oh! I'm sorry," he said. "I forgot to introduce you to Aunt Iris. Iris, say hello to your brother, Joey. Mom, this is my Aunt Iris."

Joey's jaw dropped. He scratched his head, and said, "Wait a second. Holy cow! I've seen you two before. Weren't you the two people walking on the beach at St. George Island when I was interviewing Bernie Frank?"

Poking Michael on the arm, Iris said, "I knew he had spotted us. You and your waving." They both laughed.

Joey added, "And you were at the Incline Restaurant in Johnstown when I was meeting with Rose! Am I right? That was you two, wasn't it?"

With a broad smile, Michael replied, "As well as a few other places. Yes. We were there. Oh, and mom, I needed to put the thought in Malak's head at the Chez Philippe to ask you about Shalom Chalet to save you from... well, let's just say... to save you." He gave her a sly wink. Crystal blew him a loving kiss. "Actually, Dad, we are, as you might say: co-conspirators." Iris placed her hand gently on Michael's which seemed to brighten his glow.

She said softly, "Sending the e-mail was Michael's job. That's all foreign to me. As you know, I was just a child when I made the transition. I grew up in the spirit world. After my training, my job was to teach rich and famous communicators on earth the true meaning of life once they crossed over."

Michael added, "She sent all the visitors to you, Dad. Outside of a few personal zingers, I e-mailed what she told me to write. We needed to place you in situations to receive them. All of them are her students. And when Aunt Iris tells a Carson or a Godfrey to go see someone, believe me, they go."

Iris squeezed Michael's arm, and said, "All of this — my dying as a child, my job, your choice of parents, your job — it had all been worked out and agreed to. I merely provided the rescue squad to get you back into your play. You needed to remember a promise you made once upon a time — the one many people enabled you to fulfill — a promise to use your talent for a purpose other than yourself. The Emmy? Your peers gave you that. Your *real* award is the work you performed."

Joey looked at Michael. He wanted to touch him, but he did not. Instead he simply asked, "And you, Micah? Was taking your life part of a plan as well?"

Looking squarely at his father, Michael responded, "Yes, Dad. It was. At the time, of course, I didn't know it. I just wanted to hurt you."

As he paused for a deep breath, Iris held her nephew's hand tightly and comforted him with her eyes.

"After I took my life, I had a strong compulsion to do a turn-around; to immediately reincarnate as your baby, Mom; to get another chance, another try; to make up for what I had done to me; to the both of you. But then, Dad, you went and got a vasectomy!"

He paused, looked down, then up at his folks, grinned, and said, "And while I love you with all my heart, Mom, you ain't the Virgin Mary, and I sure ain't Jesus. And, Dad, while there have been times you thought you were, I'm here to tell you that you definitely ain't..." He let his father finish the sentence. Joey loved the bit.

"Michael came across very angry," Iris said, in an assured yet mellifluous tone of voice. "I, along with some others, started working with him so he could begin to remember. The root of anger is fear. Fear, and all its siblings, is the biggest blockage to remembering the story we wrote for ourselves. Once Michael was rid of the baggage of fear he carried over, he was able to remember *his* life story, the one he wrote with your acquiescence. Eventually, everything that happened began to make sense to him so that he could move on with his story."

Joey said, "It was my frustration with not being a star, Micah. I know that now. That's why I treated you like I did. And I am so sorry, my boy." Again, Joey tried to reach over to Michael but intuitively brought his arm back.

"Dad, don't you get it? We agreed to all this. All of it! It doesn't make the hurt go away, Dad; it just explains it."

He paused, and then added, "You do want to live, don't you, Dad?"

"With all my heart and soul," Joey fervently replied. "Just as I love you, my dear son, with all my heart and soul."

At that instant, Joey suddenly felt a wave of anguish permeating his body and mind and spirit — a deep pain gripping his entire being. Tears flowed from his eyes like water gushing from a hydrant. In a state of consciousness unlike any he had ever known, he became aware of feeling, of experiencing the torment that his son had felt each time he had a confrontation with him.

Suddenly the pain was different — just as intense but different. His consciousness was now feeling, experiencing the terrible pain Crystal had felt when she lost her only child. The agony was nearly unbearable. He closed his eyes and pleaded, *Dear God, I am so sorry. Please forgive me!*

In an instant all pain was gone. He felt a kiss on his lips. Crystal's kiss.

Cris, you knew, didn't you?

Yes.

When? When did you know?

When Bernie left. I knew it then.

I guess I should have known.

I will always love you, my dearest.

He opened his eyes. He was alone, a star at last among the stars.

Suddenly, from out of the blue, he began to be subjected to a sensation of being tugged, of being pulled by an unseen force. His instinct was to resist, to oppose, to defy the power of the force drawing him toward what appeared to be an abyss.

And yet, another instinct compelled him to allow, to permit whatever was tugging on him to take him to its destination.

He made his choice: *Acceptance.*

Suddenly his warm, dark, safe, quiet environment was invaded by a cold piercing light. Not the light to which he had recently grown accustomed; this light was artificial, unwelcoming. He squeezed his eyes shut, trying to block out the terrible light and strange noise, and the unfamiliar, harsh atmosphere into which he had somehow arrived.

But soon the cacophonous din faded, and he felt comforted by the soothing touch of a woman holding him in a blanket close to her breast. He could feel her heartbeat. It was familiar.

From the distance he heard a voice coming from a box say, "Now here's a fresh new star all the way from Tennessee singing her rendition of the number one song in England: Here's Miss Dinah Shore and *We'll Meet Again.*

He saw the woman's eyes widen. She looked over toward a man standing beside her, and said, "Look Jake... the baby is smiling!"

"Don't be silly, Rachel. It's just gas."

The woman ignored her husband's comment. She focused on the small face with a blissful smile staring somewhere above.

I wonder what he knows? she thought.

The Beginning

Author's Note

In 1987, I created a radio program focusing on matters of mind, body and spirit called *Beyond Reason*. It continues to this day. We end each program with this thought: "You may not believe what you discover; but then, you may discover what you believe." That aphorism applies to this book as well.

A Particle of God is a work of fiction. It centers on my curiosity and fascination with the seemingly enigmatic system by which success—specifically fame and fortune—are meted out. Why is acclaim awarded to some and not others of equal, or superior, talent? John F. Kennedy was quoted as having said, "Life is unfair." Was he correct, or is there another perspective?

For the setting of this work, I have selected the universe of radio and television broadcasting, my universe for over forty years. I am aware that inevitable questions will arise from some readers as to whether this is really a fictional work, or if I am disguising biography? This book is not biographical. However, guided by the principal to "write what you know," it is impossible not to include aspects of what I have experienced, observed and gleaned over four decades.

Accordingly, I have generously borrowed attributes, character-istics and other qualities from people close to me, and I have augmented and embellished those traits with other characteristics, attributes and qualities to move the story forward. Thus, in this book, the characters are more than composites but less than precise. I am so deeply grateful to them for all they mean to my heart. And there are characters in this book that are pure figments. I am grateful to them as well because on some plane they exist.

I want to thank my literary agent, Devra Ann Jacobs, for her belief in this work from the first pitch, for her sage advice, and for laughing at my jokes. And deep appreciation to my publisher, John Hunt, president of O-Books, for publishing books that proliferate

Light. My thanks as well to his staff of professionals who have moved the process along. I wish also to express my gratitude to the legendary broadcasters named in this book as well as the countless others who have inspired and educated me throughout my life. Their spirit permeates this book.

Your thoughts about the ideas presented in this book are most welcome. My e-mail address is listed on my web site www.teddybart.com.

Teddy Bart
August 2008

BOOKS

O is a symbol of the world, of oneness and unity. In different cultures it also means the "eye", symbolizing knowledge and insight. We aim to publish books that are accessible, constructive and that challenge accepted opinion, both that of academia and the "moral majority".

Our books are available in all good English language bookstores worldwide. If you don't see the book on the shelves ask the bookstore to order it for you, quoting the ISBN number and title. Alternatively you can order online (all major online retail sites carry our titles) or contact the distributor in the relevant country, listed on the copyright page.

See our website www.o-books.net for a full list of over 400 titles, growing by 100 a year.

And tune in to myspiritradio.com for our book review radio show, hosted by June-Elleni Laine, where you can listen to the authors discussing their books.

MySpiritRadio

SOME RECENT O BOOKS

Suicide Dictionary
The History of Rainbow Abbey
Paul Lonely

This is a startlingly original work of sheer genius – highly recommended, if you can handle it. **Ken Wilber**, author of *The Integral Vision*
9781846940613 176pp £7.99 $16.95

The God of the New Millennium
A search for balance in an age of spin
Gregory Dark

It works, if you try. A little quiet will have you reading words that will inspire you to ask yourself the questions that matter most. Thoughts that will open your mind, set apart successful goals from the poor choices that lead to failure. Words that will clarify doubt and end negativity.
Lallouz International Magazine
9781846940637 144pp £9.99 $22.95

The Quantum Conspiracy
A Novel of Possibilities
Chuck and Karen Robison

The Quantum Conspiracy explores the global shift in consciousness that is being fueled by evolution theory, the appearance of remarkable children being born who reveal a new DNA-like shift, and the threats posed by a potential nuclear war and environmental degradation.
978-1-84694-167-2 254pp £12.99 $24.95